PENGUIN BOOKS

CAN YOU SOLVE THE MURDER?

Antony Johnston is the award-winning, *New York Times* bestselling author of more than fifty books, graphic novels, and comic series, including the popular Dog Sitter Detective murder mysteries. His graphic novel *The Coldest City* was made into the multimillion-dollar blockbuster movie *Atomic Blonde*. He is also a celebrated video-games writer, and is credited with many franchise-defining titles. Johnston is a former vice chair of the Crime Writers' Association, a member of International Thriller Writers and the Society of Authors, a Shore Scripts screenwriting judge, and sits on the Writers' Guild of Great Britain's video-games committee. He lives and works in England.

Also by Antony Johnston

The Dog Sitter Detective
The Dog Sitter Detective Takes the Lead
The Dog Sitter Detective Plays Dead

The Exphoria Code
The Tempus Project
The Patrios Network

Atomic Blonde: The Coldest City
The Coldest Winter

The Fuse: The Russia Shift
The Fuse: Gridlock
The Fuse: Perihelion
The Fuse: Constant Orbital Revolutions

The Organised Writer: How to Stay on Top of All Your Projects and Never Miss a Deadline

Can YOU Solve the Murder?

The Flowers of Elysium

• An Interactive Crime Novel •

ANTONY JOHNSTON

PENGUIN BOOKS

PENGUIN BOOKS

An imprint of Penguin Random House LLC
1745 Broadway, New York, NY 10019
penguinrandomhouse.com

Set in Laurentian Pro with Whitney and Champion Heviweight
Designed by Sabrina Bowers

LIBRARY OF CONGRESS CATALOGING-IN-PUBLICATION DATA
Names: Johnston, Antony, author.
Title: Can you solve the murder?: an interactive crime novel / Antony Johnston.
Description: New York: Penguin Books, 2025.
Identifiers: LCCN 2024058717 (print) | LCCN 2024058718 (ebook) |
ISBN 9780143138884 (trade paperback) | ISBN 9780593513026 (ebook)
Subjects: LCGFT: Detective and mystery fiction. |
Choose-your-own stories. | Novels.
Classification: LCC PR6110.O4524 C36 2025 (print) |
LCC PR6110.O4524 (ebook) | DDC 823/.92—dc23/eng/20241206
LC record available at https://lccn.loc.gov/2024058717
LC ebook record available at https://lccn.loc.gov/2024058718

First published in Great Britain by Bantam, an imprint of Transworld, a part of the Penguin Random House group of companies, 2025
Published in Penguin Books 2025

Printed in the United States of America
2nd Printing

The authorized representative in the EU for
product safety and compliance is Penguin Random House Ireland,
Morrison Chambers, 32 Nassau Street,
Dublin D02 YH68, Ireland,
https://eu-contact.penguin.ie.

For Steve and Ian

Can YOU Solve the Murder?

How to Solve the Murder

The Flowers of Elysium is no ordinary case . . . and this is no ordinary book.

Can You Solve the Murder? is an *interactive* novel. Unlike a normal book, you shouldn't read it straight through from front to back. Reading the text sequentially won't make any sense, and will spoil the experience—because this story is also a puzzle, in which YOU play the part of the detective and YOU must solve the crime by making decisions about the investigation.

Who will you interview? Which leads will you follow? What clues will you find? And, finally, who will you accuse? The choices are yours—and only by following the correct path can you solve the murder.

Here's how it works:

Numbered Sections

The story is divided into *sections*, each of which is numbered. First, pay close attention to the text, as important clues and subtle hints may be hidden within. (But be wary of red herrings . . .)

At the end of each section you will be given a choice of what you, as the detective, want to do. Each choice directs you to a different number; make your decision, then turn to the section matching that number and read on.

For example, let's say you've just read section **86** and it ends with the following options:

- To examine the body, turn to **35**
- To search the murder scene, turn to **143**

You must now decide which of those two actions to perform. If you choose to examine the body, flick backward through the book until you find section **35** and read it—remembering that you're looking for the *section* number, not the page number. If you choose to search the murder scene instead, flick forward through the book to find and read section **143**.

(These numbers are only examples, and don't reflect the actual contents of those sections within this book.)

If you're reading the ebook edition, you don't even need to flick back and forth.* Instead, simply tap the bold number **35** at the end of the option to be taken automatically to that section.

Your Detective's Notebook

Every good detective carries a notebook to record information and evidence vital to solving the case. At the back of this book, you'll find blank pages to use as your own notebook, and to record Clue Numbers.

(You'll have to supply your own pen or pencil, though. Department budget cuts seem to get worse every day . . .)

If you'd prefer not to write in your copy of this book, you can use a separate notebook or even a digital document; whatever you feel comfortable with. What's important is that you can easily write in it and review it while reading, as you'll be performing both actions many times.

Record information about the story, the suspects, your theories, and anything else you think could be significant. Solving a murder requires taking good notes, and *The Flowers of Elysium* is no exception.

Clue Numbers

From time to time, you'll be told to write a Clue Number in your notebook.

Clue Numbers consist of a letter and number, such as **C2**, **P5**, **T4**,

---

* Except in a few unique circumstances, which you may discover as you progress . . .

and so on. It's important you write these down when instructed, because later sections will ask you to check if you have a particular Clue Number in your notebook. You'll then be directed to a specific section.

(There are many different paths to take in this story, so you may sometimes be told to write down a Clue Number you already have in your notebook. This isn't an error—in fact it's a sign that you have good clue-finding skills! So don't worry about it, and move on.)

Let's say a section tells you to write **C2** in your notebook. Then, later, a different section presents you with these choices:

- If you have C2 written in your notebook, turn to **45**
- Otherwise, turn to **118**

In this example you would turn to section **45**, because you have **C2** written down. If you didn't have that Clue Number in your notebook, though, you would turn to section **118** instead.

Sometimes you'll be asked to check your notebook for *multiple* Clue Numbers. When this happens, compare them against your notes in the order listed and act on the first that applies.

For example, imagine you now have both **C2** and **T4** written down. Later, you read a section that ends with the following instructions:

Check your notebook in the following order:

- If you have P5 written down, turn to **87**
- If you have T4 written down, turn to **165**
- If you have C2 written down, turn to **45**
- Otherwise, turn to **118**

Your notebook doesn't contain **P5**, so you ignore that instruction. You do have **C2** written down—but you *also* have **T4**, and the instruction for that Clue Number precedes **C2** in the list. Therefore, in this example you would turn to section **165**.

Clue Numbers are vitally important to solving the case, and also determine your Detective Score after justice has been done, so pay close attention to them.

Can You Solve the Murder?

Remember: YOU are the Detective, and it is up to YOU to solve this dastardly crime! Attention to detail, combined with your sleuthing skills and good notes, will be required to successfully determine whodunit.

- Now begin your investigation by turning to section **1**

1

"Apparently it's a health farm these days." Sergeant McAdam weaves the car at top speed around tight, hedge-lined corners.

"I believe they prefer the term 'wellness retreat,'" you point out.

She chuckles. "Either way, I don't expect the victim would agree."

"Try to keep notions like that to yourself when we arrive, Sergeant."

Your tone is lightly admonishing, but internally you admit to similar thoughts. When you can think for more than five seconds without fearing for your life thanks to McAdam's rally-like driving, that is. She accelerates out of a bend and over a hillock, leaving your stomach somewhere on the ceiling.

This is your first case together, following her assignment to your station last week after making a name for herself in Northumbria. When you asked why she's spent her career in the English police rather than her native Scotland, she shrugged and said, "More action." McAdam is short and wiry, in her mid-thirties, with dark hair and a ruddy complexion suggesting she spends a lot of time outdoors. Reenacting Hollywood car chases, perhaps.

One final death-defying corner later, you reach the gates of Elysium: not a heavenly reward but the retreat in question, operating in the grounds and building of the former stately home Finchcote Manor. High stone walls surround the estate, broken only by a wide gate where a sign is emblazoned with the company name, bidding you to *Rediscover your place in nature and revitalize your soul* in a riot of pastel colors and painted roses.

A marked police car and two uniformed officers guard the entrance. Recognizing you, they wave you through with a nod of acknowledgment. McAdam guns the engine in response, speeding over a squat low-walled bridge that crosses a narrow river running through the grounds, before continuing up the long, tree-lined avenue to the house.

Finchcote Manor is tall and imposing, four stories of the region's characteristic pale stone in a Gothic Revival style with arched windows,

Baroque balusters, and leering gargoyles at every corner and join. An unusual ambience for a wellness retreat.

Approaching the fountain and paved circle, where more police cars are parked, you wonder where the original resident family are now. It can't have been easy giving up such a grand family home for any price.

Alongside the police cars is a forensics van, where you and McAdam don protective clothing, booties, and gloves. You nod in recognition at a tall, broad-shouldered uniformed policeman who approaches. This is Constable Zwale, a young officer you've worked with before.

You introduce him to your new partner, Sergeant McAdam. "Constable Zwale has ambitions to become a detective," you add to the sergeant.

McAdam looks the young officer up and down, appraising him. "Is that so? Then watch and learn. It's all about taking initiative, you see."

"Yes, ma'am," Zwale says. "I won't let you down."

The protective clothing doesn't breathe well—its impermeability being rather the point—so, already sweltering in the heat, you're keen to get moving.

"Lead on, Constable. Is Dr. Wash here yet?"

He nods and leads you up the steps to the main entrance. "Yes, Inspector. The white tent is already up."

Inside, the house feels very different from its classical exterior. Here old and new live side by side, demonstrated by a modern reception area of pine and shaped marble standing before a traditional wide carpeted staircase of oak and brass. The lobby is high-ceilinged and wood-lined, with a grand chandelier taking pride of place and a pleasant garden aroma thanks to a variety of plants, large and small, standing in pots around the walls. By contrast, the reception desk holds two large computer monitors, operated by a pretty young blond woman. Around you, wall-mounted TV screens advertise the retreat's courses with brightly lit videos. One screen shows a timetable of the day's activities: yoga, swimming, even flower arranging and plant care.

"Might have to pick up a brochure," Sergeant McAdam says.

"Your kind of place, Sergeant?"

She snorts. "Hardly. But my wife's birthday is coming up, and she'd love it."

"The manager's waiting for you in his office," Constable Zwale says.

"He can keep waiting for a while yet," you reply. "Let's see the body and crime scene first."

Dozens of people mill about in the lobby; some are staff, in identifiable polo shirts emblazoned with the company's rose logo, but most are guests trying to figure out what's happened. They stand aside to let you pass, whispering in hushed tones to one another and staring at your protective clothing. They know things must be serious.

Zwale leads you toward a doorway at the rear of the lobby, guarded by uniformed officers. But before you can reach it, a middle-aged blond woman wearing tennis whites and carrying a racket strides purposefully out of the crowd to block your way.

"About time, I'm sure. You're the detective, I take it?" she says to you, her expression severe.

"Detective chief inspector," McAdam corrects her.

"Yes, well. Terrible business and all, but kindly inform your chaps I have a lunch engagement."

You give her your full attention. "You have the advantage of me, Ms. . . . ?"

"Nesbitt, of course," she says with the confused air of one who expects to be recognized. "Finchcote Manor falls within my constituency."

"Carla Nesbitt, MP," McAdam explains to you, trying to be helpful. Unfortunately, it only makes the woman's eyes grow wider.

"Really! I don't hold out much hope for this investigation if you can't even recognize your own MP," she sniffs. Before you can explain that you live in a different town, she continues, "Your cops are determined to prevent us from leaving, and I won't have it."

"Ms. Nesbitt, I'm afraid that you must, as you say, 'have it.' A man is dead, and it is my job to conduct a thorough investigation and discover what happened. Just think, he might have been one of your constituents."

She takes this in. "Yes, well. He can't vote now, can he?"

"His family and friends still can," McAdam says brightly. "Not to mention everyone who hears about this case in the news. Imagine if they learned that his parliamentary representative regarded her lunch as more important than an innocent man's death."

Carla scowls at the sergeant. "Innocent! That'll be the day. Harry probably just decided enough was enough. Hurry up and get this over with, so the rest of us can move on with our lives, will you?" With that, she turns on her rubber-soled heel and walks away.

"I'm sure he spoke highly of you, too," McAdam murmurs, as you watch the MP enter the house's east wing.

Constable Zwale resumes his lead, taking you through the guarded door into a staff-only area. From here a wide rear entrance opens onto steps down to a courtyard, semi-enclosed by the house's east and west wings, which protrude at right angles from the main building. A square of neatly cut grass is divided into quarters by gravel paths running through its center and around the edges. Beyond here the grounds are wilder and more natural, with two large polytunnel greenhouses visible in the near distance.

The gardens aren't your destination at this moment, however. To your right as you reach the courtyard, close to the wall of the west wing, are more uniformed police. They guard a cordon surrounding the familiar white-canvas forensics tent, which stands on the gravel path next to the building.

It hasn't rained for several weeks, leaving the ground thoroughly dry. This is fortunate for an investigation taking place outside, even though it means standing around in the late summer sun. As it's now the first week of September, you hope the intense heat will break soon.

You walk over the grass and duck under the cordon to enter the tent. Inside you find a police photographer, a dead body, and a forensic pathologist standing over the victim.

"Victim is Harry Kennedy," McAdam says, reading from her notebook. "Fifty years old, local housing developer. Bit of a bigwig. He booked a week's treatment, staying here alone."

"And will leave it in much the same manner," the pathologist says, standing up and stretching out her back. Dr. Wash has a pristine cut-glass accent, and it's been remarked that she looks as old as she sounds—or vice versa. But with that comes decades of experience and an unflinching accuracy. You've worked together many times, and trust her findings implicitly.

You introduce them: "Dr. Wash, this is Sergeant McAdam. New transfer from Northumbria."

They exchange nods in greeting, then the pathologist stands back to give you a better view of the body. You almost wish she hadn't.

"The victim fell from the top floor, which is a fifteen-meter drop," Dr. Wash says. "The ground is hard and dry enough at the moment to be unforgiving, hence the mess."

The late Harry Kennedy lies on his back, with wide glassy eyes staring at nothing. He was probably once quite handsome, but his face and head are now badly damaged, his short hair matted with blood and dirt. A crimson pool surrounds him, seeping into the ground and soaking into a bathrobe that used to be white. Beneath the robe he wears only boxer shorts.

What stands out most, however, is something you've never seen before. A handheld gardening fork is embedded deep in Kennedy's chest.

McAdam whistles. "So much for Carla Nesbitt's suicide theory."

"Yes, that's highly unlikely for two reasons. Oof." Dr. Wash crouches over the body, groaning as her knees click in protest. "First is the obvious one. The fork entered directly into the heart, and he was likely dead before he hit the ground."

"What's the less obvious reason?" you ask.

She gently opens Kennedy's mouth, to reveal a red rose inside.

"Wonderful," McAdam says, sighing. "We've got a nutcase."

Dr. Wash gives her a disapproving look, saving you the trouble.

"You believe it was placed there deliberately, Doctor?" you say.

"I'd say so, though by whom is a mystery. You'll find a matching plant upstairs on the balcony."

"Was anything found in the pockets?"

The pathologist retrieves two clear evidence bags from a nearby folding table. One contains a nondescript metal watch. Inside the other is a plastic key card printed with Elysium branding. "I assume this opens his bedroom door, though we haven't verified that yet. The watch seems entirely ordinary."

"Nothing else? No wallet?"

"Not on his person. His phone was found on the ground outside, screen cracked and damaged badly enough that it doesn't power on. I've sent it to digital forensics."

You take all this in, trusting the doctor's thoroughness.

"Where did he fall from, exactly?"

Dr. Wash steps out of the white tent and points up to a fourth-story balcony of stone balusters. Every room on the top floor has one, all the same, and as you peer up you now notice that these rear-facing walls are much shabbier than the frontage. Stones are chipped at their corners, gargoyles have cracked faces and bodies, and several balconies have broken or missing balusters. Finchcote Manor has undoubtedly seen better days.

"Forensics have already been over the room connected to that balcony," the doctor continues, "so by all means take a look for yourself. Bit of a curious one, as it's supposed to be staff-only and was locked. I hope you don't mind heights, Inspector."

"I'll manage. Time of death?"

"Before ten forty-five this morning. That's when the manager found him and called 999. Beyond that, hard to say at this moment. Fairly fresh, though."

"Then there's only one remaining question: How certain are you that this wasn't an accident?"

Dr. Wash peers at you over her glasses. "Gardening forks are not stiletto knives, Inspector. To stab a person with one requires a forceful, deliberate act. I'm confident in my assessment."

With hands on hips, Sergeant McAdam surveys the grisly scene and shakes her head. "Aye, we're after a nutcase all right. You know, in some countries they'd send whoever did this to the electric chair."

"Thankfully not here anymore, Sergeant," you reply. "And we stopped hanging people long before you or I were born."

"Not before me," Dr. Wash says, ticking off items on a clipboard. "Even as a child I was glad to see the back of it. Surely you're not advocating for its return, Sergeant?"

McAdam shrugs. "Some people can't be cured."

"Some people also won't stop eating meat. Should we hang them, too?"

"Don't be daft, that's not a crime."

"No, merely the 'natural order,' eh? But many killers think the same way about their victims. You'd do well to remember that."

You don't yet know McAdam well enough to tell if her wide-eyed expression means she's speechless, or is about to launch into a stream of invective, so you draw things to a close and usher her outside.

"Thank you, Doctor. Do call us when you're ready at the mortuary."

You leave the tent and note the evidence marker on the grass nearby, showing where Harry Kennedy's mobile phone was found. Constable Zwale offers to lead you inside, to the balcony from where the victim fell.

"Bloody pathologists are all mental," McAdam mutters as you make your way back toward the house, still in your protective clothing. "Animal lover, is she?"

"You could say that," you reply, amused by her consternation. "Dr. Wash owns a farm filled with livestock."

"Ah. Hypocrite, then."

"On the contrary, she doesn't breed them for food. She keeps them for company."

McAdam looks at you in disbelief, then sighs.

"Like I said. Mental."

Constable Zwale has already reentered the house. You stop just before the doors, so he can't overhear what you say to McAdam.

"Sergeant, insulting the pathologist at your first crime scene here is not the kind of behavior I expect. I was assured you're a hardworking and intelligent detective, so do me a favor and live up to that reputation. Understood?"

McAdam is taken aback. Clearly, she didn't think she'd overstepped. But after a moment, she relents.

"Understood, Inspector. Best behavior it is, then."

You nod, and resume following Constable Zwale. He takes you back through the entrance hall, up the wide carpeted staircase, and along a corridor lined with rooms dedicated to massage, yoga, and similar wellness treatments. You turn a corner into the west wing, then climb two more flights of stairs while passing several therapy rooms. Finally you reach the top floor, where the room doors are numbered like a hotel.

"I wonder what the victim was doing in a staff-only area," Sergeant McAdam muses.

"Perhaps the manager can answer that," you reply. "We'll talk to him after we've looked at the scene."

Zwale stops by a uniformed officer who guards the door of room 312, marked STAFF ONLY. Farther down the corridor you see what you assume is the victim's bedroom, guarded by another policeman. As you watch, an athletic-looking tattooed man in gym clothes approaches the officer and exchanges some words. The conversation is too distant for you to hear, but it's clear the man wants to get inside the room. The officer sends him packing, though, and you make a mental note to find the tattooed man later.

"Inspector?" Zwale says, bringing your attention back to the staff-only room.

"Yes, of course. Go on, Constable."

"I thought you'd want to know that this door was locked when we arrived, and the key's missing from reception. We had to wait for the manager to come and open it."

"He's the only other person with a key?"

Zwale looks embarrassed. "Oh, I—I didn't think to ask."

"Then do it now, and be quick about it," McAdam growls.

The constable hurries away.

"Steady on, Sergeant," you murmur, giving her a look as you grip the door handle. It turns smoothly, and the door opens.

"They've got to learn," she replies. "A few choice words from my old bosses never did me any harm."

You and McAdam enter to find a musty storage room that smells of mildew and obviously hasn't been used for some time. An old vacuum cleaner stands in the corner, next to a sorry-looking mop and bucket. Metal shelving against the walls holds rusty aerosol spray cans of disinfectant and polish alongside gardening tools like spades, mallets, and trowels. An old wheelbarrow, covered in spiderwebs and filled with what appear to be disused rubber boots, occupies another corner. Lengths of hose sit atop loosely folded dustcloths and sheets, some of which are splashed with blood. A dark crimson trail of spots leads to a set of open French windows giving access to the balcony.

"What on earth was Harry Kennedy doing in here?" McAdam muses.

"Whatever it was, unless he stabbed himself in the chest, someone else was here with him. Presumably the same person who locked the door when they left."

You cross the room, avoiding the blood spatter. Even though forensics have gathered initial evidence, you'd still rather preserve the scene as best you can. You pass a large ceramic sink that contains stains of watery blood, and detect a faint scent of strawberry. Most unusual.

It seems incongruous that a storage room like this should open onto a stone balcony with fluted balusters, but it was probably once a bedroom like the others on this floor and only later repurposed for utility.

"Now, this is interesting. Look here, Sergeant."

The French windows are traditional in style, made of wood and multipaned glass. But there are blood smears on the wood, and two of the glass panes have shattered. Bloodstained shards litter the ground outside.

"Broken from the inside," McAdam says. "Suggests a struggle inside the room."

You step out, following the blood trail to the balcony railing and a red stain on the ground before the balusters. A crimson handprint marks the handrail, which is no more than a meter high. It would be easy to fall, or be pushed and lose one's balance.

"He landed face up," you point out. "That suggests he was standing here on the balcony, facing back inside, and was pushed . . . or that whoever stabbed him inside carried him outside and dropped him over the edge."

"That'd take some strength," McAdam says, following you onto the balcony. "We'll be looking for a big lad, then."

"*If* that's what happened. For now we must keep an open mind."

"Look here, the doc was right. Matching flowers."

McAdam gestures at two wide clay pots standing against the wall of the house, either side of the French windows. One contains a plant you don't recognize; from the other grows a rose bush, with distinctive red flowers.

"The Elysium sign we passed featured roses in their logo," you say, recalling the gate. "Our killer had a choice of flowers, but selected this one. I'll wager that's no coincidence."

"Aye, but we must keep an open mind," McAdam says cheekily.

Nothing else appears amiss on the balcony. There are no scuff marks or torn pieces of fabric. You'd never know a man had died here, if not for the blood and broken glass.

And his body lying fifteen meters below, of course.

You peer out along the wing, at the other rooms' balconies on this floor. The gap between them is too wide to jump, and chipped corners notwithstanding, the stone is too smooth to climb across. The killer must have exited through the door and locked it behind them.

Looking out across the courtyard, you see the evidence marker for Kennedy's mobile phone again, but now its position strikes you as odd.

"Sergeant," you say, gesturing at the marker. "How far would you say the victim's phone was found from his body?"

McAdam peers over the balcony. "Looks to be about three meters, give or take."

"Too far for a simple bounce after he fell, especially on grass. How did it get there?"

"Perhaps the killer dropped it?"

"But why not drop it alongside his body? Or simply take it with them?"

The sergeant has no answer, and neither do you.

Then you remember what Dr. Wash said about the phone being damaged, and crouch to sweep your eyes across the stone balcony floor. McAdam watches you with amusement, but after a minute you find what you're looking for.

"That's not glass from a windowpane," you say, holding a tiny shard of silver metal and black plastic in the palm of your gloved hand. "It looks more like a fragment from a broken phone. Dr. Wash said Kennedy's was so badly damaged it wouldn't power up, but falling onto grass wouldn't do that."

McAdam offers you a plastic evidence bag in which to deposit the shard. "You think it was broken here? He dropped it on the ground, picked it up . . . and then took a tumble?"

"Or the killer threw it after him."

McAdam grunts and looks over to the evidence marker. "If so, they overshot by a wee while."

On the other side of the courtyard, the east wing mirrors this one except for its lower floor. Through its windows you see a swimming pool, running almost the length of the wing.

"What do you think the view's like from there?" you wonder aloud. "Could someone in the pool have seen what happened?"

McAdam peers across the courtyard. "Maybe, if they were close enough to the windows. Worth asking."

"Let's talk to the manager first. Perhaps he saw or heard something as Mr. Kennedy fell."

You make your way back into the main part of the house, where you remove and discard your protective clothing. Returning to the entrance lobby, you find the gawping crowd has mostly dispersed. The front desk receptionist you noticed before is now circling the area with a watering can, refreshing its many plants. Constable Zwale accompanies her, talking casually. They seem to be getting on well, and smiles pass between them as they chat.

- To join Zwale and question the receptionist, turn to **23**
- To continue to the manager's office and get a report from the constable later, first write **P4** in your notebook, then turn to **135**

2

Struggling to hold your umbrella against the wind, you remove your jacket, then pass both items to Sergeant McAdam.

"What in God's name are you doing?" she cries. "You can't go in after him!"

"If I don't, he'll drown," you protest. "I won't have that on my conscience."

"I admire your bravery, but with all due respect you won't have a conscience to be troubled if you go in there. That's what strapping young constables are for!"

Zwale nods. "She's right, Inspector. Leave it to me."

There's no time to argue. Tank continues to struggle against the current and is now expending all his effort just to keep his head above water. You step back and make way for Zwale, while McAdam helps you back into your now-soaked jacket.

- Write **P10** in your notebook, then turn to **42**

"I've also received Kennedy's phone records from the carrier," McAdam says. "The only activity this morning was one call, from a local number."

"That must be the one that came after he left Alina Martinescu's massage session. How close to time of death was it?"

"Pretty close," McAdam says. "Commenced at 10:20 a.m., lasted for three minutes. That's around twenty-five minutes before his body was found, so it gives us a firm window of opportunity for the killer."

Thinking back to what the massage therapist said, though, you realize it gives you more than that.

"It's also ten minutes before Alina said he left her session. But she claimed that Kennedy didn't take a phone call while she was with him."

McAdam checks her notebook. "That's right. So either she got the time wrong . . ."

"Or she lied to us. Now, why would she do that? Find out who that local number belongs to. Could it be a building trade supplier?"

"Hold on, I'll check now."

While she accesses the police database, you wonder what this could mean. Alina either was mistaken or lied to you; and Kennedy took a phone call minutes before someone stabbed him with the intent to kill. Are they connected? Or is it just coincidence? Businessmen take phone calls all the time.

McAdam chuckles, breaking your train of thought. "Doubtful it's a supplier, unless he's running it out of his home. It's a domestic number, registered to a Robert Graham. Not far from here, actually . . . oh-*ho*. Mr. Graham lives on the Burrowlands estate."

"The estate next to where Kennedy wanted to build? That can't be a coincidence. Perhaps we should pay Mr. Graham a visit."

- Write **A8** in your notebook
- If you already have C7 written down, turn to **64**
- Otherwise, turn to **30**

4

"I wonder if you can shed some light on a curious mystery," you begin, watching her reaction carefully. As best you can through the flowers between you, anyway. "Why do you think Harry Kennedy's company would pay seven thousand pounds in consultancy fees to a firm with which they'd never previously done business?"

Carla tenses, which you're fairly sure isn't normally part of practicing yoga. "I'm afraid I can't help you there," she says, taking a deep breath.

"Really? That's unfortunate, because we've discovered Mr. Kennedy was in the habit of sending coded text messages, presumably for increased security." Suddenly, the MP's smile fades. You continue: "We've decoded one of those messages, sent to you three days before he was killed. In it Harry reminded you that he'd recently paid you the sum of seven thousand pounds, and warned you not to '*back out.*' Can you explain what he meant by that?"

Carla remains sitting in the lotus position, but judging by her expression she's no longer in her astral corolla.

"I'm sure I don't know," she says frostily. "I receive hundreds of messages every day, and my company works with people all over the country. I can't be expected to keep track of every little transaction."

- In your notebook, cross out P3 and write **C1** instead. Then turn to **95**.

5

You and McAdam move into the waiting room off the lobby to take the call without being overheard.

"Doctor," you answer, putting the call on speakerphone as the sergeant closes the door behind you. "Nice weather we're having. How is it at the mortuary?"

"Raining cats and dogs," she confirms. "The forecast says we're due something like a month's worth of rain over the next few hours. Do watch for flooding if you're out and about."

"Actually, we're rather stuck here at the manor, complete with a partially collapsed roof. Long story. So what do you have for us?"

You hear Dr. Wash typing at her computer. "I'm calling because we've had some results back from the sink in the storeroom. Remember we found what looked like evidence of blood having been cleaned up?"

"I certainly do."

"Despite that room looking unused and forgotten, it seems the sink was a different matter. There were multiple DNA profiles present in the residue. One matches our victim, Harry Kennedy. His fingerprints were also found in the room, which I expected. We believe some of the other prints we've lifted belong to third parties, but without a comparison it's impossible to say."

"What about the other DNA profiles?"

Dr. Wash hesitates. "That's where it gets interesting. We've matched one to Carla Nesbitt, which I must say came as a shock. I really can't imagine she had anything to do with Mr. Kennedy's death, though I suppose one should endeavor never to be surprised in this line of work."

"Why do you say that? Do you know her?"

"Not well, but we've met several times at local bigwig shindigs. Meet the MP, dinner with the mayor, you know the sort of thing."

You very much don't, as people tend not to invite detectives to such gatherings for fear of lowering the tone. You're not at all surprised that Dr. Wash is a regular, though, with her fine breeding and status. In another life she could have been an MP herself.

McAdam leans in and asks, "Doctor, how were you able to identify Carla's DNA?"

"She's in our files, thanks to a conviction for shoplifting many years ago. I didn't know about that, either, but I suppose we all have a past."

McAdam smiles triumphantly.

"Bad news for Carla, but good news for us," you say. "Now we know she was present at the crime scene, even if not precisely when. Doctor, you said there were multiple profiles . . . ?"

"Yes, at least one other, but I'm afraid it remains unidentified. Once again I'll need samples for comparison, and with so many people on-site I imagine that will take quite a while."

"What in God's name was going on up in that storeroom?" McAdam wonders aloud. Truth be told, you were thinking the same thing.

- Write **C16** in your notebook
- If you already have S5 written down, turn to **54**
- Otherwise, turn to **100**

"It seems quite clear to me," you say, "that Stephen Cheong didn't find Harry Kennedy's body by accident. He killed Harry, then pretended finding him was merely a coincidence."

All eyes turn to the manager.

He splutters in protest, "But I didn't do it! Why would I kill Harry?"

Why indeed? Do you have the evidence you need to make a successful accusation?

Check your notebook for clues in the following order:

- If you have S1, S4, or S7 written down, turn to **36**
- If you have S2 written down, turn to **132**
- If you have S6 written down, turn to **99**
- If you have S5 written down, turn to **190**
- Otherwise, turn to **163**

7

You place the wallet next to the laptop on the desk just as the forensics team enters. You ask them to bag up the laptop and take it to digital forensics. Hopefully they can crack Kennedy's password, so you can take a look at what he was working on.

McAdam arrives as the laptop is carried out to a waiting cart.

"Stephen Cheong said Mr. Kennedy was something of a wide boy at heart," you remind the sergeant. "Do you think he might still have been conducting business, even while supposedly on a quiet retreat?"

"I suppose wheeler-dealers never stop."

"What did you find out about his timetable?"

She shakes her head. "Not much, I'm afraid. Kennedy paid for the Lotus package—a VIP job worth nine grand per week, if you can believe that. All paid in advance, too. But for some reason he didn't take much advantage of it. Most of his sessions were massage therapy, including that one with Alina that he left early. It was his only appointment this morning, and he had nothing else booked afterward."

"Nothing at all? How much longer was he scheduled to stay here?"

"Another two days. But the receptionist says Kennedy's whole stay was like that. There are big blocks in his timetable when he attended no sessions, taking 'personal leisure time' instead."

"I wonder what he did to fill that time. Perhaps some of it was spent here on his laptop?"

"It makes you wonder why he bothered coming here at all."

"I'm beginning to think that Mr. Kennedy's visit to Elysium may have had little to do with his health, but a lot to do with whatever it was that got him killed."

You show McAdam the photo you found in Kennedy's wallet, of him and Carla Nesbitt when they were younger.

She whistles. "That puts a new spin on things, and no mistake."

Just then, your phone rings with a call from Dr. Wash.

• Turn to **91**

8

Jennifer leads Alina away through the dispersing crowd, heading toward the staff area. You leave them and turn your attention to Flora, who is being held by McAdam and Zwale. The Asian man who helped has now gone.

You direct Flora, McAdam, and Zwale to the waiting room off the lobby where you previously spoke to the widow. Rain continues falling against the windows, heavier still than when you drove here.

You close the door and lead everyone to sit down while you clear a coffee table of promotional literature and, trusting it's as sturdy as it looks, perch on it to face them.

"Mrs. Kennedy," you begin, "I must tell you you're in serious trouble. Even putting aside your assault on Alina, you compromised what might be valuable evidence in the case. So I'd appreciate an explanation."

- If you have F3 written in your notebook, turn to **114**
- Otherwise, turn to **70**

9

McAdam is about to open the door to leave, but you stop her and say, "We're not quite done here, Ms. Nesbitt."

Carla opens her eyes, sighs, and once again lowers the volume of the ocean waves. "What more could you possibly want to know?"

"Oh, there are many things I have yet to learn about this case. But I'll settle for an explanation of why you've been lying to us."

To her credit, this doesn't seem to rattle Carla at all. Years of serving in Parliament has probably inured her to being on the receiving end of such accusations.

"You'll have to be more specific than that, Inspector."

"Certainly," you say with a smile. "You told us that you and Harry Kennedy being here at Elysium simultaneously was a mere coincidence. But just two weeks ago he sent you a coded text message asking for the dates of your stay, so he could ensure his own presence at the same time. Not only that, he implied he'd threaten Stephen Cheong if the owner didn't make space for him. So please, let's try again."

"I don't know what you're talking about. Harry and I made no such arrangement."

"And your own text messages will back that up, will they?" McAdam asks.

Carla regards her coolly. "I doubt you'll ever know, because you're not going to see them."

"We can apply for a warrant."

"And my solicitor will fight you tooth and nail every step of the way to prevent this unnecessary invasion of my privacy. He's *very* good."

You adjust your angle of attack. "Ms. Nesbitt, the mere fact that Harry sent you a message in code is damning. For one thing, he must have expected you'd know how to decode it, which implies previous communication between you to arrange the method. Even putting that aside, messages are not normally sent in code unless they're sensitive and could be problematic if seen by unintended persons. Why would that be necessary between the two of you?"

Now Carla clams up. "No comment."

"What aren't you telling us about your relationship with Harry Kennedy?" McAdam asks.

"No comment. Now, I'd be grateful if you left, before I call my good friend the chief superintendent and ask why one of his officers is harassing an innocent public servant."

Once again Carla resumes her meditation. This time you take your leave, returning with Sergeant McAdam to the lobby.

"Are you thinking what I'm thinking?" she says.

"Not being psychic, I can't say. But what I'm thinking is that Carla and Kennedy are both married, and a place like Elysium would be a good cover story for them to conduct an affair away from their spouses. We know Kennedy still had a thing for Carla, so the question is: Doth the honorable member protest too much?"

"Not to mention her eagerness to point the finger at Jennifer, which could be simple misdirection."

Is it possible Kennedy was having an affair with both Carla *and* Jennifer Watts? As the MP said, he wouldn't have ordered all that Viagra for nothing. It could also explain why he left so much "personal leisure time" in his schedule.

"Oh, goodness," you say, suddenly struck by a connection. "The storeroom."

"Beg pardon?"

"The storeroom. Was it where Kennedy met his lover? Whether it was Carla, Jennifer, or anyone else, he'd want to be discreet. He couldn't use his bedroom. Anyone seeing a woman enter his room would immediately suspect. The classrooms don't have locks, so they'd be no good. But the storage rooms do."

McAdam whistles, impressed by the subterfuge. "If it wasn't Jennifer, perhaps Kennedy stole the key himself. That might explain why it's missing."

- Cross out P9 in your notebook, and write **C12** instead
- Then **add 1** to your INTERVIEW number, and turn to **65**

10

"Mr. Baker at the council planning department mentioned Ms. Nesbitt was a landlord," you recall, and decide to lay on a little more flattery. "I assume she trusts you to take care of all such business while she's working in Parliament, too? It must be a lot of work."

"That's right," Ms. Gibbs says, sitting a little straighter. "We outsource day-to-day management of tenants to the letting company, of course. But there's always maintenance to take care of, not to mention buying and selling."

"How many properties does Ms. Nesbitt own?"

She thinks for a moment. "Twenty-two. Though it'll be eighteen once these houses on Burrowlands are sold." She gestures to the printouts you saved from falling on the floor.

"Hang on—those houses are on the Burrowlands estate?" McAdam asks, taking notes. "That's right next to where Mr. Kennedy wanted to build."

"Is it?" Ms. Gibbs looks unimpressed. "Like I said, Mummy hasn't mentioned it to me. I'm sure she would have if it was relevant. You said yourself, there's very little about her life of which I'm not aware."

You have no reason to doubt that, but *very little* is not the same as *nothing*, and the secretary's tone is growing defensive. Carla told you she knew about the plans, so why wouldn't she mention them to her daughter, whom she trusts to run her business? Reading the printouts, you see that the houses are indeed on Burrowlands. They've also been on the market long enough for the asking price to be lowered twice.

"Thank you, Ms. Gibbs. I have just one more question: Where were you between ten and eleven this morning?"

"At my gym, and before you ask, a dozen other people can confirm that for you." At your surprised expression, she shrugs. "I'm no fool, Inspector. Why else would you ask?"

You thank her and leave, returning to McAdam's car. Something about this feels like it connects, but there are still too many links missing.

"Sergeant, double-check Sharon Gibbs's alibi, then dig into Carla Nesbitt's property business a little. Find out what sort of history she has, and whether she's bought Kennedy Homes properties before."

"A good thought," McAdam says, making a note. "But if she wanted to buy something on the new estate, wouldn't she try to persuade Nigel Baker to approve the plans, rather than tell Kennedy to get knotted?"

"We only have her word for it that she did," you point out. "I agree, though, it's odd that she wouldn't put pressure on the council. Something doesn't quite add up here, and I want to know what."

- Write **C15** in your notebook, and **add 1** to your LOCATION number. Then turn to **30.**

11

Zwale and the others all wait for your explanation . . . but the truth is, you're not sure you can give them one. You feel confident Jennifer did it, but you have no real evidence to back up your assertion, or to suggest what her motive was. You have your suspicions, but without evidence they're just that.

You glare at Jennifer, hoping she'll do something to give herself away or even spontaneously confess. But it doesn't work.

The moment drags on, until McAdam clears her throat. You simply tell her to arrest Jennifer, with a promise that once the receptionist is in custody at the police station you'll explain your reasoning. Disappointed, the crowd disperses from the room, whispering doubts about your deductive skills.

Constable Zwale refuses to help with the arrest, his disappointment clearly written on his face.

• Turn to **154**

12

You feel very close to learning something important, but it's not quite within your grasp.

"Assume Kennedy was bribing Carla Nesbitt, then," McAdam says. "The question is, what for?"

"Exactly. The obvious answer would be to apply pressure to the council, to give Kennedy permission to build on the floodplain. But she was adamant with us that the plan is a bad idea, and she didn't approve of it."

"She wouldn't be the first politician to do a U-turn after money changes hands. I'd say the bigger obstacle is that we've been told she hasn't applied any such pressure."

A theory coalesces in your mind.

"You're right, she hasn't. But that matches with the text message, doesn't it? 'Don't think I won't tell if you back out' is a clear threat to Carla's reputation and public standing. I wonder what she'd say if we ask her about this."

• Now return to **100**, and skip to the end of that section

13

You make your decision.

"Constable, Sergeant: take Mrs. Kennedy back upstairs, put her in the waiting room, and stay there until I return. No more following people around and threatening them."

"Understood. Come along, madam." McAdam takes Flora's flashlight, while Zwale leads the way back to the steps.

"I'm telling you, she did it," Flora Kennedy shouts as she walks away. "Make her tell you the truth!"

"I'll tell you the truth," Jennifer calls back. "Your husband couldn't keep his hands to himself! Ask any of our Roses; he tried it on with everyone like he was keeping score. Maybe your fella was a saint at home, but not here he wasn't."

Zwale and McAdam take the widow upstairs. You wait until they're out of sight, then say to Jennifer: "We don't believe Mr. Kennedy was much of a saint at home, either. Flora was looking into divorce proceedings."

The receptionist shrugs and retrieves her fallen flashlight from the ground. "Can't say I blame her. She's hardly the first woman who doesn't know what her husband gets up to when she's not around."

"Are you speaking from experience?"

Jennifer walks on through the cellar, sweeping the light left and right, looking for the generator. "I hope the fuel's still OK," she says, avoiding your question. "If I can't get this thing running . . ."

"Even if you can, will it really be enough to power the whole house?" you wonder aloud.

"No, it's only hooked up to the ground-floor circuit. But that's where all the staff offices and computers are located, so it'll keep us going for a while."

- If you have A3 or J4 written in your notebook, turn to **129**
- Otherwise, turn to **77**

14

You stop McAdam before she makes her first call.

"While you're about it, ask digital forensics to put a rush on examining the victim's phone," you say. "It was one of the only personal possessions he was carrying when he was killed."

She nods. "I'll get onto his network provider, too, and ask them for his call records."

"Good thinking, yes. I especially want to know who he was calling when he left that massage session."

- Write **A2** in your notebook
- If you already have C3 written down, turn to **51**
- Otherwise, turn to **162**

15

"All right, let's go," you say.

McAdam is already reaching into her pocket for her car keys. She tosses and catches them with a flourish.

"I'll get you home and dry, don't worry."

Dashing out of the main entrance, you're not so sure about dry, but right now you'll settle for home or even the police station. The portico is meager shelter against the burgeoning storm, and even before you run down the steps you're already half soaked.

You tumble into McAdam's car. She fires up the engine and turns the heating to maximum, which is uncomfortable but will at least help dry you out.

The windscreen wipers are running at top speed, fighting against the rain for something better than terrible visibility. McAdam pulls away with uncharacteristic slowness and you sense that for all her bluster, even she's nervous.

The one thing you don't have to worry about is pedestrians. Nobody in their right mind is walking around in this storm. So McAdam begins to pick up speed as you proceed down the long driveway toward the bridge, and the gates beyond.

The edges of the road have become miniature rivers, flowing downhill on either side of the car. You peer through the windscreen but struggle to make out anything ahead.

"Shouldn't we be near the bridge by now?" you ask, shouting to be heard over the din of the rain and blasting air of the car heater.

"I think we are," McAdam replies grimly, leaning forward and applying the brake. "Look."

Lightning flashes at the same time as a strong gust of wind rocks the car—and sweeps aside a wave of surface water, revealing the shape of the low bridge walls amid what you thought was the flooded road. It appears to have become one with the river. The recent weather has dried the ground out so thoroughly that it can't yet absorb the rain. Instead the water is rushing downhill in a deluge, making things worse. Once again you think of the floodplain next to Burrowlands, picturing water like this running onto the estate.

"Constable Zwale was right," you say. "The river has overtopped the bridge. Let's go back to the house."

"And be trapped in there with a killer?" McAdam says. "Is that wise?"

You watch the water flowing over the bridge. "I'm not sure carrying on is any wiser. Do you really think we can get through that?"

McAdam peers through the windscreen, weighing up your chances. "Looks like there's about ten centimeters of water on the bridge, but once we're through it's uphill back to the gates. It's your call, Inspector."

You've already seen that McAdam can be headstrong, so you're not surprised she thinks you can make it. You squint through the rain, just able to make out the entrance gates beyond the bridge. They're tantalizingly close . . . but perhaps literally a bridge too far. The rain is still coming down, and that ten centimeters of water now looks closer to twenty. At least being in the house with the killer would mean you can protect the other residents.

What will you do?

- To keep going across the bridge, turn to **168**
- To turn back to the house, turn to **107**

16

You've learned all you can from Jennifer for now, so you go upstairs to join McAdam in her search of Kennedy's bedroom. Walking along the corridor, though, you see the telltale signs of a forensics team already in action.

The sergeant steps out of the room, holding up a laptop inside a protective plastic pouch.

"This is the only thing of note in there. Otherwise it's just what you'd expect: clothes and toiletries, car keys, wallet, and so on." McAdam removes her nitrile gloves and hands the bagged laptop to an officer. "Get that to digital forensics, would you? See what they can find."

You're surprised to see a laptop among the possessions of a man supposedly taking a holiday. But after what you found downstairs, perhaps you shouldn't be.

"Stephen Cheong said Mr. Kennedy was something of a wide boy at heart. Perhaps he was still conducting business, even while supposedly on a quiet retreat? Look at this." You show McAdam the timetable printout. "He paid for the top VIP package—nine thousand pounds, due in advance—so that he could come and go as he pleased. But then he hardly took advantage of it, attending few sessions. Instead he spent large blocks of his schedule taking so-called personal leisure time. Do you think he might still have been conducting business, even while supposedly on a quiet retreat?"

"I suppose wheeler-dealers never stop," she says. "It makes you wonder why he bothered coming here at all, if he couldn't leave work behind."

"Indeed it does. I'm beginning to think that Mr. Kennedy's visit to Elysium may have had very little to do with his health, and a lot to do with whatever it was that got him killed . . ."

Just then, your phone rings with a call from Dr. Wash.

• Turn to **91**

17

The afternoon is getting on, but you're curious to know why this housing plan of Kennedy's seems to keep coming up in the course of your inquiries, and whether it's connected to his death. This train of thought is so engrossing it even distracts you from Sergeant McAdam's driving.

You park next to the council offices and once again step out into uncomfortable heat. Your clothes are beginning to stick to your skin, and you look forward to being able to shower off the day at home. Before then, though, there's work to do. You step inside the council building, hoping for respite.

Unfortunately, it offers little. While the walls are surprisingly bright and colorful, rather than the gray and drab place you were expecting, their paint can't hide the building's age and lack of modern amenities, including air conditioning. Sweltering, you begin to resent the uplifting decor—though not half as much as the staff, it seems.

A glum receptionist insists you wear lanyards, then takes an age printing them out, before calling a bored clerk who leads you in silence through rainbow-colored corridors lined with posters of inspirational quotes and enlarged photographs of the local countryside. You finally reach a door marked PLANNING DEPARTMENT, which the clerk knocks on listlessly before shuffling away when Nigel Baker answers, "Come!"

You open the door and introduce yourselves.

"Ah, Inspector," Mr. Baker says, nodding. "Yes, yes. Come in and take a seat."

His office is a stark contrast to Stephen Cheong's. You were expecting a mess of files, papers, and plans, but instead Baker sits at a desk containing only a laptop, desk lamp, phone, and fan. Behind him is an open window, and around the room shelves line every spare inch of the walls, packed with files and folders arranged in a precise, neat, and well-labeled fashion. This is just as well, because the fan is blowing at full blast and any loose papers would have long flown out of the open window. Still, you're grateful for the artificial breeze.

You take a seat as offered, but Sergeant McAdam remains standing and browses the shelves.

"Is it not all digital these days, Mr. Baker?" she asks.

"Yes, yes, mostly," Baker says. The man matches his office, or perhaps it's the other way around. He's tall, rail-thin, wearing shirt and trousers without a thread or hair out of place. "But the shift to digital is still ongoing, so we have many, many paper archives as you can see. Oh, please don't!"

McAdam freezes mid-action in the process of pulling an archive box from a shelf.

"I was just going to take a look," she says. "Is it fragile?"

Baker stands, steps around his desk, and gently but firmly pushes the box back into place. "Not fragile, but confidential. That shelf contains rejected plans, you see, which never went out for public consultation."

"Would that include the new Kennedy Homes plans?" you ask.

Baker returns to his desk. "It will soon, when the final decision is ratified. But I can't show you anyway, not without a warrant. They haven't yet been put to the public."

"Can you tell us why you're intending not to approve the plan?"

Baker grimaces. "The proposed site is a historic floodplain, and after consideration it was felt that the planned drainage was inadequate to compensate for its loss. The Burrowlands estate is downhill from the site, and would suffer flash flooding in the event of heavy rainfall."

"Couldn't Mr. Kennedy have improved the drainage plans and resubmitted?"

"Of course, but he didn't, and I suppose now he never will. It's a shame, as we certainly need more housing. But the location was entirely wrong, despite what he may have thought, and no matter how persuasive he may have attempted to be."

"What do you mean by 'attempted'?"

"Mr. Kennedy had a certain charm, Inspector, which he regularly used to try and get his way. But that sort of thing won't wash in this department, I assure you."

- If you have C3 written in your notebook, turn to **158**
- Otherwise, turn to **90**

18

The room waits for you to explain why you accused Flora . . . but the truth is, you're not sure yourself. You feel confident she did it, but you have no real evidence to back up your assertion, or suggest what her motive was. You have your suspicions, but without evidence they're just speculation.

Perhaps you hoped that accusing Flora would cause her to spontaneously confess, but if so it hasn't worked.

The moment drags on, until McAdam clears her throat. You tell her to arrest Flora, with a promise that once the widow is in custody at the police station you'll explain your reasoning. Disappointed, the crowd disperses from the room, whispering doubts about your deductive skills.

- Turn to **154**

19

You decide to have another chat with Stephen Cheong. Jennifer calls his office, but there's no answer, so suggests you try the garden.

"When he's not inside, he's often caring for the flowers," she explains.

"Don't you have gardening staff for that sort of thing?" you ask.

"Stephen used to run a nursery. It's how he was able to conceive of floral wellness. So he spends a lot of time tending to the plants himself and overseeing the staff. You can borrow an umbrella if you like."

Jennifer indicates a stand of colorful umbrellas, branded with the Elysium name and rose logo, near the front entrance. Taking one each, you and Sergeant McAdam head to the rear courtyard. You unfurl the umbrella, step out into the driving rain, and immediately almost lose it to a crosswind. McAdam meanwhile is already walking ahead, head down and umbrella braced. You regain control of your brolly and dash after her, hurrying toward the gardens. You pass the white forensics tent, still in place under the balcony from which Harry Kennedy fell, even though the body is no longer there. Through the windows on the other side of the courtyard is the swimming pool, where an instructor teaches a seniors class.

"Could be worse," McAdam says, nodding in their direction. "They're even wetter than us."

"At least they're dressed for it," you grumble.

You reach the gardens, noticing that many of the plants look in poor condition and there are bare patches in the beds. Stephen said the weather was making things difficult, and it seems he was right. A good thing they have the polytunnel greenhouses, then, which you noticed when you first arrived at Elysium. You notice movement inside the nearest and largest polytunnel, so make directly for it.

Hurrying inside and grateful to be under cover, you close your umbrella and leave it by the door. McAdam simply drops hers on the ground, still open.

The polytunnel stretches back almost fifty meters, with row after row of growing plants arranged on either side of a central aisle. Many are raised beds, each containing dozens of identical pots, though the pots and flowers differ greatly in size from bed to bed. The taller plants are staked out in ground beds, mounds of soil held in place by wooden borders. Metal sprinkler pipes crisscross overhead, spraying a fine mist of water over particular sections.

You see three other people in here: two gardeners and Stephen himself. The manager stands before a raised bed of flowering plants, with his fingers deep in the soil.

"I suppose we were all hoping for rain, but not like this," you say, making conversation as you approach.

He nods. "From one extreme to another. It's no good for anyone."

McAdam gestures at the overhead sprinklers and jokes, "Wouldn't it be quicker to just take the roof off?"

Stephen doesn't see the funny side. "This is a controlled environment. Exposing these plants to seasonal weather would kill them within a week."

"The flowers outside don't appear to be doing much better," you say. "Whatever the opposite of green fingers is, I have it, but it doesn't take a gardener to recognize things drooping and wilting. At least these inside plants look healthy."

Stephen sighs and wipes sweat from his forehead with his sleeve. "Like I said, things have been rough for the past couple of years. But we manage, thanks to these greenhouses."

"And thanks to high-paying customers like Harry Kennedy? Those Lotus packages aren't cheap."

"We charge rates in line with the market," Stephen says defensively.

"Except you didn't charge Mr. Kennedy at all, did you?" McAdam says. "We were told all fees are due in advance, but there's no record of him paying you a penny. How do you explain that?"

Stephen shrugs. "Sometimes we gift complimentary packages to people we hope will become regular Friends. It's hardly unusual in the hospitality business."

"Really?" McAdam says skeptically. "Because we can't find any record of you doing it before."

"Come now, Sergeant," you say mischievously. "Don't forget Mr. Destroyer's free upgrade."

"Oh, that's right," she says, watching Stephen's reaction. "In the same week as Kennedy's freebie, too. What a coincidence."

- Have you decoded the *third* text message retrieved from Harry Kennedy's phone? If so, write **P1** in your notebook. Then *multiply* the number found in that message by *14* and turn to the corresponding section.
- Otherwise, turn to **103**

20

An image comes to mind of Dr. Wash's mortuary table and the circular burns on Kennedy's back.

"Did Harry Kennedy make a complaint about being burned during hot stone therapy?" you ask.

Jennifer looks at you with surprise. "No, and neither has anybody else, as far as I know. Our therapists are all professionally qualified. They would never let a stone hot enough to burn get near a client's skin."

And yet . . .

- Turn to **113**

21

"Why didn't you tell us this before?" you ask.

Alina shrugs. "Because it looks bad, yes? I can't risk losing this job, Inspector. I need the money."

"Surely there are other places you could work."

"I don't want to move away."

"Away from your sister, you mean?" Alina looks at you with surprise. "When we spoke to her yesterday, she said she followed you here to England."

Alina's eyes flash angrily. "You should not talk to her. You have no right!"

McAdam steps in to calm her down. "She's not in trouble. We actually went to talk to her husband, Robbie—we didn't know he was married to Roxana until we got there."

"But she did mention something interesting," you say. "Yesterday you told us Harry Kennedy left your session at ten thirty to conduct a phone call."

Alina looks confused by this apparent change of subject. "Uh, yes. That's right."

"You're absolutely sure he didn't have a call while he was in here with you?"

She turns away to place the hot stones back on the heater, avoiding eye contact. "No. I mean, yes, I'm sure. No phone call."

"So how do you explain your sister's confirmation that she called him at ten twenty, and that Mr. Kennedy's phone records show he neither made nor took any further calls before he died?"

Alina hesitates, then puts away the tongs and looks defeated.

"Yes, OK. His phone rang while he was on the table. I told him this was a place of relaxation and he should turn it off, but he would not. So he took the call, and I kept working. I could tell he was arguing with a woman, but it wasn't until he called her 'Roxana' that I knew it was my sister. And then I realized who he was."

"What do you mean?" McAdam asks. "Surely you already knew Mr. Kennedy's name."

She shrugs. "I didn't know he was the same useless bastard Kennedy who built her house. Why should I?"

A picture starts to form in your mind. "And he in turn didn't know you were Roxana's sister, did he? But I bet he soon found out . . . when you *deliberately* burned him with the hot stones. It wasn't an accident, was it?"

Alina hangs her head. "No. I lost my temper. But that—that pig, he was a criminal! A no-good bastard man who lets a baby sleep in a house with leaking windows. Roxana has been fighting him for months, but he will not repair the house. I'm not sorry for what I did."

"That's the real reason he left early, isn't it?" McAdam ventures. "Just like our friend a minute ago—he stormed out after you burned him."

Alina nods silently.

• Turn to **87**

22

"It's quite simple," you say. "You're an inveterate liar, Mr. Destroyer. I'd wager that's really why you changed your name, too. You're not a multimillionaire; you didn't sell your prior business to Google for a fortune; and you're not a renowned tech mogul with investors falling over themselves to fund you. In fact you're a con man, taking money from gullible investors and then pocketing it for yourself. Your Wikipedia page is nothing but a fiction, and appears to be largely self-written. Is that why you're a regular here at Elysium? Looking for more marks like Harry Kennedy?"

"I told you, Harry was my friend," Tank growls.

"I doubt he was anything of the sort, or that he was as gullible as you hoped. He agreed to a mutual investment with you, supposedly willing to give you tens of thousands in funding, and in return you'd do the same for him. But the truth is that neither of you had the money you were promising the other, did you? You played a game of chicken with money, both waiting for the other to move, both equally desperate. I think Harry Kennedy was the first to realize it, and threatened to expose you to your other investors. Of course, you couldn't allow that . . . so you lured him into the storeroom and permanently silenced him."

A collective gasp goes up around the room.

You continue: "Alina saw you arguing with Kennedy after he left her therapy session, placing you on the upper floors of the house. Nobody saw you enter the pool, and you claim not to know when you did even though there's a clock on the wall. We also now know you had ample motive to want Harry dead."

Tank glowers at you, and for a moment you fear for your safety; he may be a fraud, but his size and strength aren't.

"One thing I do know is that you don't have a shred of evidence," he says slowly, "because I didn't do it. Harry didn't threaten me with anything, and I didn't kill him. He had no money either! He sent me begging emails, you know!"

"Yes, we've seen them. That's the real reason you tried to get inside his room, isn't it? You weren't looking for a water bottle. You wanted to steal his laptop, in case it contained evidence implicating you. But my officers prevented you, because they know their duty." You turn to McAdam. "Sergeant, kindly do yours and arrest Mr. Destroyer."

- Turn to **131**

23

You approach Constable Zwale and the receptionist.

"Here's the DCI now," the constable says, introducing you. "Inspector, this is Jennifer Watts, the receptionist. She was here this morning."

"Apparently you were asking about the key to room 312?" she asks.

"The storage room on the top floor, yes. It looked like it hadn't been used in some time."

Jennifer nods. "That's right. We use different rooms for equipment storage now, so nobody's been in 312 for a couple of years. That's why I was surprised when I saw the key wasn't here."

"When did it go missing? Was it definitely here yesterday?"

She shakes her head. "Sorry, I couldn't really say. I noticed it was gone after you all arrived and wanted to get inside the room, but . . . here, look."

Jennifer waters the final plant on her rounds, then walks back to the front desk and bids you to follow. Stepping behind the desk, she takes a ring of keys from her waistband. One of them opens a locked metal cabinet under the desk, inside which dozens more keys of different shapes and sizes hang on labeled posts.

"It's kept there," she says, pointing to 312's empty spot at the back of the cabinet. "Like I said, it hasn't been used in ages. I make a note of the keys that get borrowed, but nobody asked for this one. It just . . . vanished."

"Who has a key to this lockbox?"

She shrugs. "Me and Stephen, the manager. He has spares of every key."

"Including to 312 itself?"

"Yes. That's how we got the room open for your officers." Jennifer locks the cabinet and returns the key ring to her waistband.

So it's unlikely the manager would have stolen this key, when he had his own—unless the purpose was to divert suspicion away from himself. Assuming the key was stolen, though, it suggests Kennedy's murder may have been planned rather than a spur-of-the-moment event.

You continue on to the manager's office.

- Write **J1** in your notebook, then turn to **135**

24

"Were you really good friends, though?" you ask. "Or were you simply using each other for your individual purposes?"

"I don't know what you mean," Carla says.

"I think you do. Harry Kennedy wanted you to persuade the council planning department to approve his housing plan for the new estate next to Burrowlands. He even paid your company Standard Umbrella seven thousand pounds, money he could scarcely afford, as an incentive. But you still haven't intervened with the council. Why is that?"

Carla sniffs. "I know nothing about that payment. The day-to-day operation of my business is handled by my daughter. I'll ensure it's returned to Harry's company—sorry, Flora's company now, I suppose."

"That doesn't explain why you haven't spoken to the planning department yet."

"I've told you already, I disagreed with Harry over his plans. The field he intended to build on is a floodplain."

"That's right. Without adequate drainage, paving over that land would redirect any heavy rainfall onto Burrowlands itself—where you happen to own several houses. Houses you're currently trying to sell."

The MP shrugs. "Am I? My company regularly buys and sells houses. As I said, I don't handle the day-to-day aspects."

"So you say. But I believe you were waiting until those houses sold before talking to the council. Once the value of your own properties wouldn't be affected, you could pocket Mr. Kennedy's 'incentive' and do his bidding."

"I've never heard such nonsense."

"But things were dragging on too long, weren't they? Harry Kennedy started to worry that you'd simply taken his money and run, knowing he couldn't say anything because it would be an admission of bribing you. Desperate times, though, call for desperate measures. He threatened you with exposure, which would lead to a big scandal. You'd find yourself in the headlines for all the wrong reasons.

"So you lured him into the storeroom, killed him there, then shoved him off the balcony before returning to your Tai Chi class. Your DNA was found in the sink of room 312, presumably from where you washed off Kennedy's blood."

"You killed him over seven grand?!" Flora cries at the MP.

"I didn't kill him at all!" Carla yells in response, before regaining her composure. "This is a preposterous fantasy, and I won't dignify it with a response."

"You don't have to. Sergeant, arrest Ms. Nesbitt."

• Turn to **196**

25

"Thank you for speaking to us, Ms. Nesbitt," you say, ushering her to the door. "We appreciate your candor, and I'm sure it will help us get to the bottom of whoever killed Harry Kennedy."

"I certainly hope so," she replies. "You and your chaps have been a curse on Elysium ever since you arrived. The sooner you arrest Flora and go away, the better."

Perhaps you were naive to think Carla would have accepted your thanks with grace.

"I hardly think we can be blamed for the weather," you say diplomatically. "But you can rest assured—"

Just then the main entrance bursts open and a very wet Constable Zwale enters, dragging an equally sodden Tank Destroyer with him. The men collapse inside the lobby, so you rush to their aid, handing them spare towels from the pile Jennifer collected earlier.

Zwale takes deep, gasping breaths, while Tank coughs and moans pitifully on the floor.

"What happened, lad?" McAdam asks.

"He tried . . . to swim . . . the river," Zwale replies between breaths, toweling himself down. "Almost drowned . . . I had to . . . jump in after . . . and pull him out."

She looks at both men and whistles. "A wonder you're still alive. You did a brave thing, lad. I'll make sure the brass hears about it."

You help Tank to sit upright and begin drying himself.

"Mr. Destroyer, what could have prompted you to do such a

thing? Why were you running away? Is there something you need to tell us?"

The mogul rubs his eyes with the towel and looks at you fearfully. "I didn't kill Harry. I was trying to get away from Stephen. He killed Harry, and if I'm not careful I'm next!"

"Why would you think that? Even if Stephen did kill Harry, surely there's no reason—"

But before you can finish, a loud scream reverberates through the lobby, then is suddenly cut short.

• Turn to **69**

26

"Were you running a class yesterday morning between ten and eleven?" you ask, even though you already know the answer.

"Oh yes," Bill replies. "All morning, every morning. When the weather's good, we go outside and practice on the lawn. Get the grass under our feet."

"Except today, it seems."

He chuckles. "There were far more interesting things going on in here, weren't there? I'm trying to get everyone back together now, but it's like herding cats."

"Think back to yesterday morning, if you would. Did Carla Nesbitt take your class?"

Bill considers for a moment. "I think so. She's there most days. Is it important?"

"We're just trying to establish everyone's whereabouts when Mr. Kennedy met his unfortunate end."

"Oh, I see!" The instructor looks shocked, as if it had never crossed his mind Carla might be a suspect. "Well, let me think . . . oh, that's right. Yes, she was definitely in the class yesterday morning."

McAdam, taking notes, grunts. "I suppose that checks out, then."

"Yes," Bill continues, "I remember because she took a toilet break, which was a bit annoying. Even our seniors normally know to go before the class starts. It interrupts the flow of *chi* in the *tantien*, you see."

"Does it, now?"

He gives a self-deprecating smile. "That's what I read in a magazine."

"Hang on," you say, as McAdam remains poised over her notebook. "When exactly did Carla take this break?"

"Oh, now you're asking." He puffs out his cheeks. "It would have been . . . about half past ten, I think. Midway through the session. I noticed because it was unusual for her, but she was right at the back, so it didn't disturb the others. I don't think anyone else would have even noticed, really."

You exchange glances with the sergeant.

"How long was she gone for?"

"That's another reason I remember it," Bill says. "It was a good five minutes. I started to wonder if she'd come back at all, but she did eventually."

"And how did she seem when she returned?"

"A bit flustered, like she'd run there and back."

"That didn't strike you as odd?"

Bill shakes his head. "No, the toilets are up on the first floor. It's another reason most people go before we start."

McAdam raises an eyebrow. Carla could indeed have been running "there and back" . . . but not to the toilets.

• Write **C6** in your notebook, then turn to **81**

"We could always ask someone," you suggest.

"Great idea," McAdam says, making for the nearest driveway.

"No, not at random," you say. "Our mystery caller lives on this estate, remember? The man who phoned Harry Kennedy shortly before his death."

"Of course," she says, quickly checking her notebook to hide her embarrassment. "Robert Graham. Number 27, which is . . ." She scans around, checking the house numbers, then points. "Right over there, I should think. Round that curve."

McAdam strides across the road, trying to make up for her oversight by now being decisive. It's a trait you've seen before in officers wanting to be the "perfect" copper. But such a thing doesn't exist, and the obsession can hold them back from promotion. You know you're not perfect, and can't do everything; that's why you surround yourself with, and rely on, officers who can compensate for your weak areas. To you, that's the mark of a good leader. You hope that in time McAdam will learn that lesson.

You find Number 27 exactly where she predicted. The sergeant is already at the door and leaning on the bell before you catch up with her, trying not to move too quickly in this heat. The last thing an interviewee wants is to be faced by a sweating detective.

A young woman opens the door, balancing a child on her hip. She wears jogging bottoms, a T-shirt, and a light cardigan, with her dark hair tied back in a ponytail; the universal ensemble of tired young mothers.

"Hello?" she says, cautiously.

McAdam presents her warrant card and introduces you both. Before she can ask for Robert Graham, however, the young woman interrupts:

"What's wrong? Has something happened to Alina?"

"Alina?" you repeat, noting her Eastern European accent.

"Yes, Alina Martinescu. My sister."

• Write **A1** in your notebook, then turn to **152**

28

"You saw him first, Constable. Off you go."

"I've only just got dry from the last time . . . !" he protests. "Anyway, you said you wanted me to go with Jennifer to the generator."

The receptionist smiles at him. "Don't use me as an excuse," she says. "I'll be fine."

Constable Zwale sighs and jogs to the main entrance.

"Don't come back without him," McAdam calls cheerily after the departing constable.

Meanwhile, you usher the suspiciously friendly Carla Nesbitt into the waiting room. McAdam follows, closing the door behind her to give you all some privacy.

You look out of the windows, which yesterday morning afforded an attractive view of a bright and sunny estate. Now, with the power out and storm clouds overhead, you can barely see one another's faces.

"So," Carla asks plainly, "what are your suspicions? What have you found?"

"We've identified a number of people who had both the motive and opportunity to kill Harry Kennedy," you say, being careful not to get too specific. "I think you can probably guess who they are."

"I'd rather you told me."

"No doubt, but I must remind you that you also remain a suspect in this case."

Carla seems genuinely shocked that she's still under suspicion. "Ridiculous," she says. "I was doing Tai Chi on the lawn when Harry was killed."

"Ms. Nesbitt, I'm a simple woman," McAdam says. "So can you explain why we found your DNA in the old storeroom where Mr. Kennedy met his end?"

The question throws her off balance, though only for a moment. MPs have lots of practice at being subjected to unexpected awkward questions, after all. Her friendly, conciliatory demeanor hardens into an icy crust.

"Which storeroom would that be?" she asks.

"It's 312, on the top floor. A room that, until recently, was always locked."

"Well, I'm sure I don't know. Do they store tennis equipment there? I've touched many things in the house and grounds."

"But your DNA wasn't found on a tennis ball," you say. "It was found in the sink, along with some of Mr. Kennedy's blood. Despite how you've presented your relationship with him, we know he remained fond of you. The photo archive we found on his laptop, of you together in your younger days, speaks volumes. So I'd appreciate an explanation."

She locks eyes with you, as if daring you to voice your suspicion, but you know the way to make someone talk is to leave a silence that they feel compelled to fill. Even an MP isn't immune to that.

"OK, fine," Carla finally says, breaking eye contact. "I suppose this will come out eventually anyway, but can you please keep it to yourself for now?"

"I make no promises," you reply, "but we're always discreet."

Carla looks skeptically at Sergeant McAdam, then back at you. Unexpectedly, tears form in her eyes and she takes a deep breath.

"Harry and I were . . . involved. The storeroom was our secret meeting place."

You wish you were more surprised by this revelation. "And your DNA in the sink . . . ?"

"Well, the room isn't furnished with an en suite," she says, hardness returning to her voice.

"But you presumably didn't want to be seen going in and out of each other's bedrooms, so you made do. How did it work?"

Carla sighs. "We prearranged times, then Harry would go first to unlock the room and wait for me. He was hardly in any classes, so nobody wondered where he was. Then, during my personal leisure time, I'd reserve a meditation room but not use it."

"Instead, you'd go to the storeroom and . . . be *involved* with Harry Kennedy."

She nods silently.

Yesterday you thought it was selfish of Kennedy to book a massage session but only use half of it. Now you find Carla Nesbitt regularly booked a private room and didn't use it at all. Perhaps they were made for each other.

"And how did he come by the key to the storeroom?" you ask.

Carla shrugs. "I have no idea."

Check your notebook in the following order:

- If you have C14 written down, turn to **142**
- If you have C4 written down, turn to **184**
- If you have C1 written down, turn to **55**
- Otherwise, turn to **93**

29

"It's quite simple," you say, addressing the crowd. "What many of you may not know is that Alina's sister, Roxana, has been in a dispute with Harry Kennedy for months. Roxana and her young family live in a Kennedy Homes house, which has developed leaking windows he apparently refused to fix."

Flora sniffs. "The houses on Burrowlands are beyond the defects insurance period. Repairs are not our responsibility."

"Nobody mentioned Burrowlands, Mrs. Kennedy," McAdam points out. "So it's interesting that you knew which houses we meant. Common problem, is it?"

"Not at all," Flora says dismissively. "I'm familiar with both the complaint and complainant. I didn't know her sister worked here, though. My God, did she really kill Harry just because her sister's too stupid to understand the law?"

"No!" Alina protests. "Though maybe I wanted to. You are a criminal just like him."

Not wishing to see Flora give Alina a second black eye, you step between the women.

"Unfortunately, the issue of your sister's house is not a criminal matter," you say to Alina. "You lied to us about the time of their phone call, because you didn't want us to make the connection between your sister and Kennedy. But that call happened while he was still on your massage table. You overheard him talking to Roxana and realized who he was, didn't you? Knowing that he'd made your sister's life hell, you were incensed with anger and deliberately burned him with hot stones. We discovered the marks on his body at the postmortem."

A collective gasp goes up around the room.

"But it's what happened next that led to his death. Harry Kennedy stormed out of the room, and you were worried he would tell Stephen. We've already heard accusations that the manager has a tendency to let people like Mr. Kennedy do whatever they want, up to and including groping the staff." You frown at Stephen Cheong, who has the decency to look distraught, but says nothing. "So when Harry Kennedy left, with literal proof on his body of what you'd done in anger, you panicked. Afraid that he'd complain and Stephen would fire you, you followed and killed him, then claimed to have stayed in your room the whole time."

"It's not true!" Alina protests. "You said he was killed in that storeroom, but I don't have a key. How would I get in?"

"We can find that out down at the station. Sergeant, arrest Ms. Martinescu."

• Turn to **185**

Sergeant McAdam sits with her hands on the steering wheel, patiently waiting for you to make a choice from the many places this case could lead. She taps her fingers to an imaginary drumbeat, no doubt "listening" to something loud and raucous in her head. You're grateful she keeps it in there.

"Where to next?" she asks. "Or do you want to call it a day?"

(If this is your first time reading this section, write ***LOCATION: 1*** *in your notebook. You will only have time to visit two of the locations below, so choose wisely.)*

- If your LOCATION number is now 3, turn to **94**

Otherwise, choose from one of the following options:

- To visit the Burrowlands housing estate, turn to **62**
- To visit Carla Nesbitt's constituency office, turn to **160**
- To visit Flora Kennedy's solicitor, turn to **125**

31

You decide it's time to drop this particular bombshell on Stephen.

"Three weeks ago, an unknown person sent Harry Kennedy a text message. It was in code, so the information contained within must have been sensitive. We've now decoded it, and it seems the sender witnessed someone they call 'Flower Boy' buying four pallets of goods from a nursery, while trying not to be seen. Can you explain that?"

Stephen's expression is carved from stone. "No, I can't. Can you?"

"Mr. Cheong, by your own admission you're struggling to grow flowers. For most wellness retreats this might not be a concern, but your entire business is centered around floral therapy, isn't it? Using flowers that you proudly claim are grown here on the premises. That is, as you told us, your company's 'unique brand promise.'"

"Look around you," Stephen says. "Every flower you see in Elysium has been plucked from either our gardens or a greenhouse bed."

"But where did it grow to begin with? Your 'Friends' might not be pleased to learn your stock was bought wholesale from a nursery before being planted here. They might even call it fraud. And if Harry Kennedy had found out . . ."

"What might you do to protect your reputation?" McAdam completes your thought.

You begin walking through the rows of plants in raised beds, as if looking for evidence. You don't expect to actually find any, but it'll increase the pressure on Stephen Cheong. People say all sorts of things when they're anxious.

The manager paces after you, seeming to have finally understood what you're implying.

"No, no, hang on," he says. "I didn't kill him! It was me who found Mr. Kennedy, remember? Why would I call 999 if it was me who did it?"

"Perhaps to give yourself deniability," you point out, "exactly as you're now doing. You're also the only other person with a key to room 312."

"I already told you, I was walking back from the greenhouse when I found Mr. Kennedy. I was nowhere near him when he died."

"So you claim," McAdam says. "But can anyone corroborate that? Were any of your gardeners here with you?"

Stephen looks pained. "No. I was alone."

"Exactly. You'll forgive us for not taking your word for it."

- Cross out P1 in your notebook, then turn to **103**

You take up position at the poolside spot where Tank will turn for another width.

"Mr. Destroyer," you call out to him as he approaches.

He reaches the edge and rotates his body. For a moment you think he's going to continue swimming and avoid you, although that's hardly a long-term plan given the pool only has one exit. But then he stops and smiles, treading water.

"Inspector. And your lovely sidekick, too. What a treat."

"We'd like to ask you some questions."

Tank floats, hanging on to the poolside. "I'm an open book. Ask away."

"On dry land, if you don't mind."

"Oh, you're no fun. I was hoping to persuade your sergeant to join me in the water."

He rolls his eyes in mock disappointment, but pulls himself out of the water all the same. There's no denying Tank is in great physical shape, and he knows it. With water dripping from his tattooed muscles, he walks to a nearby lounger and begins to towel himself down, maintaining eye contact with Sergeant McAdam.

"Doing anything later, gorgeous?" he asks her. "Bring your handcuffs up to my room, you can arrest me all you like."

You almost laugh, but you suspect that this unsubtle flirting is performative, to make McAdam uncomfortable and distract you both from questioning Tank. To her credit, she doesn't rise to the bait and maintains her composure.

"Depends on whether I'd have to bring up that parcel Mr. Kennedy ordered," McAdam says. "What did you know about that?"

"Harry was a handsome fella, Sergeant, but he wasn't my type," Tank replies. "Those little blue pills were as much a surprise to me as they were to everyone else. Including his wife, apparently. What'll become of her, I wonder?"

"That's not your concern," you say. "If I were you, I'd worry more about your own position."

- If you have T3 written in your notebook, turn to **127**
- Otherwise, turn to **161**

You begin: "You know, looking back I'm surprised at your reaction to Harry Kennedy's death when we first encountered you yesterday. At that time you were dismissive and suggested there was no love lost between the two of you."

Carla unhooks herself from the lotus position and stretches out her legs on the floor. "What's your point?"

"Well, to start with, why didn't you mention that you and Harry had previously been close?"

"Who told you that?"

McAdam holds up her phone and swipes through images from the archive found on Kennedy's laptop.

"These were on Mr. Kennedy's computer," you explain to Carla. "They suggest a very different picture to the one you painted."

She shrugs. "That was all a very long time ago. We were young and stupid, which is something of a tautology, isn't it?"

"So it's all behind you now? Water under the bridge?"

"Something like that."

You reach into your pocket and produce the photo of Carla and Kennedy you found in his wallet. "Harry was carrying this on his person right up until the day he died."

Carla takes the picture from you and gazes at it in silence. For the first time, perhaps lost in memory, she looks saddened by Kennedy's death and runs a finger over the old photograph. Then she composes herself and hands the picture back to you.

"All right, yes, we were an item. It was fun until it wasn't, and in the years since our relationship has been strictly professional. He builds houses, I sometimes buy them, and that's the end of it."

"It doesn't quite explain your earlier attitude."

"Really, Inspector, have you never had a bad breakup? One that made it difficult to even be in the same room as your former lover?"

You pocket the photo. "It seems Harry Kennedy didn't feel the same way."

Carla takes a deep breath. "I always suspected he carried a torch for me, to be honest. Or perhaps he just wanted to get his leg over one last time. But I've been married now for twenty years."

She stares at you defiantly, almost daring you to contradict her—but you don't have the evidence to do so.

- Write **C9** in your notebook, then turn to **144**

34

By now Jennifer has finished cleaning the skin around Alina's black eye. She gives the therapist a reassuring hug. "No broken skin, love."

Another member of staff, a yoga instructor judging by her outfit, arrives carrying a makeup bag, and proceeds to work on covering the massage therapist's injury.

"Did Harry Kennedy harass you as well, Alina?" you ask. "Is that why you reacted the way you did to Mrs. Kennedy's accusation just now?"

She sighs. "He was a no-good pig. I was glad he left early, so I didn't have to see him anymore. The handsome ones are sometimes the worst, you know."

- If you have T3 written in your notebook, turn to **140**
- Otherwise, turn to **173**

35

You instruct McAdam to pull over, and get out to look at the field. The fence runs along its full length beside the road, barring access. But the far side backs onto a livestock field, separated by a tall hedgerow . . . with a wooden stile cut through it.

It takes five minutes to walk to the livestock field, which you're relieved to see contains only sheep, no rampaging bulls or skittish horses. Despite this, McAdam is nervous and wary, staying close to you. The sheep scatter out of your way, retreating to watch from a safe distance.

"They're more scared of you than you are of them, Sergeant," you reassure her.

"Easy for you to say," she replies, stepping gingerly around sheep droppings.

You climb over the stile leading to the field on which Harry Kennedy wanted to build, pausing at the top to take in the lay of the land. Straightaway you notice that, despite much of the region's grassland having paled and begun to burn from weeks of baking hot weather, these fields remain lush and green, all but confirming it as a floodplain.

The sheep field is the highest point in the immediate area; the floodplain lies beyond at a lower elevation, and on the other side of the road the Burrowlands estate is lower again. Rain running from here will naturally collect in those lower areas. You're no expert, but it's easy to see that if the floodplain were built over with insufficient drainage, water from the higher field would roll straight over it and continue on to the estate instead.

Stepping down into the floodplain, you find the ground gives a little under your feet.

"Not as dried-out as we might have thought," you remark. "In wet seasons this probably turns into a bog."

Keeping to the relatively firm ground of the perimeter, you walk around the area. Long grass and tall wildflowers bloom across the field, especially in the wet center.

"Would have been a big job draining this and then building on it," McAdam says. "Never mind flooding the next estate, do it wrong and you'd be in subsidence hell. No job for an amateur, that's for sure."

"Indeed," you agree, "but perhaps one for a cowboy. This field is probably dirt cheap, for all of those reasons, which would have been attractive to Kennedy given his current money problems."

"Aye. Buy this for a song, drain it in the spring, then pave over everything and throw up some houses over the summer. You probably wouldn't notice anything wrong until a few years later."

She's right, but the first step would be gaining approval of the plan. Kennedy didn't have that, and didn't seem likely to get it any time soon.

"I think we've seen enough. Let's take a look around Burrowlands itself."

You climb back over the stile, passing still-curious sheep, and scrape the mud from your soles on a wooden post before returning to the car.

• Write **P2** in your notebook, then turn to **191**

"Fraud and blackmail," you say simply. "Floral therapy, with flowers grown here on-site, is Elysium's 'unique brand promise' as Stephen puts it. But he's been struggling to grow enough flowers because of the poor weather. Going without isn't an option, so instead he's been buying plants and precut flowers from a nursery, to pass off as his own."

Stephen says nothing, waiting for you to provide evidence.

You oblige. "We know this because we found an invoice from a local nursery, made out to Stephen personally so as to hide it from Elysium's accounts, for more than a thousand pounds' worth of plants and flowers." You turn to address the manager himself. "Our working theory is that Harry Kennedy found out about this fraud and was blackmailing you over it. That's why you gave him a free VIP stay at Elysium, and let him behave like a brat.

"But then you sensed an opportunity to rid yourself of this turbulent businessman. You weren't in the polytunnels yesterday morning at all. You were here in the house, and saw Harry leave Alina's session early. You lured him into the storeroom, then silenced him once and for all. The rose in his mouth was a poetic symbol of why Harry Kennedy had to die."

Constable Zwale holds up his phone, showing the photo he took of the invoice in Stephen's desk drawer.

"Hold on," the manager says. "You . . . sneaked into my office and searched through my drawers? Without asking permission? Did you even have a warrant?"

"It's a crime scene," McAdam says dismissively. "We don't need one."

"Actually, I'm pretty sure you do," Tank says from the crowd. "Besides, Harry wasn't killed in Stephen's office, was he? So that's not a crime scene."

The room devolves into heated arguments over whether or not a warrant was required; you ignore them and direct McAdam to arrest Stephen Cheong.

It's a decision that soon comes back to haunt you.

Tank is right that Stephen's office wasn't itself a crime scene. You did indeed need either a warrant or his permission to search it, but had neither. While you didn't personally direct Constable Zwale to undertake the search, you condoned it and even tried to use what he found against Stephen.

At the police station, his solicitor wastes no time pointing out that your case hinges on an illegal search. When you counter that you have other evidence, and can almost certainly find more now that you know where to look, the solicitor declares it all "fruit of the poisoned tree"—anything else you turn up is contaminated by this earlier illegal action. The prosecution adviser agrees, and you're left with no alternative but to release Stephen without charge.

Upon learning what's happened, your detective chief superintendent hauls you, McAdam, and Zwale over the coals for your careless and, frankly, corrupt behavior. You were so eager to make an arrest that you became willfully blind to the consequences of the actions you permitted, and let the actions of a senior officer exert a bad influence over a young constable. You may not have personally done anything illegal, but you were the senior investigating officer so the responsibility falls on your shoulders.

The superintendent not only removes you from the case, he places all three of you on suspension pending an inquiry. Harry Kennedy's murder may yet be solved . . . but not by you.

Later, you consider how things spiraled out of control. Surely the seeds of your mistake were planted early, when you let McAdam get away with illegally searching Flora's car. If you hadn't done that, Constable Zwale wouldn't have assumed you'd approve of him doing the same in Stephen's office.

Were you right to accuse Stephen, but undone by your own corruption? Or was the killer someone else altogether anyway?

- To find out, don't despair. Simply wipe your notebook (and your conscience), return to **1**, and try again.

For now, though, this is . . .

THE END

37

Of course, if Sergeant McAdam's suspicion is correct, and Jennifer took the missing key in order to kill Kennedy herself, she would naturally deny sleeping with him. If only you could find that key . . .

- Turn to **136**

38

"We know you were more than just friends," you say. "In fact you and Harry Kennedy were lovers, as you've already admitted to us."

A collective gasp goes up around the room.

"You, Carla?!" Flora Kennedy cries. "How could you? How could you?"

McAdam places a sympathetic hand on the widow's shoulder, as all eyes turn to Carla.

"No comment," the MP says, her lips pressed into a firm line.

"We don't need one," you say. "We know you and Harry Kennedy arranged to 'coincidentally' be here simultaneously, as a way to spend time together without your spouses knowing. In public you kept up a pretense of disliking each other so that nobody here would suspect. You even saw an opportunity to reinforce Flora's suspicion that Jennifer was the one sleeping with him."

"I told you it wasn't me," the receptionist says quietly.

"No, it wasn't. But you were another target in their plan, Ms. Watts. Sneaking around this house wasn't difficult thanks to the lack of security cameras, which also helped Carla steal the key to the storeroom."

Jennifer turns to the MP, aghast. "You did that? But how?"

"She's been here often enough to observe your routine, and know that 312 hasn't been used for a long time," you explain. "Carla watched to see where you stored your key ring every night, then used it to open the lockbox and steal the room key before giving it to Harry. When we first entered the room, I noticed the door handle operated smoothly and quietly—which is to be expected from a door used regularly, not one supposedly unopened for several years." You return to addressing Carla. "But something went awry. Did you think one of the staff might suspect what was going on and expose your affair? Or were you simply worried Harry would feel compelled to confess to Flora?"

"Where are you going with this nonsense?" Carla asks impatiently.

"To murder, Ms. Nesbitt. You knew that if your relationship with Kennedy was revealed you'd find yourself in the headlines for all the wrong reasons, fending off calls to resign. Depending on your husband's attitude toward such matters, you might also be facing divorce."

The MP regards you with contempt. "Do you really think I'd kill Harry for that? Why wouldn't I just tell him it's over?"

"Because then he'd have even less reason not to go public. He could even sell that story for a tidy sum to the press, which would go some way toward solving his cash-flow problems. So you took a break from your Tai Chi class, lured him into the storeroom, stabbed him, then shoved him off the balcony before returning to the lawn. Your DNA was found in the sink of room 312, presumably from where you washed off Kennedy's blood."

"That is a preposterous fantasy. I won't dignify it with a response."

"You don't have to. Sergeant, arrest Ms. Nesbitt."

• Turn to **196**

39

"Are you sure? Because we have a witness who saw you arguing with him in the corridor yesterday morning, not long before his body was found," you say. Tank glares at you, wide-eyed with anger. "In fact, you may have been the last person to see Harry Kennedy alive."

Tank seethes with suppressed rage, and given his physique you can't help wondering how easily he could overpower someone.

"That bloody therapist, isn't it?" he says.

"You were seen chasing after him," you reply, ignoring his question. "Not something that would easily slip one's mind."

He takes a deep breath to control his anger. "Yes, all right. I told you, I wanted my gym gear back. That hydration vessel was *very* expensive, and he wasn't using it."

You exchange a look with McAdam. "We didn't find anything like that in Mr. Kennedy's room, did we, Sergeant?"

"Definitely not." She turns back to Tank. "If that's all you were arguing about when he told you to get lost, why did you claim not to have seen him?"

"Because I knew you'd think it meant I did Harry in," Tank sneers. "I've dealt with you lot before. No imagination."

"If you were lending him your possessions, you must have been friends," you suggest. "It seems unlikely you'd do that for someone you barely knew."

"I'm a generous spirit," he says defiantly.

• If you have T3 written in your notebook, turn to **127**
• Otherwise, turn to **161**

40

While McAdam goes upstairs to search the victim's room, you walk to the reception desk and ask Jennifer to access Harry Kennedy's timetable.

"He bought our Lotus package," she says. "Is there anything in particular you're looking for?"

"I'd just like to see what he'd attended so far, and what he was due to attend. What's the Lotus package?"

"All of Elysium's options are named for plants. Lotus Flower is our VIP package, allowing Friends to personalize their timetable and choose their sessions in the moment, with priority access."

"Priority access? So he could decide at the last moment to, say, attend a yoga session, and even if it was full you'd be obliged to fit him in?"

"That's right. For our best Friends, we accommodate every need." Jennifer says this with a bright smile that doesn't quite reach her eyes.

This means Kennedy's schedule isn't so much a timetable as a record of where his fancy took him at any given time. That could be very useful.

"How much does the Lotus Flower package cost, out of interest?"

"Nine thousand per week," Jennifer says without hesitation. "With payment due in advance."

For a moment you're speechless, which is probably just as well given what you might say otherwise. If the victim could afford that kind of expense on a whim, his financial records should make for fascinating reading.

"Which sessions did Mr. Kennedy choose to make the most of his stay?"

Jennifer scans her computer screen.

"Let me see . . . a lot of massage therapy. That's always popular. Several pollinated baths. One corollic yoga session, early in the week, but no more after that. Same goes for plant Pilates, homeopathy class, floral swim, Tai Chi on the lawn . . . just one session of each."

"Does that mean he tried them, but didn't like them?"

The receptionist shrugs. "It might. With Lotus Friends we only offer scheduling guidance if they request it. Otherwise we let them choose as they wish. Let's see, what else . . . several meditative aromatherapy sessions. He reserved the tennis courts a few times. Everything else was personal leisure time."

"What does that mean?"

"That he didn't take part in an arranged session. Many of our Friends like to take a walk around the gardens or relax in a hot tub when they're not in a timetabled period. Some of our group bookings get together and play cards, that sort of thing."

You wonder if this was a dead end after all. Perhaps you should have searched Kennedy's room instead. But there's something odd about him coming here in the first place, then paying all that money but not using his stay to the fullest. Besides, in your experience, tracking a victim's movements is often the key to solving their murder.

"Did he book a tennis court for yesterday evening? Around seven o'clock?"

"Oh, there's no need that late in the day. Not many people play after dinner."

"How about this morning? He had a massage session from ten till eleven, but where was he due to be afterward?"

Jennifer checks the schedule and shakes her head. "Nowhere. That session with Alina was his only appointment today."

"Is that unusual? Even for a 'Lotus Friend'?"

She shrugs. "Mr. Kennedy was rather, um, spontaneous. There were several occasions when I had to find last-minute massage therapists for him."

Spontaneous . . . or impulsive? Could that be part of an explanation for why Kennedy was in the storeroom?

Jennifer gives you a printout of Kennedy's schedule, confirming everything she told you.

- Write **J4** in your notebook
- If you already have A2 written down, turn to **150**
- If you have T6 written down, turn to **86**
- Otherwise, turn to **16**

41

"Isn't it obvious?" you say. "Harry Kennedy was killed by someone most of the people here never even think about. Someone who can come and go as she pleases unnoticed because she's a permanent fixture: Jennifer Watts."

"But that's not true!" she protests. "I mean, OK, it's true people don't notice me. But I didn't kill Harry. I had no reason to."

Constable Zwale looks as shocked as everyone else in the crowd. "She's right," he says, "Jennifer had no motive to kill Harry Kennedy. You must be wrong."

"Be quiet, Constable!" McAdam barks.

This is why you didn't dare share your suspicion with Zwale. He's clearly become fond of Jennifer over the past couple of days.

"I'm sorry, Constable, but I believe she did. Allow me to explain . . ."

Do you have the evidence you need to make a successful accusation? Check your notebook for clues in the following order:

- If you have J2 or J5 written down, turn to **176**
- If you have J3 written down, turn to **115**
- Otherwise, turn to **11**

42

"All right, Constable, get him out of there," you order. "Now!"

Zwale dives into the rushing water without hesitation. Whatever the young officer's faults, there's no questioning his bravery.

Tank continues struggling against the current, barely a quarter of the way across the river but expending all his energy merely to stay afloat and keep his head above water. With powerful strokes, Constable Zwale reaches the tech mogul and immediately wraps an arm around him, positioning both men on their backs. Rather than fight against the current Zwale lets it carry them downstream, focusing his strength on returning to the bank of the swollen river. You and McAdam keep pace, jogging alongside them as, inch by inch, the constable brings them closer.

Finally, they're close enough for you to help. Abandoning umbrellas to the wind, you take McAdam's hand in yours while she reaches out with the other for Zwale and Tank, clutching at the constable's shirt. Working together, you drag both men to the riverbank. Zwale pushes Tank ahead of him, leaving McAdam to pull the half-drowned man from the water while the constable hauls himself out.

Tank retches and vomits water onto the grass. Zwale doubles over, hands on knees, gasping for air. You make a mental note to ensure he's recognized for his actions today.

At this moment, though, the more urgent task is to get Tank and yourselves out of the rain. With McAdam and Zwale supporting Tank, you all stagger back to the house and up the steps, collapsing inside the entrance lobby.

Jennifer Watts immediately takes an armful of towels from her clean stack and hands them out. You receive one with thanks, though it'll take more than a towel to dry out your sodden clothing.

"I'll try to get that generator going. Don't worry about me, Joseph," she says to Constable Zwale. "I'll be fine on my own."

As McAdam, Zwale, and you all towel off, you address Tank. "Suppose you tell us who the devil you were running from? You said 'he' would get you next?"

"Stephen Cheong, of course," Tank replies between shivered, gasping breaths. "He killed Harry . . . and now he's after me to clean up the loose ends . . . First he cut the power, then . . . he came after me with a hammer . . . You have to arrest him!"

"Hold on there, slow down," McAdam says gently. "Are you saying Stephen attacked you?"

"He tried to . . . I came out of my room, and Stephen ran . . . down the corridor at me holding a hammer . . . that's why I scarpered!"

A crowd is beginning to gather around you, curious to know what happened. Constable Zwale stands, taking the initiative, and asks them to move back. He tells them it's to give Tank some recovery room, but he makes sure everyone is far enough away to be out of earshot.

McAdam looks skeptically at Tank. "Can you explain why Stephen would attack you?"

The tech mogul brings his breathing under control, then sighs. "Because only Harry and I know that Stephen's been buying flowers and plants from a local nursery, but telling everyone they're home-grown. Harry asked me to keep an eye on him, and I saw it with my own eyes! Stephen's a rotten fraud. That's why Harry got a freebie, and I was upgraded, because he threatened to tell you lot otherwise. But Stephen killed him to shut him up, and I'm next," he wails.

"But why would Stephen deliberately cut the power?"

"I don't know, ask him," Tank replies. "If you can find him. He's insane!"

"More importantly," you say, "how did Harry know about the fraud? By all accounts, he'd never set foot in this place before. What led him to suspect Stephen lied about the flowers? Did you tell him?"

Tank looks confused. "No, I had no idea. It was a couple of months ago, while we were negotiating our mutual investments. Harry mentioned Stephen out of the blue, and said next time I stayed here I should watch him, and follow him if he took the van out. Sure enough, two o'clock in the morning he sneaked out. Didn't want a soul to see him. But I did. Now are you going to arrest him, or what?"

"I don't think his flower antics are really our domain."

"Not that, you idiot! He killed Harry, and tried to attack me!"

That was loud enough to be heard by the gathered onlookers. They begin to whisper, wondering who he's talking about. You decide to nip this in the bud.

"Mr. Destroyer . . . what you saw was Stephen Cheong rushing to repair the hole in the roof. He nailed a temporary piece of board over it to keep the rain out. He wasn't running *at* you with a hammer; he was running *past* you with a hammer."

Tank regards you with suspicion. "I still think he killed Harry," he says quietly.

"That's your prerogative, I suppose. But you also have questions of your own to answer."

- Write **S2** in your notebook, then check your other notes in the following order:
- If you have F5 written down, turn to **146**
- If you have T7 written down, turn to **112**
- Otherwise, turn to **170**

43

McAdam puts away her phone. "The very helpful real estate agent confirms all four houses are owned by a single company, called . . . Standard Umbrella."

"Carla Nesbitt's company. The same one to which Kennedy Homes recently made a large payment. Now isn't that interesting?"

Why is Carla so keen to sell the houses? Do they also have leaking windows, and she wants to get rid of them? Or is she looking to turn a profit? Not that those reasons are mutually exclusive. Prices in this country only ever seem to rise, and the MP wouldn't be the first or last landlord to sell up and take the money.

These questions, not to mention asking what the payment from Kennedy was actually for, are matters you can put to the MP next time you see her. For now, though, it's time to move on. You wanted to see Burrowlands with your own eyes, and you've satisfied that curiosity.

- **Add 1** to your LOCATION number, then turn to **30**

“Are you sure? Because we have a witness who saw you arguing with him in the corridor this morning, not long before his body was found.” Tank glares at you, wide-eyed with anger. “In fact, Mr. Destroyer, you may have been the last person to see Harry Kennedy alive.”

Tank seethes with suppressed rage, and given his physique you can’t help wondering how easily he could overpower someone.

“That bloody therapist, isn’t it?” he says.

“You were seen chasing after him,” you reply, ignoring the question. “Not something that would easily slip one’s mind.”

He takes a deep breath to control his anger. “Yes, all right. I wanted that gym gear back. I told you, it’s expensive and he wasn’t using it.”

McAdam obviously doesn’t believe him. “Really? If that’s all you were arguing about when he told you to get lost, why tell us you hadn’t seen him?”

“Because I knew you’d think it meant I did him in,” Tank sneers. “And I was right, wasn’t I? I’ve dealt with you lot before, you know. No imagination.”

That would have been quick thinking, considering that until two minutes ago Tank thought Kennedy had killed himself. Is that due to his sharp computer-whiz mind . . . or is he simply lying? Either way, it doesn’t seem like you’ll get any more information from him at this time.

“Thank you, that’s all for now,” you say, turning to leave. Then you pause and ask: “Actually, there is one more thing, if you’ll forgive my curiosity. What prompted your choice of the new name?”

A sly smile forms on Tank’s face as he gathers his yoga mat and vine cuttings.

“Long story. Let’s just say it involves a bachelor party with some old school chums, a decommissioned tank range in Dorset, and a little too much champagne.”

McAdam snorts. “How the other half lives, eh?”

You thank Tank for his time and let him return to the class next door.

- Write **T6** and **T8** in your notebook
- If you've already questioned either Alina or Carla, turn to **120**

Otherwise, choose one of them to interview:

- To question Alina the massage therapist, turn to **48**
- To question Carla the MP, turn to **177**

45

"If Carla and Kennedy met here secretly," you wonder aloud, "how would they have found any time alone?"

"What do you mean?" McAdam asks.

"We know Harry Kennedy hardly attended any classes apart from massage sessions, where the presence of a therapist would stymie any secret activity. But whenever he and Carla encountered each other around the house or grounds, they traded insults—presumably to maintain the illusion that their relationship was fractious, and being here simultaneously was a coincidence."

She considers this. "Out of hours, perhaps? The guests stay on-site, so maybe they waited till everyone else was asleep before meeting up."

"Bedroom visits would be risky, even in the early hours. Where could—?" Then the answer strikes you. "Of course. The disused store-room. There were the sheets on the floor, remember."

McAdam nods. "Did Kennedy himself somehow have the key to 312?"

"Perhaps. A room like that, supposedly never used and permanently locked, would make an ideal place for secret meetings."

You resolve to confront Carla with these questions the next time you talk to her.

- Now return to **100**, and skip to the end of that section

46

"I've made up my mind," you say. "We'll collect the CCTV evidence now, then visit Elysium later and confront Flora Kennedy with it. We can check on the parcel at the same time."

McAdam grumbles, but drives away in the direction of the police station. Halfway there, though, you receive another call from Constable Zwale.

"What is it, Constable?" you say, answering.

"Inspector—I'm sorry, it's—I couldn't stop her . . ." He sounds even more panicked than before.

"Calm down. What's happened?"

Zwale exhales loudly. "We've just arrested Flora Kennedy. For assault, and possible manslaughter."

McAdam slams on the brakes, pulling the car over to the side of the road.

"Manslaughter? What the hell happened?" she asks.

"The parcel, ma'am. Turns out it was a batch of mail-order Viagra. Flora lost it, accused Stephen Cheong of running a brothel, and they argued . . . Then she attacked him, and he slipped and smacked his head on the reception desk."

You picture the scene in your mind, recalling the shaped marble of the desk in the lobby.

"Call an ambulance, Constable. Immediately."

"I already did, just in case," he says with a heavy sigh. "But I called Dr. Wash, too. There's . . . there's a lot of blood."

McAdam is already turning the car around, activating the "blues and twos"—flashing blue lights concealed behind the car's front grille and an accompanying police siren. You barely hear it; you feel faintly nauseous, replaying your decision to leave things in Zwale's hands over and over in your mind. The constable is still talking on the phone, but his voice sounds muffled and distant.

McAdam is an excellent driver, and even in the wet conditions you arrive at Elysium less than half an hour later, parking next to an ambulance. You dash up the front steps and into the lobby, where uniformed officers have set up a cordon to keep onlookers at bay. The paramedics are already preparing to leave. At your inquiring look, one of them shakes his head.

Dr. Wash and a photographer step around the body of Stephen Cheong, lying prone on the lobby floor.

With so many witnesses to what happened, Flora Kennedy's conviction in the weeks that follow is a foregone conclusion. Your fate, however, remains undecided.

The detective chief superintendent reprimands you for leaving a volatile situation in the hands of a young constable, something McAdam warned you wasn't a good idea. You're confined to your desk while an inquiry is held into the matter, and another inspector is called in to take over the Elysium case.

Harry Kennedy's murder may yet be solved . . . but not by you.

- You can now wipe your notebook, return to **1**, and try again.

For now, though, this is . . .

THE END

47

You read the decoded message again, wondering what it could mean.

"Three weeks ago, an anonymous person sent Harry Kennedy a message about a 'flower boy' buying four pallets of . . . something . . . from a nursery."

"Presumably not children," McAdam quips.

You frown at her off-color humor. "Don't give up your day job, Sergeant. No, the obvious answer is flowers. And 'trying to be invisible' implies whoever it was didn't want to be seen."

You both ponder this for a moment, before realization hits you.

"Remember the invoice that Constable Zwale found in Stephen Cheong's office? It was from Green Fingers Nursery."

"Flower Boy," McAdam says, understanding. "Someone saw Stephen buying flowers, ready to pass them off as his own. But why would anyone be watching him in the first place? They'd have had to suspect something was up."

"I'm sure they did. Look at the first part of the message again."

"'You were right,'" she reads. "Of course. It suggests Kennedy had his suspicions, and asked this anonymous sender to keep an eye out."

"Not only that, but asked them to encode the message upon sending, ensuring nobody else could read it." You recap what you now know. "Stephen Cheong has been secretly buying in flowers and passing them off to guests as his own. Somehow Kennedy came to suspect this, and had someone watch Stephen. Sure enough, they observed him making a big purchase at the nursery and texted Kennedy to let him know. That gives him a hold over Stephen, something that could very easily turn into threats or blackmail. It might explain why Stephen gave Kennedy the Lotus package for free."

"Blackmail, eh? One of the oldest motives for murder you'll find. Like I said before, we're all carrying secrets. There isn't much a person won't do to protect them, especially when his livelihood's at stake."

That's true. Could Stephen have killed Kennedy to prevent his secret from being revealed?

"One question left to answer, then," McAdam says. "Who sent this text?"

"Actually, Sergeant, I think there are two questions. The identity of the anonymous sender is certainly one. The other is, how come this message was sent three weeks ago?"

She looks confused. "I don't follow."

"Harry Kennedy had never been here before, and by all accounts wasn't normally one for wellness retreats in the first place. How did he even know who Stephen Cheong was, let alone suspect him of lying? And why would he care?"

"I've no idea. Go on."

You laugh. "That's just it, I don't know either. But hopefully we can find out . . ."

• Write **S7** in your notebook, then return to **100** and skip to the end of that section

48

A passing member of staff directs you to the break room, in the non-public area of the ground floor. You enter to find a plain and utilitarian room of tables and benches that, you note with interest, is completely free of flowers. Evidently the blessings of floral healing don't extend to the staff, and by the looks of things neither does the maintenance budget. Paint peels from the room corners, while the dinged and scratched furniture has seen better days.

You find Alina sitting in a corner and sipping coffee. She's slim and quietly spoken, with a stillness interrupted only when she tucks a stray dark hair behind her ear or sips her coffee. You and Sergeant McAdam introduce yourselves and sit with her to gently ask questions.

Alina tells you she's originally from Romania, where she trained as a massage therapist. She came to England five years ago, with her younger sister Roxana following soon after and eventually marrying an Englishman. Alina has been working here at Elysium for three years.

"Are you also married?" you ask. "Do you have a family who can take care of you after today?"

Alina shakes her head. "Roxana is my family. We look after each other."

Not wanting to press further, you let the subject pass and move on.

"Mr. Kennedy had a session with you this morning, is that right?"

"Yes, from ten till eleven. But he left early, at half past, because he had a phone call."

"You mean someone called him during the session? So he had his phone with him?"

She shakes her head. "No. I mean, yes, he had his phone. I never saw him without it, you know? But he just said he had to go."

"I wonder why he didn't just book you for half an hour. Why waste an appointment like that?"

Alina shrugs. "It made no difference to him. His package is all-inclusive, so he lost nothing by leaving early."

Perhaps not, but booking a full session with no intention of using it may have denied someone else an appointment. It suggests Kennedy had a selfish streak. You wonder how much that package costs.

"Did you see Mr. Kennedy again after he left?" you ask.

"Only when he went into the corridor. I saw the tattoo man, Tank, chase after him."

"You mean Tank Destroyer? Chasing after him, you say?" Stephen said the tech mogul and Harry Kennedy were friends. Tank may have been the last person to see the victim alive.

"Yes. He called to him, and they talked. I didn't hear what, but Mr. Kennedy didn't want it, you know?"

"I'm a simple woman, Ms. Martinescu," McAdam says, "so I'm confused. Why didn't you try to persuade Mr. Kennedy to finish his session?"

"It's not my place," Alina says. "Stephen wants us to call them Friends because the house is theirs while they stay. They come and go, you know?"

"So if you didn't go after him, what did you do with that spare half-hour?"

The therapist looks worried. "I—I stayed in my room and took a break. I didn't want Stephen to know."

"It's hardly your fault if a client leaves early, though, is it?" McAdam says.

"No, of course," Alina replies quickly. "But I should have told Jennifer I was free to see someone else. Stephen likes us to always be working, for the house to be busy. It's expensive to run."

You suspect the key to repeat business is letting people like Harry Kennedy do whatever they want rather than drag people into sessions they're not interested in, but maybe Stephen Cheong knows different.

"Is there anything else you can think of? Did Mr. Kennedy say or do anything odd during your session? Besides leaving early."

Alina shakes her head. "No, sorry. It was just a massage, you know? I didn't see him again until . . . Stephen was shouting. Then we all saw him, on the ground."

The therapist doesn't seem to know any more, so you leave her in the break room.

- Write **A5** in your notebook
- If you've already questioned either Carla or Tank, turn to **120**

Otherwise, choose one of them to interview:

- To question Carla the MP, turn to **177**
- To question Tank the tech mogul, turn to **73**

49

"It wasn't a question of need," you say. "It was a question of desire . . . both unrequited and illicit."

Understandably, that grabs the attention of the assembled crowd. Everyone leans forward a little.

"The illicit desire was between Harry Kennedy and Carla Nesbitt. Previously young lovers, they'd secretly rekindled their spark and arranged to 'coincidentally' stay here at Elysium at the same time. We even have a text message between them as evidence of this arrangement."

A collective gasp goes up around the room.

You continue: "The unrequited desire, on the other hand, was Flora Kennedy's. Why else seek a divorce, but for the oldest reason there is? She discovered her husband was unfaithful, and to make things worse, the other woman was someone Flora herself knew."

Flora scowls at Carla Nesbitt, who reddens.

"Is it true?" Flora says. The MP remains silent.

"Don't pretend you didn't know, Mrs. Kennedy," McAdam growls. "That's why you killed your husband, isn't it? You found out he was sleeping with his old flame, and the green-eyed monster did the rest."

"But I swear I didn't know Harry was here. Besides, how could I have got here without being seen? Check the CCTV cameras in town—they'll show me driving home from my solicitor's office."

McAdam nods. "They do . . . before you divert to come in this direction. There's a ten-minute gap until you return on camera, at which point you're heading away from the manor and back to your house."

"Well, I took a scenic route," Flora says, close to tears. "I had a lot on my mind. But none of it involved killing Harry! I didn't know he was sleeping with . . . her." She spits out the last word like an insult, and Carla flinches.

"I don't think so," you say. "The CCTV puts you close by, with enough time to sneak through the house—where there are no cameras at all—and kill your husband, before returning to your car and driving home."

Finally, Carla Nesbitt speaks up. "That sounds like a lot of effort, Inspector. Does Flora really look like a woman who'd do that? No offense, Flora," she adds.

"Still waters run deep, Ms. Nesbitt. Earlier today, Mrs. Kennedy climbed out of a window to escape confinement. And the more unlikely the plan, the better chance it won't cast suspicion."

Flora Kennedy moans quietly and bursts into tears. You're not convinced they're any more real than her alibi.

"Also, there's the matter of the rose placed in the victim's mouth. A flower . . . or should I say *flora*."

The widow sniffles. "You can't possibly think that points to me. Why . . . why would I leave a clue like that?"

"Some criminals subconsciously want to be arrested and punished," you say. "And I'm happy to oblige. Sergeant, arrest Mrs. Kennedy."

• Turn to **172**

50

Something stirred in your brain when you rescued the printouts from falling to the floor, and now you realize what it was.

"Can I see those houses for sale again?" you ask.

Ms. Gibbs passes them to you, smiling. "Looking to buy after all?"

"I'm afraid not . . . but they do look familiar. Where are they situated?"

"Oh, those are on Burrowlands. Four of them, all for sale at a very reasonable price. I'm sure they'll move before long."

Just as you thought. They're the same houses you saw for sale earlier. You also notice they've been on sale long enough that the asking price has already been lowered twice.

"You're aware Mr. Kennedy wanted to build his new estate next to Burrowlands."

"Did he?" Ms. Gibbs looks unimpressed. "Like I said, Mummy hasn't mentioned it to me. I'm sure she would have if it was relevant. You said yourself, there's very little about her life of which I'm not aware."

You have no reason to doubt that, but the secretary's tone is growing defensive.

McAdam picks up the thread, laying on a little more flattery. "So in addition to running your mother's company while she's in Parliament, she also trusts you to handle her properties? That's a lot of responsibility."

"It is," Ms. Gibbs says, sitting a little straighter. "We outsource day-to-day management of tenants, of course. Standard Umbrella isn't a letting company. But there's always maintenance to take care of, not to mention buying and selling."

"What sort of relationship does Standard Umbrella have with Kennedy Homes?"

Ms. Gibbs looks momentarily disgusted. "None at all. Mummy sometimes buys houses Mr. Kennedy builds, but that's the extent of it."

"Thank you, Ms. Gibbs. Just one more question: Where were you between ten and eleven this morning?"

"At my gym, and before you ask, a dozen other people can confirm that for you." At your surprised expression, she shrugs. "I'm no fool, Inspector. Why else would you ask?"

You thank her and leave, returning to McAdam's car. This feels like a significant breakthrough.

"Standard Umbrella, eh?" the sergeant says, making notes. "So now we know who Kennedy paid that seven grand to. What kind of consultancy would Carla Nesbitt be doing for him?"

"I doubt it was any kind of consultancy at all," you say. "The question is, what *was* it for? Hush money, perhaps? Or an incentive to do something on his behalf?"

"Aye, like convince the council to approve the plans . . . except we know she didn't do that."

McAdam is right. There's obviously a connection here, but too many links remain missing.

"Double-check Sharon Gibbs's alibi, then find out what you can about Standard Umbrella and its history. It might be interesting to know how many Kennedy Homes properties Ms. Nesbitt has bought before, for example."

"There's a thought. If she wanted to buy something on the new estate, though, why tell Kennedy to get knotted?"

"We only have her word for it that she did," you point out.

- Write **C1** in your notebook, and **add 1** to your LOCATION number. Then turn to **30.**

51

McAdam pauses.

"Should I call the council as well, do you think? See what was going on with that housing estate scheme the victim was involved in?"

"Good idea. Contact the planning department and find out if Carla Nesbitt really was blocking those plans." You think about what that could mean. "It may not be connected, because if Kennedy was sufficiently angry about that I'd expect him to be a killer, not the victim. Nevertheless, there's still so much we don't know at this stage. Learning about his business plans might give us a better picture of the man himself."

McAdam nods and begins making calls.

- Write **C7** in your notebook, then turn to **162**

52

Your thoughts return to blackmail. You already know that Harry Kennedy learned Stephen Cheong was buying in flowers to pass them off as grown on-site, and that Harry got Tank Destroyer involved, too. Now, hearing Carla Nesbitt talk about it, you realize this could be how Kennedy came to suspect the manager in the first place.

What you know about Kennedy suggests he probably wasn't above indulging in a spot of blackmail. If he had Stephen Cheong over a barrel, it would explain how he was able to book a place despite Elysium being busy, and why he was given the Lotus package for free.

Most importantly, it would give the manager a powerful motive to protect his business by silencing Kennedy. Perhaps permanently.

• Write **S6** in your notebook, then turn to **25**

You address Sergeant McAdam and Constable Zwale. "Take Mrs. Kennedy to the waiting room we used before and see what sense you can get out of her. Remind her that we have grounds to charge her with assault. That might give you some leverage."

The constable and sergeant lead Flora away, while you dash after Jennifer and Alina.

For a moment you fear you've lost them, but then you see their figures through a gap in the dispersing crowd, heading toward the staff area. You follow them into the break room, marveling again at the contrast between the flower-filled public areas and this stark, nondescript room with peeling paint. Jennifer guides Alina to a table with benches on either side, where they're joined by another female member of staff.

"Are you going to arrest her?" asks Jennifer when she sees you enter behind them. "Because it didn't sound like you were." She walks to the kitchenette area, takes a first aid kit from inside a cupboard, then returns to the table and tends to Alina's rapidly darkening black eye with antiseptic wipes.

"Would that satisfy you?" you ask. "It won't heal that injury."

"That's not the point," the other staffer says, scowling at you. "She's dangerous. She probably killed Mr. Kennedy, and now she's attacking us, too!"

Alina winces from the wipe's antiseptic sting. "I don't want to cause trouble. I shouldn't have said what I did."

"Rubbish," Jennifer says. "Don't start blaming yourself. She's the one who threw a punch. All you did was tell the truth."

You stay at the opposite end of the bench, trying to remain casual.

"You didn't mention Harry Kennedy had wandering hands before," you say to Jennifer.

She shrugs. "Didn't seem important. He's dead, so he can't do any more harm now. But ask any of the female staff; he was handsy like a bloody octopus. Look at that timetable I gave you. All his appointments were with different women because he burned through the Roses like tissue paper."

"And what about you, Ms. Watts? Did he . . . ?"

The receptionist laughs bitterly. "Only once. I told him where to get off."

"Did you report Mr. Kennedy's behavior to Stephen?"

The other staffer sighs. "What's the point? The rich clients do whatever they like, and because he's desperate for their money Stephen does nothing about it. It's just part of the job."

"Then why not work somewhere else? Surely it's not like this at every wellness retreat?"

All three women look at you with the same silent, skeptical expression.

- Write **J5** in your notebook
- To ask Alina if Kennedy also harassed her, turn to **34**
- To ask about Elysium's financial troubles, turn to **194**

54

"One other thing I do have is a result from that key you found," Dr. Wash adds.

You're surprised. "I didn't even realize that had been returned to the lab. The constable I gave it to must have just made it out before the storm."

"Well, we can move fast when we need to. The key had been washed before being placed in the soil where you found it, but some traces of blood remained. I haven't had time to do a DNA test, but I can confirm that the traces match Harry Kennedy's blood type."

"Just like the blood on Stephen's clothes."

"Indeed."

That suggests the key was either on Kennedy's person when he was killed, or—more likely—handled by his killer after the fact, and then washed in the storeroom sink. Was that killer Stephen Cheong? He's the only suspect who had Kennedy's blood on him.

• Turn to **100**

55

You flip through your notebook, making connections.

"So not only did Mr. Kennedy recently pay you seven thousand pounds, but he did so while you were having a secret affair. I can understand why you'd want to keep the matter quiet."

"I knew nothing about that payment," she says haughtily. "I wasn't even aware of it until Sharon informed me it had been deposited. I've already ordered her to return it on the company's next payment run."

"It's billed as a consultancy fee," you say, pressing the matter. "For what, I wonder? We already know you don't approve of Kennedy's plan to build on the floodplain next to Burrowlands—where, let us not forget, you own several properties—and you refused to intervene on his behalf with the council planning department. So what exactly were you being consulted on?"

"I've already told you: nothing. Anyway, I doubt anything will happen on that field now. Flora will probably sell the company off as soon as the will is executed."

"Would that displease you?" McAdam asks. "Its new owners might not be inclined to give you a few grand in bribes."

Carla shoots daggers at the sergeant. "I've done nothing wrong."

- Turn to **93**

56

You read the decoded message and ponder what it means. Check your notebook in the following order:

- If you have P1 written down, turn to **31**
- If you have P6 written down, turn to **78**
- If you have S1 written down, turn to **121**
- If you have T6 written down, turn to **195**
- Otherwise, turn to **105**

57

You ask Jennifer where you can find Alina. She checks her computer. "Alina's in 208—that's her usual therapy room—but she's with a Friend."

"When will Ms. Martinescu be free?" you ask.

Jennifer checks the timetable. "She's booked up for the rest of the morning, and all afternoon, too. You'll have to catch her at lunchtime."

"I'd rather not. Remind us where to find room 208, if you'd be so kind."

"I told you, she's with a client."

"And the inspector told you we don't want to wait," McAdam growls. There's no denying her attack-dog nature can be useful sometimes.

Jennifer reluctantly gives you directions. The first-floor rooms you pass are generally wide and airy, with large windows—no doubt very pleasant on a summer's day, but somewhat gloomier now, with rain clattering furiously against the glass. The second-floor rooms are smaller, their doors closed by default for privacy.

You find 208 and knock, then enter without waiting. A man lies face down on a massage table, wearing only jogging bottoms, with small round stones placed on his bare back. Alina stands over him holding a pair of metal tongs. Behind her you see more stones, all rounded and polished, sitting on a small heater. The high-ceilinged room is dimly lit by lamps, with no windows allowing daylight. An abundance of plants and flowers line the walls, making it feel cramped.

Alina looks up in surprise and says, "I'm busy. I'll talk to you later." Although the bruise from Flora's earlier punch has been covered well with makeup, you can see a slight swelling around the therapist's eye.

"I'm afraid that's not possible," you say. "Please step outside so we can talk. Your Friend looks very comfortable. I'm sure he can wait for a few minutes."

"No," Alina insists, placing her hands on her hips. "I'm telling you, I'm busy. Ask Jennifer to make an appointment."

The man on the massage table raises his head to look you and Sergeant McAdam up and down, then grunts. "Police, is it? It's never 'a few minutes' with you lot—*aaaah*!"

The man hisses in pain, startling Alina. Using the tongs, she quickly removes the stones from his back and apologizes.

"See!" she says to you angrily. "You're distracting me. You should wait till I've finished."

"I think maybe we already are," the man says, grimacing in pain. Pushing himself upright, he takes a bathrobe from a hook, wraps it around himself, then shoves past you to leave.

But before he stood up, you saw that two of the stones had left small, circular red marks on his back. You and McAdam share a look. She closes the door as you begin to question the therapist.

"Alina," you say, "we found three burns on Mr. Kennedy's body, all in a row down his spine. I was baffled as to what could have caused them, but now it seems quite obvious they were from hot stones. Did you cause them?"

"Anyone could have done that to him," she says defensively.

"Our pathologist has determined they were made shortly before his death, and his only appointment yesterday was with you."

The therapist exhales, her shoulders sagging. "All right, yes. It was an accident. But it was just a small burn, I promise. It didn't kill him."

- Write **A4** in your notebook, then check it in the following order:
- If you already have A1 written down, turn to **21**
- If you already have A8 written down, turn to **108**
- Otherwise, turn to **119**

58

You reach out and remove the central plant blocking your view of Carla, placing it on the floor.

"Shortly before he died, Harry Kennedy paid seven thousand pounds in consultancy fees to a firm with which he'd never previously done business: Standard Umbrella. I understand you're familiar with them?"

Carla eyes you carefully. You can almost see cogs whirring behind her eyes as she tries to guess how much you already know. Finally, she counters your question with another question.

"What makes you think I know anything about it?"

"Perhaps because you haven't been entirely truthful with us about your relationship with Mr. Kennedy." Her eyes widen in surprise. "We know you're a landlord with many properties, including several on the Burrowlands estate that you're now trying to offload in a quick sale. Houses that, if Kennedy's new plan had been approved, would be in the path of that potential flooding you told us about. How many of the properties you own were originally purchased from Kennedy Homes?"

This is a gamble, because McAdam hasn't yet had a chance to look into Carla's property business. But you're confident it will pay off . . . and it does.

"Maybe a dozen, over the years," Carla says at last. "Harry had many faults, but he knew a good development site when he saw one."

"Apart from the floodplain next to Burrowlands, presumably. Standard Umbrella is your company, isn't it? You know we can just call Companies House to check your firm's records if need be."

Carla pauses to take a swig from her water bottle.

"Mine and my husband's. We use it to manage the property portfolio, among other things."

"Such as?"

"I make many public appearances, Inspector," she says dismissively. "I'm in demand."

"I'll say. So let me ask you again, and this time I'd appreciate an answer. Why did Mr. Kennedy pay you seven thousand pounds?"

- Turn to **82**

You look around the room, wondering if there's anything else to find.

- If you have T8 written in your notebook, turn to **104**
- Otherwise, turn to **7**

You nod in approval. "Well done for showing good initiative, Sergeant. This is valuable information that could help uncover other leads in the case." You turn to Zwale and ask pointedly, "Don't you agree, Constable?"

Zwale's disagreement is written all over his face. You understand; he's young and keen, wanting to make a good impression. But everyone knows a little rule-bending now and again is simply how police work gets done. He grudgingly acquiesces to your authority.

"Yes, of course," he mumbles. "I understand."

Sergeant McAdam nods, satisfied.

• Write **P12** in your notebook, then turn to **139**

61

The room waits for you to explain why you accused Alina . . . but the truth is, you're not sure yourself. You feel confident she did it, but you have no real evidence to back up your assertion, or suggest what her motive was. You have your suspicions, but without evidence they're just speculation.

Perhaps you hoped that accusing Alina would cause her to spontaneously confess, but if so it hasn't worked.

The moment drags on, until McAdam clears her throat. You tell her to arrest Alina, with a promise that once the massage therapist is in custody at the police station you'll explain your reasoning. Disappointed, the crowd disperses from the room, whispering doubts about your deductive skills.

• Turn to **154**

62

Burrowlands is a half-hour drive through town, and you sit in gridlock twice during the journey. Sergeant McAdam insists it's the shortest route and would take even longer if you circumvented the town.

When you finally break out of the traffic and approach the estate, you first pass a wide, flat field of tall grass and wildflowers, elevated slightly from the road and closed off by a chain-link fence. A sign attached to it informs you that the land is under offer. It doesn't mention Kennedy Homes, but this must be where Harry wanted to build his new estate.

"Almost there," McAdam reassures you.

"So I see," you murmur. "In fact, I was just thinking it might be helpful to take a quick look at where Mr. Kennedy wanted to build. It's right here."

"The floodplain? If you want to take a wander, now's the time. Not much danger of needing wellies at the moment, but there's rain forecast for tomorrow."

- To take a diversion and look at the floodplain, turn to **35**
- To continue directly on to Burrowlands, turn to **191**

The room waits for you to explain why you accused Carla . . . but the truth is, you're not sure yourself. You feel confident she did it, but you have no real evidence to back up your assertion, or suggest what her motive was. You have your suspicions, but without evidence they're just speculation.

Perhaps you hoped that accusing Carla would cause her to spontaneously confess, but if so it hasn't worked.

The moment drags on, until McAdam clears her throat. You tell her to arrest Carla, with a promise that once the MP is in custody at the police station you'll explain your reasoning. Disappointed, the crowd disperses from the room, whispering doubts about your deductive skills.

• Turn to **154**

64

For a moment, all is silent in McAdam's car as the sun beats down through the windows, testing the air conditioning. In your mind, you run through the places you'd like to visit to continue the investigation. But before you can tell the sergeant to begin driving, her phone breaks the silence, buzzing with a call from an unknown number. She answers on speakerphone, placing the phone between the two of you on the dashboard.

"Sergeant McAdam speaking."

"Hello, hello. This is Nigel Baker. I'm a supervisor in the council planning department. I understand you were asking about Kennedy Homes' submitted plans for a new housing estate. May I ask why?"

"Mr. Baker, I'm sorry to inform you that Harry Kennedy was found dead this morning under suspicious circumstances. We're looking into his recent activities, to understand what happened."

The line falls silent for long enough that you start to wonder if Mr. Baker has hung up on her. Then he exhales loudly.

"Well, well! I'm sure I don't know anything about a death. But if you want to talk further, I can spare you ten minutes if you pop round right away. From tomorrow I'm on holiday for the next two weeks."

Once again, you wonder whether this mysterious housing scheme ties in to Kennedy's death, or if the whole thing is a diversion. But if you don't act now and it turns out to be important, you might be kicking yourself until the council supervisor returns from holiday.

"Thank you, Mr. Baker," McAdam says. "We might well do that. Goodbye." She ends the call and starts the car. "So, Inspector, what's our first port of call . . . ?"

- If you wish to take Nigel Baker up on his offer and visit the council's planning department, turn to **17**
- If you think the housing scheme is a diversion and want to follow other, more important leads, turn to **30**

(If this is your first time reading this section, write ***INTERVIEW: 1*** *in your notebook.)*

"I can see you're itching to put someone under the spotlight," McAdam says. "Who's the lucky suspect?"

- If your INTERVIEW number is now 4, turn to **123**

Otherwise, choose from one of the following options:

- To interview Alina Martinescu, turn to **57**
- To follow up with Carla Nesbitt, turn to **183**
- To talk with Stephen Cheong again, turn to **19**
- To discuss matters with Tank Destroyer, turn to **116**

66

"It's quite simple," you say. "I believe your motive was one of the oldest there is: jealousy."

Tank looks confused. "Why would I be jealous of Harry? He had nothing I wanted."

"Materially, perhaps. I think you were jealous of his affair with Jennifer Watts."

A collective gasp goes up around the room, and all eyes turn to the receptionist.

"But we weren't," she protests. "Harry wasn't my type at all."

"His wife believes otherwise," you point out, "and one assumes she would know. Then Tank discovered the truth and became jealous. Was he also sleeping with you, Mr. Destroyer? Or did you only wish that were the case?"

"I'm not going to dignify that with an answer," he replies. "I don't even know if Harry was bi."

"But you would say that, wouldn't you?" McAdam points out. "And the inspector's right, jealousy is one of the oldest and strongest motives in the book."

You nod in agreement. "Mr. Destroyer, Alina saw you arguing with Kennedy after he left her therapy session. That places you on the upper floors of the house. Nobody saw you enter the pool, and you claim not to know when you did even though there's a clock on the wall. Finally, we also now know you had a powerful motive. Sergeant, arrest him."

• Turn to **131**

67

"Doesn't look like this is stopping any time soon," someone says, and the crowd still gathered in the lobby murmurs agreement. People press against the doors and windows to marvel at the storm and watch lightning flash across the sky.

"They're right," McAdam says. "We're basically trapped here now. Damn it, it's my wife's birthday tomorrow."

"I'm sure you'll be home by then, Sergeant. Surely this storm won't last more than a few hours."

"Aye, but I still need to call in at Tesco and buy her some flowers."

"My, how romantic. Perhaps Jennifer Watts can find some for you that aren't too wilted."

To your horror, McAdam seems to take this idea seriously. Still, you're confident you made the right decision to stay inside—and not just for your own safety.

"Look at it this way," you say, keeping your voice low. "We may be trapped, but so is Harry Kennedy's killer. I'm sure they're in this house."

"So you know who did it?"

"I'm not a hundred percent sure yet," you admit. "But I have a strong suspicion, and with nobody able to leave any time soon, we might have enough time to become sure. The storm could work to our advantage."

"We should warn everyone to be careful," McAdam says, but you stop her before she can call out to the crowd.

"No, Sergeant. If I'm right, I don't think anyone else is in danger. There's no sense in making people even more worried than they already are. Besides, if we announce there's a killer in the house, we'll be inundated with false accusations and unreliable witnesses faster than you can say 'Whodunit.' Let's keep our powder dry for now."

She grumbles. "Easier said than done in this weather."

Your phone rings, and taking it out you're pleasantly surprised to see a call from Dr. Wash.

• Turn to **5**

68

"Thanks for your time, Mr. Proctor," you say, hurrying to the door and signaling for Sergeant McAdam to follow. "We'll be in touch."

You take the stairs at a clip and reach reception just as Flora opens the door to enter. McAdam takes the initiative, blocking the doorway. When the widow steps back, startled, the sergeant presses forward and you follow. Just like that, you're all standing outside the building.

"Mrs. Kennedy," you say politely, "how nice to see you again. Do you have an appointment with Mr. Proctor?"

"I was just coming to inform him of my husband's death," she replies. "Though it looks like you beat me to it."

"I had the constable drive you home for a reason. You needn't worry about informing people; that's our job."

You're already feeling the heat, standing out here, but Flora seems unperturbed. It's as though she has an internal icebox.

"That's as may be," she says, "but there are arrangements to be made, which Mr. Proctor will have to carry out."

"At least he won't have to go to the trouble of drawing up divorce paperwork," McAdam says.

It's a risky strategy, and Flora adopts a confused frown in reply. "Whatever do you mean?"

"Is it not true you were considering divorcing your late husband?"

"No, it is not. If you must know, I've been inquiring about divorce procedure on behalf of my sister. Harry and I were very happily married. Now, if you'll excuse me—"

She tries to step around you, but you block her again. "Not so happily married that he told you the truth about the company's finances, it appears. You claimed Kennedy Homes is a prosperous business, but it's actually in serious debt. Did your husband keep that from you?"

Flora looks deeply unsettled by this news. "I don't . . . debt? Really? But Harry always had . . . no, surely you must be mistaken."

"I'm afraid not. You've inherited an albatross, Mrs. Kennedy."

She looks about to say something, then changes her mind. "I can't really think about this at the moment, Inspector. I have arrangements to make, and an appointment with my solicitor. Please excuse me."

With that, Flora Kennedy steps around you for good and reenters the building.

You and McAdam watch her go, before returning to the sergeant's car. Once again you're grateful to be out of the afternoon heat, and you both spend a moment in silence, letting the air conditioning cool you down. If the car had a built-in shower, right now you'd take it.

Finally, your thoughts return to the case. "Flora seems rather less distraught than when we saw her last," you say. "Remarkable self-possession, wouldn't you say?"

"Aye, though she seemed genuinely surprised by the state of the business. I suppose it makes sense Harry would have kept it to himself, so as not to upset her."

"Perhaps he thought building the new estate would turn the business around, so she'd never know and he could avoid an uncomfortable conversation."

"Only if the council approved the plans," McAdam points out.

She's right, and you already know that would have required intervention from Carla Nesbitt. Intervention that wasn't forthcoming.

However, this is all getting away from Flora Kennedy's potential role in her husband's death. You don't believe the tale about her sister wanting a divorce, but if Flora was planning to divorce Harry anyway, why go to the trouble and risk of murder?

Neither you nor McAdam can answer that question—yet.

- Write **F1** in your notebook, and **add 1** to your LOCATION number
- Then turn to **30**

69

Constable Zwale's head whips around. "I think that came from the cellar. Jennifer's down there!"

The door to the staff area is ajar. Zwale is already running through it, with McAdam hot on his heels. You call a uniformed officer to keep an eye on Tank, then follow them both.

With the power off it's dark inside the staff-only area, with only a few windows to let in the gloomy storm light. But Zwale and McAdam between them make enough noise for you to easily find them, and soon you see them up ahead, standing before another open doorway leading to total darkness.

Zwale reaches for his flashlight, then remembers he's not wearing his uniform. McAdam uses hers instead. The beam reveals stone steps beyond the doorway, leading down.

"After you, lad," she says, rather unnecessarily as the constable is already quickly descending the steps, calling out Jennifer's name.

You switch on your phone flashlight and follow, carefully taking the steps into the cellar. Ahead of you McAdam lights Zwale's path, revealing empty wine racks and dusty shelving in the cavernous, arched space. Farther into the darkness you see two beams of light in the corner of the room. One lies on the floor, unmoving, pointed at bare bricks. The other shines directly in the terrified face of . . .

"Mrs. Kennedy!" Zwale calls out. The flashlight beam shifts, and in the light from your phone you see it's held by Jennifer. The receptionist looks furious.

"She attacked me!" Flora cries, relief flooding her face. "Arrest her!"

"Rubbish," Jennifer snarls. "She came at me, and I defended myself. It's her you should arrest!"

Zwale separates the women. "We already did, remember? Mrs. Kennedy, you really have to stop wandering around like this. Now, what happened?"

"Maybe I wouldn't need to wander around if you did your job properly," the widow growls. "While you were all wasting time, I worked out that Jennifer here killed Harry. She was sleeping with him, then realized she could be fired for it, so she killed him to keep it quiet. She knew about that storeroom, she has the keys, and she knows where everyone is all the time. It's obvious."

"Except for the minor fact that I *wasn't* sleeping with him," Jennifer protests. "Believe me, your husband was not my type."

"Mrs. Kennedy," you say, "even supposing you're right, you should have come to us, not taken matters into your own hands. You're already in trouble. Is it true you attacked Jennifer first?"

Flora struggles against Constable Zwale's grip, groaning in frustration. "I didn't 'attack' her. I just wanted to scare her, and make her tell the truth."

"For heaven's sake," McAdam sighs, exasperated. "Can we at least get that generator up and running before we start concocting half-baked theories?"

You take a deep breath. This business in the cellar has certainly put a spanner in the works. Is there anything relevant to the case in what Flora says? Or should you focus your attention on other avenues of investigation?

- Write **J3** in your notebook
- If you already have S2, S6, or S7 written down, turn to **199**
- Otherwise, turn to **13**

70

Flora looks downcast as you begin to ask questions. "Can you explain the accusations you made when you saw the contents of that parcel? Why would you immediately assume your husband was having an affair with one of the Elysium staff?"

"Why else would he send that stuff here?" she says, not looking at you. "That one on reception is just his type, too. Young, blond, boobs."

It's hardly an unusual taste, and would have described Flora Kennedy herself in her prime. Perhaps that recognition is why she accused Jennifer.

"Was your husband in the habit of sleeping with other women?"

"It wouldn't be the first time," she says, sighing. "I'm sorry, I just lashed out in the heat of the moment. And then when that girl said those things about Harry . . ."

McAdam interjects, "You know, we have CCTV footage of your car heading in this direction yesterday morning. So I'll ask you again: Did you come here after meeting with your solicitor? Did you confront your husband and demand a divorce?"

Flora's face becomes an impassive mask.

"No comment."

- If you have F1 written in your notebook, turn to **198**
- Otherwise, turn to **175**

71

"I looked up Mr. Destroyer," McAdam says as you approach the swimmer. "Forty-two years old, birth name Thomas Ball. He made a fortune during the second dot-com boom, whatever that was. He ran some kind of website, a resource for computer programmers."

"He doesn't look like a stereotypical nerd," you point out.

"No, and I bet most of them don't have his money either. According to his Wikipedia page, he sold the business to Google for eight hundred million dollars. Nice work if you can get it."

"How does that relate to his new name?" you wonder aloud, standing at the poolside spot where Tank will turn for another width.

"Mr. Destroyer," you call out to him as the swimmer approaches.

He reaches the edge and rotates his body. For a moment you think he's going to continue swimming and avoid you, although that's hardly a long-term plan given the pool has only one exit. But then he stops and smiles, treading water.

"Inspector. And your lovely sidekick, too. What a treat."

"We'd like to ask you some questions."

Tank floats, hanging on to the poolside. "I'm an open book. Ask away."

"On dry land, if you don't mind."

"Oh, you're no fun. I was hoping to persuade your sergeant to join me in the water."

He rolls his eyes in mock disappointment, but pulls himself out of the water all the same. There's no denying Tank is in great physical shape, and he knows it. With water dripping from his tattooed muscles, he walks to a nearby lounger and begins to towel himself down, maintaining eye contact with Sergeant McAdam.

"Doing anything later, gorgeous?" he asks her. "Bring your handcuffs up to my room, you can arrest me all you like."

You almost laugh, but you suspect that this unsubtle flirting is performative, to make McAdam uncomfortable and distract you both from questioning Tank. To her credit, she doesn't rise to the bait and maintains her composure.

"Tell you what," she says, "why don't we begin with your name. What prompted you to change it?"

A sly smile forms on Tank's face. "Long story. Let's just say it involves a bachelor party with some old school chums, a decommissioned tank range in Dorset, and a little too much champagne."

McAdam snorts. "How the other half lives, eh?"

With Tank now at ease, you turn to more pertinent questions. "Where were you yesterday morning between ten thirty and eleven?"

Immediately he stiffens, wary and defensive. "Here, more or less. I went for a run, came back, jumped straight in the pool for a dozen lengths, then had a shower and went to my room. I was there until Flower Boy started shouting and screaming."

"And by 'Flower Boy,' I assume you mean Stephen Cheong."

"The very same."

"Did you see him find the body? These windows afford a view of the courtyard."

"Nope. Look, I don't know exactly what time I was swimming. I haven't worn a watch since I retired."

"And you were alone in here?" McAdam asks.

"Yes. I mean, I passed a few people here and there on the way, but there's never anyone else in the pool at that time of the morning. It's why I like it."

"I thought you just said you didn't know what time it was."

Tank glares at the sergeant, and something tells you there'll be no more mock flirting. Evidently the mogul has no alibi for the time of Harry Kennedy's death.

"Let's go back to this morning's parcel," you say. "Did Kennedy mention to you that he was expecting it? What was the nature of your relationship?"

"What business is that of yours?" Tanks says, offended.

"When it comes to murder, everything is our business. And you seemed very keen to get inside his bedroom yesterday, when I saw you arguing with the officer guarding the door."

Tank frowns. "I loaned Harry some gym gear while he was here, that's all. A hydration vessel and a fitness band monitor."

"So you were good friends, then? How close were you, exactly?"

He glares at you for a tense moment, then relents. "We weren't sleeping together, if that's what you mean. I didn't know Harry all that well, we only met this week, but I do like a troublemaker. We'd agreed to invest in each other's business. Me in his new housing estate, him in my new AI startup. That's Artificial Intelligence, by the way," he adds condescendingly.

You wonder about the alleged mutual investment. From what you know of Kennedy's financial status, he was in no position to invest in anything, let alone a risky tech startup. Notwithstanding Tank's prior success in business, Kennedy hardly knew him. Why would he agree to fund Tank's business?

"When did you last see Harry Kennedy?"

"The night before he . . . well, the night before. We played tennis, took a hot tub together, then went to bed. *Not* together," he adds.

- Write **T6** in your notebook, then check it in the following order:
- If you have A5 written down, turn to **39**
- If you have T3 written down, turn to **127**
- Otherwise, turn to **161**

72

She makes a quick recovery, but it seems clear that Flora Kennedy doesn't know what you're talking about.

"You didn't know the council wasn't going to approve the new estate?" you ask.

"Um . . . Harry hadn't said anything to me yet. I'm sure he would have once he returned home."

"Can you think why your husband wouldn't have told you about that?"

She gazes out of the window. "Harry often protected me from the rough and tumble of business, Inspector. I helped him with big ideas, but I didn't get bogged down in the nitty-gritty of running the company."

You wonder what other secrets Kennedy kept from his wife.

• Turn to **134**

73

Stephen said that Jennifer the receptionist could tell you where to find Tank Destroyer, so you turn to her. She checks his current session booking and directs you to a room on the first floor. Along the way, Sergeant McAdam looks up the tech mogul on her phone.

"Birth name Thomas Ball," she relates. "Forty-two years old, made it big during the second dot-com boom, whatever that was. He ran some kind of website, a resource for computer programmers." She whistles. "According to his Wikipedia page, he sold it to Google for eight hundred million dollars. Nice."

"How does that relate to his new name?" you wonder aloud. McAdam has no answer.

You approach a bright, sunlit room where an instructor leads a group of Elysium's Friends in a yoga class. Strong floral scents surround you upon entry; colorful petals are scattered on the floor, and each practitioner's yoga mat is surrounded by cuttings of a flowering vine.

"Well, I never did," murmurs McAdam.

"So this is corollic yoga," you reply. "*Corolla* is simply another word for the petals of a flower, you see."

"No wonder Stephen Cheong is concerned about the health of his plants."

You know better than most that appearances can be deceptive, but even if he wasn't the only man taking the class you're confident you could pick Tank Destroyer out of the crowd. Tanned and muscular, his arms and chest are covered with tattoos of intricate patterns, abstract shapes that flow into and around one another. His neatly trimmed beard and bald head frame a deeply lined face, and one of his eyebrows is pierced.

Then you realize that not only does he stand out, but you've seen him before. It's the same man who was arguing with the officer outside Harry Kennedy's bedroom earlier.

You apologize to the instructor for interrupting, and invite Tank to the room next door. It has the same layout and large, sun-gathering windows overlooking the manor grounds, but it isn't in use. Tank brings his yoga mat and cuttings with him, laying them on the floor before he proceeds to continue practicing yoga while you talk. Sergeant McAdam closes the door behind you all, for privacy.

"Mr. Destroyer, what was your relationship to Harry Kennedy?" you ask.

"He was a good laugh," Tank says, stretching on the mat. "Not that I don't like the peace and quiet here, but it's nice when someone comes along and shakes things up a bit."

"Shakes things up how?"

Tank shrugs. "People treat this place like a monastery. But Harry didn't take things too seriously. He was a bit of a troublemaker."

"What did the other guests—sorry, Friends—think of that?"

"Can't say I cared enough to notice."

For a man who apparently comes here regularly, the tech mogul seems singularly uninterested in what goes on at Elysium.

"When was the last time you saw Mr. Kennedy?" McAdam asks.

"Last night. We played a game of tennis, took a hot tub, then went to bed. Separately," he adds, winking at her, "in case you were wondering if you've got competition." McAdam rolls her eyes.

"Would you have preferred it to be together?" you ask. "I saw you earlier, attempting to get into his bedroom."

Tank frowns. "I loaned Harry some gym gear while he was here, that's all. It's got nothing to do with his death, but your copper wouldn't let me go in and get it back."

"You will, when our investigation is complete," you reassure him. "What should we be looking for? T-shirts? Jogging bottoms?"

He switches position, arching his back in what looks like a very uncomfortable manner.

"Try a *very* expensive hydration vessel and a fitness band monitor. I don't want any of your lot nicking them, either. I know what you're like."

"Our officers work to the highest standard," you say. "If those items are in his room, they'll be cataloged and stored until we can safely release them. Now, can you tell us what you and Mr. Kennedy discussed last night? Anything significant?"

Tank shrugs, an impressive physical feat in his current position. "Business. Investments. Cars. Normal stuff."

"And there was nothing unusual about his behavior? Did he say or do anything odd, or out of character?"

"Quite the opposite, I'd say. A row with Nesbitch, tennis and tub with me, then off to bed. Textbook."

McAdam tuts quietly at the derogatory nickname.

"Do you mean Carla Nesbitt?" you ask.

Tank laughs. "Who else? You know she threatened to block his plans for a new housing development, right? Next to the Burrowlands estate. She's been spouting some nonsense about a 'floodplain.' New construction would really benefit the town, but that's what politicians do, isn't it? They stand in the way of good men trying to do good work."

"Are you speaking from experience?"

He adopts a one-legged pose, with arms outstretched. "You're a sharp one, Inspector, I'll have to watch myself around you. So I might as well tell you since you'll find out soon enough—we were going to invest in each other's business." Tank's expression turns serious. "That's why I don't understand why he'd jump off a building. When I left him yesterday, he was in a good mood."

"He didn't jump," you explain. "I'm sorry to have to tell you that Mr. Kennedy's death wasn't an accident. He was murdered."

Tank tumbles to the ground, his balance lost. His hands fly to his mouth in shock.

"No way! Oh my days!"

You continue, "Therefore, I must ask where you were between ten thirty and eleven this morning?"

Immediately he stiffens, wary and defensive. "A few places, actually. I went for a run, came back, jumped in the pool for a dozen lengths, then had a shower and went to my room. I was there until Flower Boy started shouting and screaming."

"'Flower Boy'?"

"You know, the head honcho. Stephen Cheong."

"Did you see him find the body?" You recall your earlier thought about potential witnesses among the swimmers. "The pool windows afford a view of the courtyard."

"Didn't see a thing."

"What time did you start swimming, exactly?"

"I don't know. Since I retired, I don't wear a watch."

"Were you alone? Was anyone else in the pool?" McAdam asks.

"No. I passed a few people here and there on the way, but there's never anyone else in the pool at that time of the morning. It's why I like it."

"I thought you just said you didn't know what time it was."

Tank glares at the sergeant in reply.

"You also said you're retired," you point out. "So how come you have a business for Mr. Kennedy to invest in?"

He sniffs. "Nobody ever really retires in tech. I'm building an AI-powered startup—that's Artificial Intelligence, by the way—and Harry saw the potential. Now, is there anything else? Or have you spoiled my day enough already?" Tank asks.

"One more question, if you don't mind. Was yesterday the last time you spoke to Harry? Or did you see him again this morning?"

"Not a peep since last night," Tank says, frowning.

- If you have A5 written in your notebook, turn to **44**
- Otherwise, turn to **178**

74

You recall your encounter with Carla's daughter at the MP's office, and a theory forms in your mind. "Thinking about the timelines, here . . . is it possible that Harry Kennedy is Sharon Gibbs' father? Could that give her a motive for murder?"

"In what way?" McAdam asks.

"I'm not sure. Protecting her mother, somehow? If Harry Kennedy truly was a liar and a cheat, it's not a huge leap from there to something worse."

She sighs. "It's an idea, but I had uniform follow up, and Sharon Gibbs's alibi checks out. The gym security cameras have her in sight until ten forty yesterday morning. There's no chance she could have got here in time to kill Harry Kennedy."

How disappointing. Could the possibility of Sharon secretly being Kennedy's child be relevant anyway? You're not sure.

- Turn to **149**

75

"Particularly," McAdam continues, "as the only named investors in his AI startup are all strictly small-time."

You eye McAdam, impressed. "I didn't realize you were in a position to know."

She taps her phone and grins. "I may not be a computer whiz, but I can use a search engine. Turns out these people are easy enough to look up; like I said, most of them love the spotlight. Even the small-timers plaster themselves all over the place."

"Presumably attempting to move up into the big leagues. But if Tank is already a proven success, and his new venture is a hot new thing, why aren't those big-league investors already involved?"

McAdam shrugs. "Maybe we should ask the man himself."

• Turn to **117**

76

McAdam arrests Stephen, and when the storm clears you take him to the police station. But things soon fall apart.

Although you have a solid motivation for Stephen wanting to kill Harry Kennedy, what you lack is real evidence. Forensics can't place him in the storeroom; nobody appears to have seen him in the house that morning at all, let alone with Kennedy; and his solicitor argues that Elysium is in sufficient financial trouble that the bank will probably foreclose on it within a month or two anyway. Exposing Stephen's fraud might have hastened that event, but only by a few weeks.

The case is a bust. Losing faith in you, the detective chief superintendent reassigns you to a different, simpler case and calls in another inspector to take over the Elysium killing. Harry Kennedy's murder may yet be solved . . . but not by you.

Later, you consider what went wrong. Were you right to accuse Stephen, but simply didn't collect enough evidence? Could he have killed for some reason other than covering up his fraud? Or was the killer someone else altogether?

- To find out, don't despair. Simply wipe your notebook, return to **1**, and try again.

For now, though, this is . . .

THE END

77

As you walk on through the cellar, past empty shelves storing nothing but dust, you consider what Jennifer said about Harry Kennedy and try to fit the pieces together.

"So Kennedy really did try it on with every female member of staff?"

"He really did," the receptionist confirms. "Especially the massage therapists. So predictable."

"But not anymore," you point out. "You could say the problem has been solved."

To your surprise Jennifer laughs, then quickly stifles it.

"Inspector, if you think Harry Kennedy was the only man who got handsy with the Roses, you're more naive than you look. The big spenders do whatever they like around here."

"Surely you could complain to the management?"

"Stephen? He's the one who lets them get away with it. Doesn't want to risk them taking their money elsewhere, does he?"

- Write **A3** in your notebook, then turn to **166**

78

"I'm afraid the third degree is set to continue," you say. "One might even call it a fourth degree . . . which would be appropriate, as that was how many pallets you saw Stephen Cheong buying from the nursery, wasn't it?"

It's a gamble. Digital forensics have been unable to trace who the encoded text message came from, but Tank is the only person whom you've heard refer to Stephen as "Flower Boy."

He hesitates, presumably trying to calculate how much you know, but your accusation is too specific. Tank relents, letting out a low whistle.

"I suppose I'm impressed you figured it out. It was me who gave Harry the encoding app to begin with, you see. Something I've been tinkering with in my spare time. Did you figure out how to use it?"

"I have no idea what 'app' you're talking about, Mr. Destroyer. I simply worked out the cipher code and translated the message."

To your surprise, he laughs. "Ha! Now I'm even more impressed. Bravo, Inspector, bravo."

"The message," McAdam says, steering the conversation back on track. "Why send it to Harry Kennedy? What's it all about?"

Tank leans back and folds his hands behind his head. "Your boss seems to have it all figured out. Why don't you explain, Inspector, and I'll tell you if you get anything wrong?"

The ploy is obvious; having been found out, Tank is trying to regain the upper hand by establishing himself as the man in charge, without giving away any further information. But you have him cornered, and can bide your time.

"You observed Stephen Cheong secretly buying flowers from a nursery. We already know he's struggling with his crop this year, because of poor weather. But Elysium's 'unique brand promise' is that they grow all their own flowers for the therapy they provide. That's why he was 'trying to be invisible,' as you put it in the message. If anyone found out he was buying in flowers and passing them off as his own, it could ruin the company's reputation. How am I doing so far?"

"Carry on," Tank says, smiling.

"For that I'll need your assistance. You see, I understand why Stephen would want to keep his purchasing secret . . . but not why you were watching him in the first place, or why you informed Harry Kennedy, who by all accounts barely knew Mr. Cheong."

McAdam groans. "I think I've just worked it out. Blackmail."

Tank claps his hands in delight. "Looks *and* brains! You really must give me your number, Sergeant."

You ignore his attempt to divert the conversation again. "Of course . . . Stephen gave Harry Kennedy his Lotus package for free, and upgraded you, in return for your silence. A pity for you that it's over, really."

"It doesn't have to be," Tank says, with a trace of concern in his voice. "You don't have to say anything to him."

"Mr. Destroyer, what you've just told us—"

"Whoa there, I haven't told you a thing. You're the one who's done all the talking, remember? Keep my name out of it."

"That will be hard to do, now you've admitted you sent the text message. This evidence suggests a strong motive for Stephen Cheong to want Harry Kennedy dead."

Tank sits bolt upright on the lounger. "Exactly! And if you tell him I spilled the beans, he'll come for me next!"

"You're a big lad," McAdam says, gently provoking him. "Can't you look after yourself?"

"No amount of working out will stop you from getting stabbed."

"There's a police presence throughout the house, Mr. Destroyer. You're perfectly safe." Tank doesn't seem very reassured.

"Who first suspected this was going on with Stephen?" you ask. "You or Harry Kennedy?"

"Harry," Tank admits. "After we first met, I sent him the app so we could talk privately."

"Hold up," McAdam interrupts. "Did you give it to Carla Nesbitt, too?"

Tank looks like he'd rather give the MP a punch in the kidneys. "No chance. I suppose he might have passed it on to her himself, though. Why, was she using it?"

"We're exploring all possibilities," you say noncommittally. "Please carry on. You were talking privately with Harry . . . ?"

"Yeah. When I first mentioned Elysium to him he wasn't very interested, though. Then, out of the blue a few weeks later, he said he thought Stephen was up to no good and I should keep an eye on him the next time I came here. Harry had a hunch he might sneak off when nobody was watching. Sure enough, one night I saw Stephen looking shifty, then get into an unbranded van and drive away. So I followed him."

"To the nursery, where you saw him buying flowers and sent the text," McAdam says. "Presumably Harry Kennedy then demanded freebies from Stephen in return for his silence. Why didn't he ask for money? He could have used it."

"Stephen's got no bloody money. This place runs on a shoestring."

You wonder if that's the only reason. Was there something else that made a luxury stay at Elysium worth more than money to Harry Kennedy?

- In your notebook, cross out P6 and write **S2** instead. Then turn to **89.**

79

Constable Zwale approaches, ready to update you.

"I spoke with Jennifer—Jennifer Watts, that is, the receptionist. She was very helpful. Apparently the key to room 312 is normally behind her desk, in a locked cabinet. She noticed it was missing this morning after we arrived, but isn't sure when it was taken."

"She doesn't do a daily check?"

"It seems not. She said the storeroom hadn't been used in years, so she didn't keep track of that particular key."

You consider this news. "So the key could have been taken at any time prior to this morning, days or even weeks ago. That doesn't help us much, does it?"

"No, sorry. She did say there are only two keys to that room: the one missing from the cabinet and the manager's own. No other duplicates."

It's unlikely that Stephen would have stolen the key when he had his own—unless it was to divert suspicion away from himself, of course.

McAdam sighs. "That's a dead end, then. Thank you, Constable."

As Zwale returns to his duties, you decide on your next course of action.

- To question Alina the massage therapist, turn to **48**
- To question Carla the MP, turn to **177**
- To question Tank the tech mogul, turn to **73**

You stand in the entrance lobby and gaze at the fallen chandelier. This has been one of the most puzzling cases of your career. It's led you down many different paths. But now, at last, you feel you've reached the correct destination.

"You've got that faraway look," McAdam says. "What's on your mind?"

"Murder, Sergeant. Its motive, method, and malefactor."

"I'm a simple woman, Inspector. Big words like that are beyond me."

You know by now that Sergeant McAdam's "simple woman" is an act she performs to lull people into underestimating her. Perhaps in time she'll stop performing it around you, but it serves her well when dealing with suspects.

"After everything that's happened here since yesterday morning,

I'm confident I know who did it," you say. "I also believe I know why and how. Let's get everyone together."

"Where?"

You look around at the lobby, with its incongruous clash of old and new. It seems entirely fitting. "Where better than here? Gather all the staff and management—plus Flora Kennedy, Tank Destroyer, and Carla Nesbitt. They all need to hear the truth."

McAdam dashes off to round people up, enlisting Zwale in the effort. You watch over Flora Kennedy while they do, but after her escapade in the cellar the widow isn't going anywhere. If she was in trouble before, she's in even hotter water now.

Soon, everyone you requested has crowded into the lobby. Their assembly has also piqued the curiosity of many Friends, who stand watching from the stairs and doorways. Whispers and speculation move through the crowd like waves, wondering why you've called them here—and, given the recent drama that's engulfed Elysium, what could possibly happen next. You stand before them with Sergeant McAdam at your side, while Constable Zwale and other uniformed officers keep an eye on the doorways.

"Thank you for coming," you say, ready to sate their curiosity. "I asked you here because it's important for you all to understand how and why Harry Kennedy died, not to mention who did it."

"So you know?" asks Bill Cheong, the Tai Chi instructor. "You've worked it out?"

"I have. And the key to it all lies in motivation—not just the method by which Mr. Kennedy was killed, but the reason it happened. First, though, let's recap the events of yesterday morning. There's a lot of potential contradiction in everyone's stories, but I believe there are certain things we know for sure. The following facts are beyond dispute."

A silence falls across the room. Everyone hangs on your words.

"Harry Kennedy had a massage therapy session booked from ten till eleven, where he was attended by Alina. At some point during that hour he received a phone call, though there is a dispute about whether it happened during the session, prompting him to leave, or shortly after he'd already left."

Alina looks slightly embarrassed, but offers no clarity.

You continue: "Regardless, he left Alina's room at ten thirty, cutting the session short by a full half-hour. Tank was passing, on his way upstairs to get changed for a swim. He saw them both as Kennedy left the massage room."

Tank and Alina look at each other and nod. "I saw her in the doorway," the tech mogul agrees. "She was definitely there."

"And I saw you chase after Harry," the therapist counters. "Not long later, he was dead."

"Indeed," you say. "Alina retreated to her room to avoid Stephen seeing her unengaged. No manager likes the thought of their staff standing idle, even when the customer is responsible."

"It's a bad look," Stephen says. "Besides, there's always something around here that needs to be done."

You continue: "At this point we must divert into speculation. The next fifteen minutes, between ten thirty and ten forty-five, are crucial . . . but largely unknown, at least in terms of the six established suspects. At some point Tank went for a swim in the pool . . . but he can't say when, and nobody else saw him enter."

"I got in directly after speaking to Harry in the corridor," Tank protests. "It's not my fault nobody else was around, is it?"

"What did you speak to him about?" Carla Nesbitt asks.

"That's none of your business, Nesbitch."

The MP recoils, offended by Tank's hostility.

"Really, Mr. Destroyer," McAdam says disapprovingly, "there's no call for language like that."

You try to wrestle the moment back under control. "As for you, Carla, you were—"

She interrupts you, determined to speak for herself. "I was doing Tai Chi on the lawn, with Bill," she says defiantly. "He can attest to it."

The Tai Chi instructor shrugs. "I can also 'attest' that you took a bathroom break at half past ten."

The MP glares at him, silently fuming.

You pick up the thread again. "Meanwhile, Alina was in her work room. Nobody else was there with you, is that right?"

"No. I mean, yes, nobody was with me. I read a book and waited for my next appointment, you know?"

"But that appointment never came, thanks to the discovery of Harry's body . . . by Stephen, who claims he was working in the polytunnels before returning to his office to have a phone call with the bank."

"There's no 'claim' about it. I was there, cultivating."

"Was anyone else with you?"

The manager hesitates. "Not at that time of the morning. I often work alone in the greenhouses."

You turn to Jennifer Watts. "Much like Jennifer works alone at the reception desk, don't you? So nobody can verify for how long you're away when you take a vaping break."

The receptionist looks confused. "What's that got to do with anything?"

You let her wonder a little longer and turn to Flora. "Mrs. Kennedy had an appointment with her solicitor at nine thirty. From there she drove home, but CCTV shows her taking a diversion in this direction, and there are ten minutes when her car disappears from local cameras. Enough time, especially in a Ferrari, to pay a visit here but still be home by eleven."

"Don't you think someone would have seen me?" the widow protests. "For a start, I would have had to get past that young woman . . . oh."

You smile, watching her defiance slip away as she realizes. "The young woman who may well have been on a break at that time, you mean? There's no CCTV here in Elysium, either. Perhaps you have a knack for avoiding cameras . . . and people."

Finally, you return to Stephen Cheong.

"What couldn't be avoided is the discovery of Harry Kennedy's body itself. Regardless of where you came from, Stephen, you found him lying in the courtyard. His watch had stopped at ten forty-three, the time he hit the ground, and you raised the alarm two minutes later at ten forty-five. People came rushing to see what had happened. The police were called." You look at each of the suspects in turn. "And at that point, one of you believed you'd got away with murder."

"Belief is a powerful thing," McAdam says, "but it doesn't change facts." Whatever disagreements you may have had during this case, you're glad to know that she now stands firmly beside you.

The room falls silent again, listening to the deluge pelting hard against the windows. A low rumble of thunder murmurs in the distance.

"So who did it, then?" Bill Cheong cries, speaking aloud what's on everyone's mind. "Don't just stand there, tell us!"

You're ready to make an accusation. But do you have enough evidence to close the case on your prime suspect?

- To accuse Alina, turn to **155**
- To accuse Carla, turn to **197**
- To accuse Flora, turn to **124**
- To accuse Jennifer, turn to **41**
- To accuse Stephen, turn to **6**
- To accuse Tank, turn to **109**

81

You let Bill Cheong return to his work so you can follow up with Jennifer Watts, but she's no longer at the front desk.

"She was just here a minute ago," you say, looking around in vain. "Where could she have gone?"

Then you hear laughter from the direction of the main entrance. Two voices talking, one low, one high. And the deeper voice sounds familiar . . .

You step out under the portico, which is barely wide enough to keep the rain from the front door. With every passing minute, the sky darkens and the downpour becomes heavier. Under the shelter you find Jennifer talking with Constable Zwale—in fact, judging by their closeness and exchanged smiles, they appear to be flirting.

You clear your throat. The constable jumps, startled, and hastily stands to attention as if he's back in police college.

"What are you doing out here in this weather?" you ask.

Before Zwale can stammer out an answer, Jennifer raises a device to her mouth, inhales, then exhales a billowing cloud of strawberry-scented mist.

"No vaping inside," she explains with a shrug.

Your mind goes back to when you first entered the storeroom. There was a faint scent of strawberry there.

"Ms. Watts, when was the last time you were in room 312?"

"Yesterday, when you lot asked us to unlock it. The key wasn't in the lockbox, so I went to find Stephen and we opened it together. Why?"

"You're sure you didn't go in before then?"

She shakes her head. "Not for months."

It's a plausible story, and would explain the scent of strawberry being present. But it might already have been there, if she killed Kennedy. Blowing more into the room yesterday would have concealed that fact.

You turn your attention to Zwale. "Constable, shouldn't you be driving Mrs. Kennedy to the police station by now?"

"I thought I'd wait for all this to clear first," he says hastily, gesturing at the rain. "She's secured in the waiting room, she's not going anywhere."

At that moment, a wave of water spills down from the portico roof and splashes on the manor's steps. You certainly wouldn't like to drive in this. You would have preferred if Zwale had asked you first, but at least the constable is showing some initiative.

"Also," he says before you can pass judgment, "Jennifer had something interesting to say. Go on, tell the inspector what you told me."

- If you have T2 written in your notebook, turn to **148**
- Otherwise, turn to **126**

82

"All right," Carla says, sighing. "Yes, Kennedy Homes made a payment to Standard Umbrella. But I swear I wasn't expecting it. Go ahead and check our accounts; you'll find we raised no invoice for that sum. I was intending to return it in full on the company's next payment run, but then Harry . . . well, you know. Really, this is all most inconvenient."

"Slightly more inconvenient for Harry Kennedy," McAdam mutters.

You don't doubt that there was no invoice, but you remain equally skeptical of Carla's insistence that she knew nothing about the payment. Nevertheless, without documentation you can't prove otherwise.

"What about the houses for sale?" you ask. "It's quite a coincidence that you happen to be selling up while Mr. Kennedy was planning his estate next door."

"An estate that hasn't been approved by the council," she reminds you. "The truth is, Inspector, I'm simply tired of the landlord business. It's exhausting."

"But surely a letting agency takes care of day-to-day management," McAdam says. "You just sit back and take the rent money."

Carla shoots her a venomous look. "There speaks a woman who's never had to fork out for a new boiler, or chase a builder around while her tenants are threatening to sue because a roof slate moved half an inch."

"My heart bleeds," McAdam says, unconvincingly.

"I assume you're speaking from experience," you suggest to Carla. "You have my sympathies."

"Thank you. Trust me, the money isn't worth it."

You smile. "Oh, I didn't mean about the houses. I meant about Harry Kennedy."

- If you have C5 written in your notebook, turn to **33**
- Otherwise, turn to **187**

83

"You've answered your own question," you say. "A divorce could take months, even years, to finalize. At the end of it you might get half of Kennedy Homes to yourself. But the business was already in dire straits, with very little money in the bank. Everything was riding on this new housing plan, which seems to be going nowhere."

Flora protests. "I had no idea about the financial troubles. Harry told me the business was doing well. I wasn't involved in the day-to-day."

"Do you expect us to believe you simply took him at his word? A man you admit you were planning to divorce? Even if you did, your solicitor certainly wouldn't. I think you discovered that Kennedy Homes was in trouble—perhaps also that Harry paid a large sum he could barely afford for a mysterious 'consultation'—and decided enough was enough. After all, even if you came away owning more of the company in a divorce, your ex-husband would still be running it."

"Running it into the ground," the widow grumbles.

"Perhaps. But with him dead you inherit the entire business, which you can now run as you see fit. What's more, you admitted earlier that you came here yesterday morning."

A collective gasp goes up around the room.

"I also told you I turned around and left when I realized I was being a fool," Flora says, close to tears. "I had a lot on my mind, but none of it involved killing Harry!"

"Didn't it?" you say. "You had sufficient motive to want your husband dead. We only have your word for it that you didn't sneak through the house—where there are no cameras at all—and kill him, before returning to your car and driving home."

Carla Nesbitt speaks up. "That sounds like a lot of effort, Inspector. Does Flora really look like a woman who'd do that? No offense, Flora," she adds.

"Still waters run deep, Ms. Nesbitt. Earlier today, Mrs. Kennedy climbed out of a window to escape confinement. And the more unlikely the plan, the better chance it won't cast suspicion."

Flora Kennedy moans quietly and bursts into tears. You're not convinced they're any more real than her alibi.

"Also, there's the matter of the rose placed in the victim's mouth. A flower . . . or should I say *flora*."

The widow sniffles. "You can't possibly think that points to me. Why . . . why would I leave a clue like that?"

"Some criminals subconsciously want to be arrested and punished," you say. "And I'm happy to oblige. Sergeant, arrest Mrs. Kennedy."

- Turn to **172**

Reading the decoded message, you understand now that not everything you've been told is true.

- If you have P9 written in your notebook, turn to **9**
- Otherwise, turn to **165**

"It's quite simple," you say. "I suspect you're not the multimillionaire you claim to be at all. Perhaps you once were but lost it, or perhaps you never had it to begin with. Either way you're now small-time, desperately in need of cash and taking small-time investors' money. Is that why you're a regular here at Elysium? Looking for businessmen like Harry Kennedy, whom you can persuade to invest in your startup?"

"There's nothing illegal about that," Tank says.

"No, there isn't. And when he agreed to a mutual investment with you, I'm sure you were overjoyed. But you were both still waiting for each other's payment, weren't you? Playing a game of financial chicken."

"These things take time. There are contracts to be drawn up."

"But you can't draw money into existence. How did you feel when you discovered that Kennedy didn't have the cash he'd promised you? I imagine you were furious. All that time and energy spent convincing him to invest, when it was a lie. He was trying to con you."

Flora Kennedy gasps, though you suspect it's more for the benefit of the assembled crowd than from any genuine surprise.

You continue: "Alina saw you arguing with Kennedy after he left her therapy session, placing you on the upper floors of the house. Nobody saw you enter the pool, and you claim not to know when you did even though there's a clock on the wall. We also now know you had ample motive to want Harry dead."

Tank glowers at you, and for a moment you fear for your safety; he may be a fraud, but his size and strength aren't.

"One thing I do know is that you don't have a shred of evidence," he says slowly, "because I didn't do it. Harry didn't threaten me with anything, and I didn't kill him. No, he didn't have the money—yet. He even sent me begging emails, you know. But he would have got it eventually. I believed in him."

"I don't think you did. Those emails are the real reason you were trying to get into his room, aren't they? You weren't looking for a water bottle. You wanted to steal his laptop, in case it contained evidence implicating you. But my officers prevented you, because they know their duty." You turn to McAdam. "Sergeant, kindly do yours and arrest Mr. Destroyer."

- Turn to **131**

86

"I assume Tank Destroyer also has the Lotus package?" you ask.

"He does this week," Jennifer says. "Stephen gave him an upgrade."

"Upgrade? I was under the impression Mr. Destroyer was a wealthy man, and one of your regular high-paying customers."

The receptionist sighs. "I'm sure he's got money, but he doesn't spend much of it here. Normally Tank has the standard Rose package—that's more of a pay-as-you-go program, with a lower standing fee—but there was a note on his booking this week to upgrade him gratis. Stephen sometimes gives the regulars special treatment."

"How much does the Rose package cost?"

"A hundred pounds per day," she says. "Paid in advance, again."

You once heard someone remark that the rich stay rich because they don't give it away. Perhaps that explains why a multimillionaire tech mogul spends the bare minimum on his stays at Elysium. Is the fact it's called *Rose* significant? The flower keeps cropping up in this case: the Elysium logo, the flower in the victim's mouth, Stephen's nickname for his female staff, and now a package name. How is it all connected?

- Write **T2** in your notebook, then turn to **16**

87

"Did you already know about Mr. Kennedy's . . . issues with the other staff?" you ask. "As I understand it, you were the last remaining therapist with whom he hadn't had a session until yesterday."

"Of course I knew. The women, we all talk to one another."

The room falls silent. You can think of only one more question at this time.

"Ms. Martinescu—Alina—why did you leave Romania?"

"To work. The pay is better here, and it's good for Roxana, too. She married an Englishman, and now they can raise Valeria where she is safe."

"Isn't Romania safe?" McAdam asks.

Alina regards her with lidded eyes. "Not for us."

- Write **A7** in your notebook, and **add 1** to your INTERVIEW number
- Then turn to **65**

88

Moving silently, you press your ear to the door and listen to the conversation on the other side. To your surprise, you realize Tank is talking to Flora Kennedy.

"I don't care what you know or don't know," he says angrily, "I want that money. I'm owed it!"

"Rubbish," Flora replies. "Even if Harry really did make a promise, which I doubt, that's not the same as owing you. If you think I'm going to honor it, think again. There's no money anyway."

"Then find some! Just because Harry died before he could pay me, the debt doesn't vanish."

"It's not a debt! Show me paperwork, and then we'll talk. Until then, get lost."

The conversation ends, and you hear footsteps moving away.

You open the door as casually as you can, pretending that you have no idea anyone was on the other side. Tank is already walking up the wide staircase on the other side of the lobby. Flora is nowhere to be seen.

"Well, well," McAdam says. "How many multimillionaires do you know who go around shaking down widows?"

"More importantly," you ask, "why is Flora Kennedy wandering around freely?"

You walk down the corridor to the staff-only room where Constable Zwale was holding the widow. He stands outside the door, wearing the civilian workout clothes Jennifer gave him to replace his uniform.

"Constable, where's Mrs. Kennedy?"

Zwale seems confused by the question. "In here," he says, thumbing over his shoulder. "I stood outside to give her privacy while she changed into dry clothes, but I've been here ever since."

You open the door into the small room, which is lined with shelves holding folded piles of Elysium-branded shirts and exercise clothes. Unfortunately, they're not currently suitable for wear—because a window on the back wall is open, allowing heavy rain to blow in and around the room.

Zwale begins to apologize, but you wave it away.

"Don't blame yourself, Constable. I don't think any of us would have expected Mrs. Kennedy of all people to pull off a daring escape. She won't go anywhere in this weather, so let's just focus on finding her again."

• Write **F5** in your notebook, then turn to **137**

"There's a financial riddle here," you say to Tank. "If you were investing in Kennedy Homes, where's the money? We've seen the company's records, and there's no incoming cash from anyone. Why should we believe you?"

"Obviously because we hadn't exchanged yet," Tank replies condescendingly. "You don't just shake on it and hand over a hundred grand, Inspector. There are contracts to draw up, lawyers to pay."

"But he didn't have the money you wanted from him. Kennedy Homes was in dire financial straits. Did you know that? Didn't it concern you?"

Tank laughs. "I'm not short of investors, Inspector. Everyone wants to get in on AI these days, it's the hot new thing. I knew Harry would come forward with the money when he could. Now, are we done here? I'd like to finish my swim."

There isn't much more you can ask Tank at this time, but something about his manner suggests he hasn't told you the whole story.

"Not quite. I'd like to go over yesterday morning again. You said you finished a run before coming to the pool, correct? While you were outside, did you see or hear anyone or anything unusual? Someone acting oddly, perhaps, or something out of place?"

"Nothing," Tank says. "I ran circuits of the grounds, came back—"

"Did you see Stephen Cheong? He was in the gardens, apparently."

"Can't say I noticed. I get into a zone when I'm running."

"Did you return via the front entrance, or the courtyard?"

"Front," he says without hesitation. "I remember because I walked through a cloud of that awful woman's strawberry smoke."

"Jennifer Watts's vaping device." McAdam nods. "So she would have seen you? She can corroborate your whereabouts?"

Tank thinks, then shakes his head. "I didn't actually see her. But nobody else uses that horrible stuff."

You feel the conversation has run dry, and that's all you'll get from Tank for now. You let him return to his swim, while you and McAdam exit the pool area.

"Check up on that AI business of his, would you, Sergeant? There's something about Tank's story that still doesn't sit right with me. I wonder how much he needed Harry Kennedy's money."

McAdam shrugs. "I'm surprised he needs investors at all. He's worth millions."

"True. But while I may not be an entrepreneur like Tank, even I know a smart businessman doesn't gamble with his own money."

- Write **T7** in your notebook, and **add 1** to your INTERVIEW number
- If you already have T2 written down, turn to **193**
- Otherwise turn to **65**

"Now that I think about it," Baker says, "Carla Nesbitt did recently ask me about Mr. Kennedy's plans. But her inquiry concerned deadlines."

"Deadlines?"

"The date of our final decision, the proposed building schedule, and so on. I assumed she was thinking of buying some properties should the plans be approved. She's a local landlord, you see. But I informed her the plans were likely to be rejected in their current state."

"Did you tell her why?"

"I don't recall, sorry. It was an impromptu conversation following a council meeting, not an official correspondence."

You thank Baker for his time and return to McAdam's car, grateful to be leaving the suffocating building. It's still no cooler outside, but at least the air moves. You haven't learned much from the conversation, though it reinforced some things about Harry Kennedy. One question that comes to mind is, why was Carla Nesbitt asking about the deadline for Kennedy's housing plan? She didn't advocate for it to the council, so what difference would the deadline make to her? Could she be involved in some other way she hasn't told you about?

The sun creeps lower in the sky, and there are still several places you'd like to go before the day is out. You must hurry.

• Write **P7** in your notebook, then turn to **30**

91

"Doctor," you answer. "What news?"

"The kind that involves a postmortem," she replies drily. "I've completed my preliminary, so come down to the mortuary when you're ready and I'll run through it with you."

"No time like the present. Expect us shortly."

You end the call, and McAdam raises a questioning eyebrow. "Off to see Dr. Posh, are we?"

"I don't think she'd appreciate being called that. Now, let's see what Harry Kennedy was able to tell the good doctor after a proper examination."

You instruct Constable Zwale to ensure the uniformed officers take statements from everyone on the premises as soon as possible. You can't force people to stay for long, so time is of the essence.

Leaving Elysium and Finchcote Manor behind for the moment, you take Sergeant McAdam's car to the mortuary. She speeds away with screeching tires, turning on the stereo to blast loud rock music. The singer sounds like he's being tortured on a rack.

"Mr. Kennedy is already dead, Sergeant," you shout, clinging to your seat for dear life. "That won't change, no matter how quickly we arrive."

"You sound like Emma," McAdam says with a chuckle, easing off the accelerator and turning down the music. "She says I should have joined the traffic division."

"It does rather feel like you're training for it. What does Emma do?"

McAdam smiles. "Runs the household, keeps everything shipshape. A bit easier now the bairns are at school, but there's still lots to do, and Champ to look after, of course. That's the dog," she explains.

"I see. Yes, I can definitely picture that. What kind of dog?" In your mind's eye you envision the sergeant proudly holding a Rottweiler, or perhaps a Dobermann.

"Welsh Corgi," she says. "Aye, he's a handful."

That'll teach you to make assumptions. You travel the rest of the way in a comfortable silence, over the river and out of town. The fields and verges are starting to brown from the relentless heat of the past few weeks. Soil lifts in sparse clouds, stirred by passing cars. Surely the weather must break soon, and bring some welcome rain.

Soon McAdam turns into the car park of an unassuming single-story building on the edge of town. The only clue to its nature is a van wrapped in paramedic livery, near what might otherwise be mistaken for a warehouse-style roll-up door.

You park and enter, thankful for the mortuary's carefully controlled climate. After signing in you proceed to Dr. Wash's lab, where the body of Harry Kennedy, now cleaned and naked, lies on the central metal table under a crisp white sheet.

Behind a perspex screen, the doctor sits at her computer eating a salad.

"Be with you in a moment," she says. "I assumed you'd want these results as soon as possible, so I delayed my lunch."

"That looks suspiciously healthy, Doctor," you remark. "What is it?"

She smiles. "Fresh kale, edamame beans, and carrot with a ginger soy sauce. Delicious."

McAdam curls her lip with distaste. "Sounds like something your farm animals would eat. Give me a burger any day."

Dr. Wash laughs around a mouthful of food. "So you've heard about my farm, eh? Maybe I'll whip some up for George when I get home."

"George? Is that your husband?"

"No, Sergeant, he's a British Alpine goat. My eldest, in fact, who in his dotage has settled into the role of sheep guardian." She pushes her half-finished salad aside, places a cap over her short white hair, and steps out from behind the screen to wash her hands. "Now, as for your body. The first thing I should say is that I may have been hasty in my earlier assessment."

"How so?" you ask. "Surely you're not now calling it suicide."

Dr. Wash walks to Kennedy's body and removes the sheet. The blood has been rinsed from his wounds, but they remain extensive, and combined with the lab's perpetual acidic smell of strong disinfectant, it's enough to turn your stomach.

"No, but I can't say for sure if it's the fork that killed him," she explains. "There's no question that death was by exsanguination, but whether from the stab wound in the chest, or the head wound from hitting the ground, is impossible to conclude. As you can see, the fall did extensive damage to his head and face. He might even have been struck on the head beforehand, but any evidence of that may have been lost following the impact with the ground."

Dr. Wash indicates the areas she's talking about, and Sergeant McAdam peers closely at Kennedy's head. You stand back a little, quite prepared to take her word for it.

"There's something else, too. I didn't see it until I cleaned the body."

With the help of an assistant, she turns Mr. Kennedy over to reveal his back. Three small circular red patches follow the line of his spine.

"What is that?" asks McAdam.

"They appear to be mild burns," Dr. Wash says. "Very recently antemortem, too. I'd say he sustained them no more than six hours before death."

You peer at the circles, wondering what might have caused them.

"Is there anything else? Defensive wounds?"

"Again, hard to say definitively. There was dirt and grit under the fingernails, which appears to be of the same type found on the balcony from which he fell. But grit is grit, so I doubt we can prove that conclusively. As for wounds, there are recent lacerations, but only on one side."

She lifts Kennedy's right forearm, showing you a series of slashes and bruising.

"You don't think those are defensive?" you ask.

"A gardening fork isn't sharp, per se," she explains. "Sharp at the points, obviously, but it possesses no real edge. These cuts are much more consistent with a slicing blade of some kind. But while that implies defensive wounds, it's highly unusual to find them on only one arm."

You puzzle over this for a moment, then remember the bloodstained shards of glass. "The French windows leading to the balcony were smashed. Could these cuts have been caused by jagged glass?"

Dr. Wash looks again at the wounds and nods, satisfied. "Yes, that would explain it."

"Good. Did you get anything from his watch?"

"Just an ordinary watch, which stopped at ten forty-three when it struck the ground. We also confirmed that the key card was for his bedroom. Nothing unusual there."

"Let's put all of this together in a rough hypothesis," you say. "Kennedy was stabbed inside the room, hence the blood on the floor and trail leading outside. He staggered toward the French windows, falling into them and smashing the glass panes, cutting his arm. He continued outside to the balcony, where he left a bloody handprint on the handrail. Then he fell over the balustrade to the ground. His killer returned inside, washed themselves in the sink, then left and locked the door, taking the key with them."

Sergeant McAdam nods. "It's also possible Mr. Kennedy was pushed into the doors, and then again over the balcony, rather than fell."

"True," you concede. "There's still a lot to be explained, including why his phone landed three meters away, and at what point a rose was placed in his mouth. But this is a start. Wouldn't you agree, Doctor?"

"Confirming the hypothesis is your job," Dr. Wash replies, unwilling to be drawn into speculation. "Mine is done, and there's not much more I can give you other than to say Kennedy was in typical health for a man in his fifties with a poor diet. Nonetheless, while his heart and liver weren't in great shape, he wasn't facing any immediate illnesses or major issues."

"Is the rose in his mouth notable?"

The doctor picks up a metal examination tray, holding the rose in question. "An everyday rose," she says. "Freshly picked, probably from the plant on the balcony as we've already surmised. It's a little crushed, suggesting it was there when he fell and affected by the impact. Unusual and macabre, certainly. But it didn't materially contribute to his death."

You peer at the rose, willing it to give up its secrets. If plants could talk . . .

"Is there anything else?" you ask.

"Only that I've run a blood group analysis on the clothes the manager gave us, and confirmed the blood on them likely belonged to the victim."

"It's a match, then?"

"Yes, and of a relatively rare type, too. Harry Kennedy's blood group was A-negative, which occurs in less than ten percent of the UK population. I can't be definitive without a DNA test, of course, but in the circumstances I'm willing to state it's highly likely the blood on those clothes belongs to the victim."

"Wouldn't be the first time a killer pretended to 'find' the body so they could explain why they're covered in blood," McAdam suggests. She's right, and Stephen Cheong must remain on your list of suspects.

"Thank you, Doctor. We'll leave you to finish your lunch."

Before you leave, though, the pathologist pulls you aside and asks quietly, "How's it going with the new recruit?" She nods in the direction of the door, through which Sergeant McAdam has already exited.

"She's hardly new," you say. "McAdam had a good record in Northumberland, in terms of closing cases. So far today she's been up and down; missing things here and there, but sometimes insightful, too. I hope things will settle down."

"Yes, well. You know I give as good as I get, Inspector, but one doesn't normally expect insults from the constabulary within ten seconds of meeting."

"I suspect we can put that down to nerves, Doctor. I'm keeping a close eye on her, never fear. I'm willing to judge the sergeant on her results, rather than her demeanor."

"Just make sure that if she goes down in flames, they don't burn you alongside her." Dr. Wash holds the door for you.

You exit the mortuary to find Sergeant McAdam waiting for you outside, in the hot afternoon sun.

"All good?" she asks as you cross to her car.

"Yes, though I must warn you that if you keep taking the bait she'll keep winding you up. Don't be fooled by her accent; Dr. Wash has spent her career around plainspoken coppers, and knows exactly which buttons to push."

McAdam snorts. "I just don't see why she bothers to keep farm animals if she won't put them to use? That's good meat going to waste."

"Didn't you say you have a dog?" you ask.

"Aye. What of it?"

"Ask your children. I suspect they'll have a rather different perspective on keeping animals without 'wasting' their meat."

"That's not the same," she grumbles, getting into her car. "So where next? Back to the manor?"

"Not yet. Let's allow uniform to take everyone's statements, and let them stew for a while before we question people again. I want to use what's left of today to cast our net farther afield."

Before you can make a decision, though, you receive a call from Penny—a senior technician at the digital forensics lab.

"Penny," you answer on speakerphone, so McAdam can hear. "Any good news?"

"Not much," she replies. "The victim's phone was severely damaged, with multiple impact fractures to the body and internals. We've hooked the board up and made some very preliminary recovery, but I don't know how much more we'll be able to pull off it."

"Anything is better than nothing," you reassure her. "What have you got so far?"

"A text message, sent from the victim to Carla Nesbitt three days ago."

McAdam grins. "What does it say?"

Penny hesitates. "That's the problem. It's garbled—just complete nonsense. One of my team thinks it could be a code. It's possible, but not one I've ever seen."

"I see. Could you send it to me? And did you get any fingerprints from the phone?"

"We did, but they all belong to Mr. Kennedy. Even if there were other prints, the damage to the phone could have destroyed them."

Ambiguity seems to be a common feature of this case.

"I'm sending you the text now. Good luck."

You thank Penny and end the call. A few seconds later, you receive a text message:

Text Message #1: Harry Kennedy to Carla Nesbitt, 3 days ago

hua twif fqec cqec bieiw paewm feb oua. muw'c cqowt O fuw'c ciuu oo hua kelt uac

"She's not wrong," McAdam says, reading over your shoulder. "Total garbage."

"Or perhaps it really is a code. Which makes me wonder why Harry

Kennedy would go to such lengths to disguise a message." You make sure to keep a copy of the text, in case inspiration strikes and you're able to decode it later. "Even if it truly is garbage, we should ask Carla Nesbitt why Kennedy was texting her, of all people."

"Harassment?" McAdam suggests. "From what she said, he seems the type."

That's true, but you've never trusted obvious answers. Too often they hide a deeper truth.

"Do we have Kennedy's financials yet?"

McAdam checks her email and smiles. "Came through while we were in with the doc, as it happens. Let's take a look . . . oh-*ho*."

You lean over to see what's so impressive, and are greeted by the cells of a spreadsheet. This is a surprise, as the sergeant strikes you as the type to run a mile from nitty-gritty detail.

"Can you actually make sense of that?" you ask.

"Heavens, no," she laughs. "I asked records to provide a summary. Listen to this: Kennedy Homes is in bad shape, with very little cash to hand and substantial debts to both vendors and the bank."

"Didn't Flora Kennedy imply the business was doing well?"

"What she doesn't know can't hurt her, I suppose."

So either Flora lied to you, or Harry was hiding the state of the business from his wife. With the company in dire straits, even if the council had approved his plans for the new housing estate, how would he afford to build it? Would the bank have risked lending him even more money?

McAdam continues reading the summary. "There aren't many payments from Kennedy to service those debts . . . but then three weeks ago, the company paid out seven thousand pounds for consultancy fees."

"Is that unusual? Consultants are normally well paid."

"Aye, but apparently Kennedy Homes had never done business with this firm before. Bit odd to engage a new vendor when you're strapped for cash."

"What's the consulting company called?"

"Standard Umbrella. Never heard of them."

Neither have you, but it's worth looking into. "Is there anything else?"

"There certainly is. I asked the financial team to check on Kennedy's payment to Elysium. Turns out there isn't one. Nothing from either his personal or business accounts, not even a hold on his credit card."

"But the receptionist said that all fees are due in advance."

"Aye. A gift from the management, perhaps?"

You wonder what could prompt Stephen Cheong, a man clearly worried about his cash flow, to waive nine thousand pounds in fees.

Check your notebook in the following order:

- If you have A2 written down, turn to **3**
- If you have C7 written down, turn to **64**
- Otherwise, turn to **30**

92

"On the surface it may seem complex," you say, addressing the crowd, "but it's actually quite simple. In a way, the clue to this case has been under our noses the whole time . . . but it also goes back several years, to another country entirely."

You begin pacing in front of the fallen chandelier, each step accompanied by gusts of wind that throw hard rain against the lobby windows.

"Many of you here had reason to want Harry Kennedy dead, which greatly confused matters. There were occasions when I began to wonder if I was going down the wrong track, and overlooking the real killer. Like you, Mr. Destroyer."

Tank jerks to attention. "What? I didn't do it. I wasn't there."

"No, you weren't. Despite being the last person seen with Harry Kennedy, not to mention having no real alibi, I don't think you would have had time to kill him, run to the pool, swim for a while, and *then* jump out to attend his body with everyone else. Certainly not without anyone seeing you."

The so-called tech mogul breathes a sigh of relief.

"Of course, that doesn't absolve you of your other sins. Fraud, fakery, and who knows what other rackets . . . you're a piece of work, Mr. Destroyer, but not a killer."

At that he looks rather less relieved, but doesn't argue. You turn to Carla Nesbitt.

"How about you, Ms. Nesbitt?"

She shrugs. "I was in a Tai Chi class. Ask anyone who was there."

"But you took a break halfway through," Bill Cheong interjects.

The MP reddens. "A toilet break, yes. So what?"

"So it means you might not have gone to the bathroom at all," you explain, "but instead lured Harry Kennedy into the storeroom to kill him. We can't overlook that we found your DNA in the storeroom sink, after all. But I don't think you left it after killing him. It's there because you and Harry used that room for secret assignations."

Flora's head whips around to glare at Carla, who remains aloof.

"Nevertheless, I don't think you killed him," you say to the MP. "You're in good shape, but even you would struggle to run up three flights of stairs, kill Harry, wash, then run back down again to rejoin Bill Cheong's class just five minutes later."

Carla isn't sure whether to be flattered, insulted, or relieved. She settles for a curt nod, ignoring Flora.

"Stephen Cheong is another obvious suspect," you say, prompting a protest from the manager.

"I didn't kill him," he insists. "It was me who found him."

"A classic ruse," you explain. "Killing a person, then pretending to find their body, gives you a solid excuse for having their blood on your clothes, not to mention for leaving evidence on the victim. And there are undoubtedly some very shady things going on here at Elysium, which my colleagues in corporate investigations will be looking into once I report to them. But I don't believe you have murder in you."

Stephen looks relieved by your conclusion, then worried by your threat of sending in the corporate crime squad. As he should be.

"I also considered Flora Kennedy, of course," you continue. "The widow who now stands to inherit everything, even though she was planning to file for divorce."

Flora looks aghast. "Why would I bother with divorce if I was going to kill him?"

"A good question. But surely you know your inheritance is worthless. Kennedy Homes is poor in both cash and assets, particularly as your husband's gamble on the new estate didn't work out."

Flora sighs. "He was a sharp businessman, but *gamble* is the right word. Harry was always looking for a shortcut to the money."

"Because of that, the only way you'll get money out of the business now is to sell it, and even then it may only fetch pennies. You'd be better off selling your Ferrari . . . with which you could have driven here yesterday morning, and killed Harry before returning home." She twitches nervously. "But I don't believe you could have done it without anyone here noticing you. If you'll pardon me saying, you're hardly inconspicuous."

"She did suspect he was having an affair, though," Jennifer Watts says. "Remember how she reacted to the Viagra. And she hit Alina! You already arrested her for that."

"All true," you agree, "but it seems clear Flora blamed the women, not Harry. Besides, it wouldn't take much to gain evidence of those affairs if she'd really wanted to. Which brings us to you, Ms. Watts."

The receptionist looks shocked. "I swear I wasn't sleeping with him! He propositioned me, like he did everyone, but I sent him packing."

"We only have your word for that. I wondered for a while if there might be some truth in Flora's accusations."

"I was nowhere near the storeroom when Harry was killed. Anyway, I wouldn't need to steal the key to the room, would I? I could have just put it back in the lockbox."

"But that would immediately have brought suspicion on yourself, as one of the only two people with access to a key. Were you really at the front desk the whole time yesterday morning? Nobody would have thought twice if you'd taken a five-minute break. Everyone seems used to the scent of your strawberry vape drifting through the lobby."

Jennifer frowns. "Well, all right, yes. I did take a break, as it happens. But I went outside, not upstairs!"

"I believe you. I don't think you had sufficient motive to warrant murder, and unless you have some kind of automatic vaping contraption, you had to be down here for your strawberry scent to be present."

The receptionist sighs with relief. Then she realizes what this means, and she—along with everyone else in the room—returns her attention to Alina.

Or rather, to where Alina had been.

"*Hey! Let go of me, you pig!*"

While you talked, the massage therapist quietly retreated into the crowd, slipping toward the exit. But you were ready for this; as he's no longer in uniform, you asked Constable Zwale to blend in with the Friends. Now he grips the therapist's arm firmly.

"That just leaves Alina Martinescu," you say in conclusion. "So allow me to explain how and why she killed Harry Kennedy."

• Turn to **200**

93

Carla sighs. "Look, I apologize for putting on an act about Harry, but you must understand I can't afford a scandal. My husband doesn't know, and there's no reason he should find out."

"To what lengths would you go to make sure of that, I wonder?"

It takes her a moment to understand what you're implying. When she does, her eyes flash angrily.

"How dare you! I was nowhere near the storeroom, or Harry, when he died. I was on the lawn practicing Tai Chi, along with a dozen other people. Besides, it seems obvious to me who killed Harry."

"Oh? Pray tell."

The MP rolls her eyes. "That horrid wife of his, of course. Flora. You already saw her temper, and she suspected Harry was having an affair."

"In which she was correct, even though she thought it was with Jennifer Watts."

"For all I know, it was both of us. Harry and his wandering hands couldn't be trusted around women. It's why we split up in the first place, all those years ago."

"Yet you continued sleeping with him," McAdam points out.

Carla shrugs. "All the fun without the heartache, Sergeant. I doubt you'd understand. Flora certainly wouldn't. She's always been rather unworldly, I'm afraid."

You've already got your eye on Flora Kennedy. Could jealousy or humiliation have driven her to kill her husband?

"Was meeting you the sole reason Harry came here?" you ask. "Or did he have other business in mind, too?"

Carla shrugs. "You'd have to ask him that, though of course you can't. Harry didn't mention any other business to me. He didn't even mention Elysium until earlier this year, when it came out of the blue."

"Because he knew you were a regular?"

"I suppose someone told him. Despite your own ignorance, Inspector, I'm quite well known."

You resist the urge to retort. "What did you tell him about Elysium?"

"Heavens, I don't know. That I enjoy my time here, that I find it very relaxing—normally, anyway—and about Stephen's miraculous green fingers. I suppose it tickled his fancy, because a few weeks ago he asked when I was next visiting so he could book at the same time. I was surprised he found an opening, to be honest. As you'll have seen, it's quite busy at this time of year."

"Not only that, he didn't pay for it," McAdam says. "Stephen Cheong appears to have given Harry Kennedy a free VIP package. What can you tell us about that?"

Carla looks genuinely surprised. "Nothing at all. I didn't realize they even knew each other."

The conversation feels as though it's at a natural end, but from experience you know that's sometimes when the most interesting statements are made.

"You mentioned Stephen has 'miraculous' green fingers," you say. "What did you mean by that?"

Carla shrugs. "I'm no gardener, Inspector, but it doesn't take one to be impressed by Elysium's wonderful plants and flowers, especially when Stephen is always complaining about the weather. He works so very hard."

Write **C10** in your notebook, then check it in the following order:

- If you have S7 written down, turn to **159**
- If you have S1 written down, turn to **192**
- If you have S2 written down, turn to **52**
- Otherwise, turn to **25**

94

The afternoon sun has now become the evening sun, and checking the dashboard clock in McAdam's car, you realize how long you've been out here already. Technically your shift finished an hour ago.

"Let's call it a day so you can get home to your family," you reply to McAdam. "I'm sure Champ is waiting by the door."

"He's more Emma's dog, to be honest," she says, taking out her phone. "She's the one who feeds him, so he's glued to her legs all day. I'll just let her know I'll be home soon." She takes out her phone to send a text, and you notice her lock screen is a family picture.

"How old are your children?" you ask.

"Nora's nine, Douglas is seven." She shows you the photo: McAdam and another woman smiling alongside a fair-haired boy and an Asian girl, who holds a grinning Corgi on a lead.

"You all look very happy," you say approvingly. McAdam nods her thanks and sends the text before pulling away. Left with your own thoughts, you wonder at your reaction to the picture. Did you expect the sergeant to scowl in family photos, because of her demeanor at work? Her reactionary style of policing doesn't mean she has to be like that at home. You wonder if it could even be an outlet for things not permitted when she's around Emma and the children.

As McAdam drives you through the town's busy roads, you contemplate what you've learned today. Your hypothesis of the crime scene has held up so far, but you haven't gathered nearly enough evidence to make a concrete accusation. On the other hand, there are now several suspects in the frame for Kennedy's murder. Most of them have alibis, but you know that upon examination many alibis turn out to be nowhere near as airtight as people think.

You feel certain that the key to this case is motive. *Why* was Harry Kennedy killed? Again, you've already found several potential answers. He was evidently something of a rogue, charming people with one hand while swindling them with the other. But is there more to uncover?

Night seems to fall unusually quickly during the drive home, until you realize your eyes are deceiving you. The dim light isn't from night descending, but clouds gathering.

"That looks rather ominous," you remark. "Are we about to finally get a break from the heat?"

"The forecast is pretty grim," McAdam says. "Good thing we started today, really. Standing over bodies in the rain is never fun."

Your thoughts briefly turn to the floodplain on which Harry Kennedy wanted to build. If heavy rain does descend, the residents of Burrowlands will be relying on that field to do its job.

Fat raindrops begin bursting on the windscreen as you approach your house.

"If this turns into something, I might be late collecting you in the morning," McAdam says. "Emma won't drive in rain, so I'll have to take the bairns to school."

"Don't be too late," you say, as she pulls up outside your house. A light shower has begun to fall, so you find your keys and prepare to make a dash for the front door. "We can't keep Elysium sealed up for long. Tomorrow may be our last chance to question people before we have to let them leave."

It's too late to fix a proper dinner, so you settle for a microwave-ready meal that you find at the back of the fridge. You barely taste it anyway, as your mind is preoccupied with the case. You turn over the clues and information you've already gained, trying to fit the pieces together.

Later, trying to wind down in front of the TV, it's still on your mind. What on earth was Harry Kennedy—and his unknown assailant—doing in that disused storeroom? If it was privacy he wanted, his bedroom was just down the hallway. Does that mean his killer led him to room 312? Or perhaps he didn't go voluntarily?

Finally, you lock up and get into bed. But even then you struggle to relax.

Eventually the rhythm of falling rain does what your overactive brain cannot, and you fall asleep. But it's an unquiet slumber, and when you wake in the morning to find rain still falling, you hardly feel refreshed at all.

A shower and breakfast help. Soon you feel ready to face the world, and run through your hopes and plans for the day. You hope to hear from digital forensics regarding Kennedy's laptop; it rarely takes them long to crack a computer password. Perhaps that will give you the boost you need.

Waiting for Sergeant McAdam to arrive, you reflect on your first day working a case with her. She's headstrong and outspoken, but perhaps that could make for a good balance alongside your own approach, which is more thoughtful and considered. She asked some good questions of people, and even furnished one or two insights you hadn't thought of yourself. Her bedside manner, so to speak, needs some work, but that's an area where you can lead by example. All in all, you feel better about the new partnership this morning than you did yesterday.

Just then you hear a horn, and look up to see the sergeant's car parked outside. After shrugging on your coat you grab an umbrella, dash to the car, and quickly climb in.

"I think we've got her," the sergeant says before you can even say hello.

"Got who?"

"Flora Kennedy." McAdam holds up her phone. "The traffic camera team spent the night tracking her Ferrari. She left her solicitor's when she claims—but then she starts to head in the direction of Elysium, before disappearing from cameras for ten minutes. When they pick her back up, she's heading away again. I told you she could do it if she put her foot down. They want us to go down to the station, watch it for ourselves, and confirm timings."

So Flora Kennedy lied to you. Could this be the breakthrough you've been looking for? Before you can tell McAdam to drive to the station, though, your own phone rings. To your surprise, it's Constable Zwale.

"Constable," you answer, "what's up?"

The young man sounds frantic, raising his voice to be heard over loud background noise.

"Sorry to call, Inspector. I'm at Elysium, and there's a bit of a situation."

"What kind of situation?" You put Zwale on speakerphone so McAdam can listen in.

"Mrs. Kennedy is here, demanding to take a parcel that was delivered this morning. It's addressed to Harry Kennedy, but instead of informing us, Jennifer the receptionist called Flora and asked if she wanted to pick it up. I didn't realize what was happening until I asked why she was here, and now she insists we give her the parcel."

That explains the background noise. Now you recognize Flora Kennedy's voice, arguing with someone.

"Who would address a parcel to Harry Kennedy at the retreat?" you wonder aloud. "Hardly anyone knew he was there to begin with. Constable, do you have any idea what's in this delivery? Where's it from?"

"Difficult to say. It's not large, probably mail order. We haven't opened it yet, because I didn't want to compromise anything."

"Good lad," McAdam says. "Explain to Mrs. Kennedy that whatever the parcel is, it's potential evidence. You can't let her take it."

"I already did," he sighs. "She wasn't satisfied. I think it might help if you told her."

McAdam covers the phone with a hand and says to you, "If Flora did it, that parcel could be vital. He's right, we should go down there and help him out."

You're not so sure. "Zwale held his own with Flora when she arrived yesterday, remember. Weren't you saying he's got to learn to handle situations on his own?"

She shrugs. "Aye, but not all at once. A guiding hand never hurt, and the CCTV isn't going anywhere."

On the other hand, the sooner you confirm that the footage incriminates Flora Kennedy, the sooner you can return to Elysium and confront her with it.

You uncover the phone. "Constable, do you need our help? Or do you think you can handle the situation?"

"Um . . . I can handle it," Zwale says, with obviously forced confidence. "Leave it with me."

McAdam silently shakes her head.

- To let Zwale deal with Flora Kennedy by himself, turn to **46**
- To drive to Elysium and take control of the situation, turn to **167**

95

Check your notebook in the following order:

- If you have C1 written down, turn to **130**
- If you have C15 written down, turn to **58**
- If you have C5 written down, turn to **33**
- Otherwise, turn to **187**

96

McAdam explains: "The very helpful real estate agent confirms those four houses are all owned by a single company, called . . . Standard Umbrella."

"Isn't that the firm Kennedy Homes recently paid several grand to, for 'consultancy services'?"

"The very same, and if that's a coincidence then I'm a Venus flytrap."

"We should check with Companies House for more information about that company. There must be more to this than meets the eye."

McAdam begins tapping on her phone again. "No need, I can look it up on their website. It's all online these days."

"Yes, thank you, Sergeant. I wasn't about to drive to Cardiff and ask His Majesty's tax office in person, you know."

McAdam mumbles as she types and taps. "Standard Umbrella . . . funny name, really. I suppose it's hard to be unique these days . . . OK, here we are. Management and consulting company, otherwise unspecified. What do you want to know?"

"Let's start with the directors and shareholders."

She taps a link, then laughs. "Oh-*ho*. They appear to be one and the same, and you'll never guess who."

"You're absolutely right, because I won't try. Just tell me."

McAdam shows you her phone screen. "Not one, but *two* Nesbitts. Carla and her husband are both the directors and shareholders."

This really is a turn-up for the books. Why is Carla so keen to sell the houses? Do they also have leaking windows, and she wants rid of them? Or is she looking to turn a profit? Not that those reasons are mutually exclusive. Prices in this country only ever seem to rise, and the MP wouldn't be the first or last landlord to sell up and take the money.

For now, though, it's time to move on. You had a feeling Burrowlands could be important to this case, and what you've learned here backs that up.

- Write **C1** in your notebook, and **add 1** to your LOCATION number. Then turn to **30.**

97

"Thank you, Ms. Gibbs. Just one more question: Where were you between ten and eleven this morning?"

"At my gym, and before you ask, a dozen other people can confirm that for you." At your surprised expression, she shrugs. "I'm no fool, Inspector. Why else would you ask?"

You thank her and leave, returning to McAdam's car. Something about this feels like it connects, but there are still too many links missing.

"I don't believe for a moment that Carla Nesbitt didn't tell her daughter about Kennedy's plans," McAdam says, breaking the silence. "But why lie about it? What's going on here?"

"Damned if I know. Something about this whole case feels off, and I feel like we're missing something important. We'll just have to keep digging until we find it."

- **Add 1** to your LOCATION number, then turn to **30**

So three days before Kennedy was murdered, he sent Carla Nesbitt a message reminding her about money he'd paid her. An amount that just happens to match what Kennedy Homes paid another company for "consulting services."

- If you have P3 written in your notebook, turn to **4**
- Otherwise, turn to **122**

You turn to Carla. "As it happens, Ms. Nesbitt, you played a crucial role in exposing Stephen without even realizing."

The MP looks confused. "I have no idea what you're talking about."

"You told us you sang Mr. Cheong's praises to Harry Kennedy," you explain. "You called his ability to grow Elysium's flowers 'miraculous,' despite the terrible weather. But Harry didn't take you at your word. Instead, he suspected Stephen of deceit."

"Deceit? What do you mean?"

• Turn to **132**

100

"There's one last thing," Dr. Wash says. "Do you remember the cuts and bruising on the victim's forearm? Upon further examination, I don't believe they're from the same incident."

"What do you mean? Two sets of defensive wounds?"

"Not exactly. The cuts were sustained very shortly antemortem, as I concluded previously. But the lividity of the bruising suggests it occurred at least forty-eight hours ago, and is consistent with someone tightly gripping his arm."

McAdam doesn't speak, but silently performs a karate-chop motion and points in the direction of the lobby. You would have expressed it rather differently, but were thinking along the same lines.

"Would that take someone with a good amount of strength, Doctor?" you ask. "A martial arts practitioner, perhaps?"

"That's speculation beyond my remit," Dr. Wash replies. "But a person with that training would likely have significant gripping strength."

You thank her and end the call. Why does the evidence place both

Carla Nesbitt and Harry Kennedy in an unused and normally locked storeroom? And who else might have used that sink?

As McAdam pointed out, you're stuck here now, so you might as well get on with conducting more interviews. First, though, you want to see if digital forensics has turned up anything more, so you call Penny.

"Inspector," she answers. "I was about to call you, as it happens. We've found some interesting email threads on Harry Kennedy's laptop. One is a conversation with the Kennedy Homes solicitor, double-checking that the company isn't responsible for repairs to houses on the Burrowlands estate."

"What was the solicitor's verdict?"

"They backed him up. Apparently builders are only obligated to make repairs up to two years after construction is complete, which they call the 'defects insurance period.' That's bad news for residents of Burrowlands, as many have only begun complaining of defects in the past year. Leaking windows, jamming doors, that sort of thing."

"Bad news indeed," you agree. "It does seem that Mr. Kennedy wasn't averse to taking shortcuts in the name of profit."

Penny continues: "There's also a thread between him and someone called Tank Destroyer. According to the case notes he's a witness at Elysium, is that right?"

"More than that, he's a possible suspect. What did they talk about?"

"Technically nothing, because it's all one-way. There are almost a dozen emails, all from Kennedy to Tank, asking for investment money. They start out civil, then get increasingly angry, and Tank never replies. They're not completely unique—Kennedy sent a lot of emails asking various people for money, it seems. But in these messages to Tank he gets especially belligerent."

That's interesting. You file this away for the next time you question Mr. Destroyer.

"I've forwarded the thread to you, so you can see for yourself," Penny says. "Let me know when you've got it."

McAdam is already checking her phone. "Received, safe and sound," she says. "Penny, what about those garbled text messages? Anything more on those?"

"Actually, yes," she replies. "It turns out they were in code, after all.

We recovered an app on Harry Kennedy's phone that scrambles and unscrambles text, so that even if someone sees a message they won't be able to read it without the code cipher."

"So you have the cipher?" you ask.

"We do, and I should warn you it's quite complex. Most of the letters are a simple substitution cipher . . . except for vowels, which makes it easy to get a false positive."

McAdam begins to take notes on her phone. "How does it work?"

"Well, the basic code is a 'subtract 9' cipher. So if you have a K in the encoded message, that's the eleventh letter of the alphabet. Subtract nine and you get two, the second letter of the alphabet, which is B. So any K in the garbled text becomes a B."

"What happens if B is the letter in the coded message?" McAdam asks, brow furrowed as she types furiously. "Two minus nine is minus-seven. There's no such letter."

"The cipher wraps around the start and end of the alphabet," Penny explains. "So instead of minus-seven, you'd subtract seven from twenty-six to get the nineteenth letter, which is S."

"You said vowels were an exception," you remind her. "How so?"

Penny sighs. "That's what makes it complex. Vowels rotate, rather than subtract—but not always, depending on context. Vowels in the original message are replaced by the *next* vowel in the alphabet in the encoded message, rather than adding nine. So A becomes E, E becomes I, and so on. Which means any vowel in the message you're trying to decode could be another vowel, *or* a substitute for the consonant nine places behind it. An I, for example, could be an E, the vowel preceding it . . . or it could be a Z, the letter nine places behind it."

"Good God," McAdam says, exhaling. "How do you tell which is which?"

"By context of the letters surrounding it. I'm afraid that's the only way. Take the first word of the second message, for example. The coded text is *biwm*; if we subtract nine from everything that becomes *sznd*. But if we rotate the I vowel back a place instead, we get *send*. So in that instance it's pretty clear which is correct—"

Suddenly the call ends, cutting Penny off mid-sentence. You try to call back, but your phone won't connect.

"Sergeant, is your phone working?"

McAdam looks up from her notes. "Yes, I'm using it right—oh." She looks back at her screen and groans. "No signal."

Your phone is the same, showing no connection. "The storm must have knocked out the local cell tower. What a pain!"

Luckily, you copied out the text messages when Penny originally sent them to you, and now you know enough of the cipher to decode them fully. You look at them again:

Text Message #1: Harry Kennedy to Carla Nesbitt, 3 days ago

hua twif fqec cqec bieiw paewm feb oua. muw'c cqowt O fuw'c ciuu oo hua kelt uac

Text Message #2: Harry Kennedy to Carla Nesbitt, 13 days ago

biwm vi huaa mecib ewm O'uu veclq bog mehb, qi'uu veti byeli oua vi oo qi twufb fqec'b puum oua qov

Text message #3: Unknown to Harry Kennedy, 20 days ago

HUA FIAI AOPQC, SABC BEF OUUFIA KUH CAHOWP CU KI OWEOBOKUI OW E EEW AUAWM CQI WAABIAH. KUAPQC OUAA YEUUICB

"It really is a tricky code," McAdam murmurs. "Difficult to reverse-engineer, too."

"No doubt that's why Harry Kennedy used it. The question is whether these messages are connected to his murder."

You begin unscrambling the messages, conscious of time passing as the storm outside continues unabated.

When you've deciphered the messages, you'll see that each contains a number within the text. Multiply that number by **14** to get a new number, then turn to the corresponding section to discuss it with McAdam.

NOTE: If you already decoded one or more of the messages without

needing the cipher from Penny, give yourself a pat on the back—and you'll score additional points at the end of the book. But there is now more to be found, so multiply each number within the texts by 14 and turn to the relevant section again, paying particular attention to your notebook. After discussing each message, you'll be returned to this section.

- When you've done everything you can with the text messages and are ready to move on, turn to **143**

101

You enter the waiting room off the lobby to find McAdam, Constable Zwale, and Flora Kennedy waiting for you. Unlike the break room, this one has windows. Rain continues falling against them, heavier still than when you drove here.

You close the door behind you and take a seat. Flora holds her head in her hands, staring at the floor.

"Mrs. Kennedy," you begin, "I must tell you you're in serious trouble. Even putting aside your assault on Alina, you compromised what might be valuable evidence in the case. Can you explain the accusations you made when you saw the contents of that parcel? What makes you believe your husband was having an affair with one of the Elysium staff?"

"Affair? *Pfft.*" Flora doesn't look at you. "One-night stand, more like. She's just his type, that one."

"You mean Jennifer? Is it likely your husband would sleep with her?"

The widow shrugs. "Harry would sleep with anything young and pretty. I learned to live with it, I suppose."

"Why were you so keen to take the parcel away? Did you suspect what was in it?"

"No, but . . . Harry had a knack for embarrassing me. And I was right, wasn't I?"

"Is that why you were planning to divorce him?"

Flora's face becomes an impassive mask. "My solicitor's advised me to answer 'no comment' to such questions."

McAdam interjects, "You know, we have CCTV footage of your car heading in this direction yesterday morning. So I'll ask you again: Did you come here after meeting with your solicitor?"

"No comment."

"Mrs. Kennedy . . . did you kill your husband?"

She hesitates, then: "No comment."

You won't get anything more from her. With little choice after what she did to Alina, you get to your feet and deliver the bad news.

"Flora Kennedy, I'm arresting you on suspicion of assault by beating, contrary to Section 39 of the Criminal Justice Act 1988. You do not have to say anything . . ."

As you caution her, you're surprised to see Flora's reaction. Most people break down and grow listless upon being arrested, but Mrs. Kennedy regains her strength and poise, sitting upright with a defiant expression. A moment ago she was in despair; now she seems ready to face the world.

You direct Constable Zwale to arrange for her to be taken into custody. First, though, you check in regarding the witness statements taken yesterday.

"I'm afraid nobody saw anything," he says glumly. "Most people were in classes at that time, they weren't looking at the courtyard. As far as we know, Alina and Tank remain the last people to see Kennedy."

• Turn to **133**

102

You make your decision.

"Constable: take Mrs. Kennedy upstairs, put her in the waiting room, and stay there with her. No more following people around and threatening them."

"Understood. Come along, madam." Zwale takes Flora's flashlight from her and leads her up the steps to the house.

You turn to Jennifer. "Ms. Watts, we need to have a word with Stephen. You should be safe now, so please proceed with getting the generator up and running."

"I'll do my best," she says apprehensively, and walks on into the dark cellar.

You return upstairs with McAdam. You're already in the staff area, so it's a short walk to Stephen's office, and for once you get lucky. His office door is closed, but you knock and enter to find him at his desk. Upon seeing you, he quickly gets to his feet and moves to greet you.

"Inspector," he says, forcing a smile. "What can I do for you?"

The room is dim, its courtyard-facing windows allowing insufficient light to counter the lack of power. Deep shadows fill the crowded room, and you hear McAdam curse quietly as she stumbles into a potted plant.

"I thought we could chat about the small matter of fraud," you say. "Your fraud, that is, which now seems beyond any doubt. Your crop of flowers has been so poor that, rather than turn away customers—sorry, Friends—you've been buying in flowers from a local nursery and passing them off as your own. What's more, Harry Kennedy found out, had you followed, and I believe he then blackmailed you over it."

Despite this litany of accusation, Stephen isn't looking at you. Instead he's watching McAdam from the corner of his eye, as the sergeant prowls around the room with her phone flashlight turned on.

"Look, I really don't know what you're talking about," Stephen says, quickly shuffling to stand by the corner of his desk, directly in McAdam's path. "It sounds like someone with a grudge against me has been feeding you nonsense. You shouldn't believe everything you hear."

"I couldn't agree more," McAdam says, pointing her flashlight beam directly in Stephen's face. The manager recoils, squinting. "I prefer to rely on what I see with my own eyes. Like whatever it is you're trying to hide right now."

You're glad to see that McAdam picked up on Stephen's awkward position, which conveniently blocks you both from seeing whatever is behind that far corner of his desk.

"Stand aside, please, Mr. Cheong," you say, quietly but firmly. "In fact, why don't you just sit at your desk while we chat?"

The manager looks between you and McAdam, wide-eyed like a cornered animal. You brace yourself to stop an escape attempt . . . but then his shoulders slump and he exhales heavily, before returning behind his desk and sitting down as you suggested.

"What do we have here?" McAdam is finally able to see what Stephen was standing in front of. "Looks like the power went out at just the wrong time for you, doesn't it?"

You peer over her shoulder and smile in agreement. On the floor next to Stephen's desk is a paper shredder stuck halfway through an operation—specifically, shredding an invoice from Green Fingers Nursery.

"Oh dear," you say. "That looks quite conclusive, don't you think, Sergeant?"

"Indeed. Some might even call it damning."

Lightning strikes outside, punctuating the moment.

"All right!" Stephen cries. "God, what does it matter now? The way things are going, Elysium will belong to the bank by next month anyway."

"Is that so? There are plenty of people here. I assumed business was booming, or perhaps I should say 'blooming.'" Stephen doesn't laugh at your bad joke. "What's the problem?"

The owner-manager sinks into his chair and sighs. "Most of them are on a discount. I didn't even charge Harry Kennedy, because I thought he'd be good for repeat business."

"But that's not true, is it?" McAdam interjects. "The reason you gave him a freebie was because he threatened to tell everyone about you buying in flowers from outside."

"Well, yes, all right. But he wasn't the only one. Hardly anyone pays full price here. It's the only way I can get the punters in. Even Jennifer doesn't know."

You consider this. "I'm no business expert, Mr. Cheong, but it sounds to me like your prices are simply too high compared to your expenses. Couldn't you cut back on staff? Or drop the flowers?"

Stephen looks at you as if you suggested he fly to the moon. "The flowers are Elysium's USP." He points to the wall plaque of his company's insignia, with its rose emblem. "It's on our logo. Without the flowers, we're just another spa in the countryside. How would we compete?"

"With a good service and lower prices?" McAdam suggests cheekily.

"I can't give a good service without staff, can I?" Stephen groans and puts his head in his hands. "I should never have sold the nursery."

"Perhaps not," you say, looking out of the window. The white forensics tent in the courtyard fights against the wind, stubbornly staying put while gusts try to uproot it from the ground. "Harry Kennedy would still be alive, for one thing."

"Now hold on a minute," Stephen protests. "OK, I admit I've been buying in flowers. Yes, Kennedy threatened to expose me if I didn't give him a free Lotus package on the dates he wanted. But I didn't kill him for it, I swear! What would be the point? Like I say, the bank is breathing down my neck anyway."

"There's still the matter of your reputation. Elysium might be doomed, but if the world knows you for a fraud, establishing a new business afterward could be difficult."

Stephen glares up at you with a dark expression. Is it resentment, or defiance? Before you can decide, you're blinded as the room light flicks on. It's not even all that bright, but after stumbling around in the dark for so long, it might as well be direct sunlight.

The power has been restored—and not only to the lights. You hear a whirring sound from somewhere on the floor . . . the shredder! It's powering back up, preparing to finish the job of destroying the invoice from the nursery. Blinking to clear your eyes, you whirl around—

To see Sergeant McAdam already on the floor, holding an unplugged power cable like a trophy. The whirring sound stops, and she smiles.

"Enough shredding for one day, I think." McAdam produces an

evidence bag from a pocket. "Given time, I'm sure the lab can piece this back together."

She opens the paper collector and begins stuffing shredded strips into the evidence bag. Meanwhile, you reach down and neatly tear off the unshredded part of the nursery's invoice. Stephen moans quietly.

• Turn to **80**

103

The manager looks offended, but before he can respond you feel a blast of cold air and someone shouts, "Look out!"

You turn to see what's going on, and witness an extraordinary sight. A staffer opened the polytunnel door, preparing to leave, but a blast of wind from outside caught the open umbrella Sergeant McAdam left by the door. You watch as the brightly colored brolly floats over your heads, narrowly missing a sprinkler as it cartwheels through the air.

McAdam looks sheepish and quickly chases the umbrella, now descending upon a raised bed of plants.

"Be careful!" Stephen shouts, running after her. "Those are young crocuses, they're fragile!"

"Don't worry," McAdam calls back, and snatches the umbrella from the air just before it lands on the flowers. She immediately closes it and breathes a sigh of relief. "Sorry, everyone. I didn't expect it would . . ."

She trails off, peering down at the flowers in their plastic pots. Doubting the sergeant has suddenly developed an interest in gardening, you hasten over to join her and Stephen at the raised bed.

"Well, well," she murmurs. "What's this?"

You follow the line of her gaze to the flowers . . . and see a glint of something metallic in the soil.

Stephen moves to pull it out, but McAdam stops him. "We'll handle this, thank you."

You pull on a pair of nitrile gloves and gently brush the soil aside to reveal a silvery metal shaft. Stephen gasps.

It's a key, and attached to it is a cardboard room number tag reading "312"—the old storeroom. Despite having been buried in soil, you can clearly see some stains of blood in the metallic nooks and crannies.

Stephen stares at it in disbelief. "What the hell's that doing in here?"

"We might well ask you the same question," you say. "If this isn't the key you keep on your person, I believe it must be the one used by whoever gained access to the storeroom and killed Harry Kennedy. So, as you say: what's it doing it here?"

"Wait—you can't think I dumped it here?"

"Tried to bury it, looks like," McAdam says.

"But why would I put it here, of all the places in the manor?" Stephen protests.

"Why not?" you suggest. "Even seasoned crooks can panic in the aftermath of a crime. Especially when they have limited time to dispose of incriminating evidence. If not for a stroke of luck just now, we'd never have found it."

"No. I'm being framed," the manager says, folding his arms defensively. "Someone put that there knowing it would make me look bad."

"Oh?" McAdam says. "And who might that be?"

"I don't know! Isn't it your job to find out? Carla Nesbitt, maybe. She knows Elysium well enough by now to put all this together. You saw for yourself that anyone can walk in here."

He has a point. If someone is trying to misdirect you toward Stephen, this would be a good place . . . except they'd have no way of knowing you and McAdam would ever step inside the greenhouses. Which inevitably swings the suspicion back to Stephen himself.

At this moment you lack solid evidence either way. You place the key in an evidence bag, making sure it's sealed before you retrieve your own umbrella and leave the manager to his flowers.

The rain is still lashing outside, and the rainclouds have darkened even further in the short time since you left the house to come out here. You hurry back inside and hand the evidence bag to a constable.

- Write **S5** in your notebook
- If you already have P12 written down, turn to **147**
- Otherwise, **add 1** to your INTERVIEW number and turn to **65**

104

You recall your conversation with Tank Destroyer, and the gym gear he lent to Harry Kennedy. An expensive "hydration vessel" (presumably a posh name for a water bottle) and a fitness band, he said. But you haven't found either in this room, and given its sparseness you're sure you can't have missed them.

Did Kennedy dispose of the objects? Or is Tank simply lying? Why was he *really* trying to get inside this room earlier?

- Turn to **7**

105

You read the decoded message again, deciphering not just the words but its meaning.

"Three weeks ago an anonymous person sent Harry Kennedy a message about a 'flower boy' buying four pallets of . . . something . . . from a nursery."

"Presumably not children," McAdam quips.

"Don't give up your day job, Sergeant. No, the obvious answer is flowers. And 'trying to be invisible' implies whoever it was didn't want to be seen."

You both ponder this for a moment, before realization hits you.

"Stephen Cheong," you say slowly. "Flower Boy."

McAdam whistles. "But why would someone be watching out for Stephen at a nursery? Everything here at Elysium is grown on the estate. Stephen said it's their 'unique brand promise.'"

"Exactly. But he also complained about the recent bad weather, and said he's struggling to cope. What if he's not coping at all, and has to supplement his own crop with flowers bought from a nursery? If word got out, Elysium's reputation would suffer heavily. It might even be actionable fraud. Look at the first part of the message."

"'You were right,'" McAdam reads. "It suggests Kennedy suspected something and asked this anonymous sender to keep an eye out."

"Not only that, but asked them to encode the message upon sending, ensuring nobody else could read it."

This text message isn't itself proof. But if you've interpreted it correctly, it's damning evidence against Stephen Cheong. If Kennedy knew Stephen was buying in flowers and passing them off to guests as his own, it would give him a hold over the Elysium manager. A hold that could easily turn into threats, or blackmail—one of the oldest motives for murder there is . . .

"Just one question left to answer, then," McAdam says, breaking you out of your thoughts. "Who sent this text?"

"Actually, Sergeant, I think there are two questions. The identity of the anonymous sender is certainly one. The other is, how come this text was sent three weeks ago?"

She looks confused. "I don't follow."

"Harry Kennedy had never been here before, and by all accounts wasn't normally one for wellness retreats in the first place. How did he even know who Stephen Cheong was, let alone suspect him of lying? And why would he care?"

"I've no idea. Go on."

You laugh. "That's just it, I don't know either. But hopefully we can find out . . ."

• Now return to **100**, and skip to the end of that section

106

"We know you took an unscheduled break during your Tai Chi class yesterday morning," you say, nodding toward Bill Cheong. "In fact, Mr. Cheong says you were gone for at least five minutes, at the same time when Harry Kennedy was being murdered in the storeroom."

Carla regards you with contempt. "I'm a middle-aged woman, Inspector. The need to 'go' can strike without warning, I assure you. Is that really all you have?"

"Not at all. We also know you have a previous criminal record . . . which is how we identified your DNA in the sink of room 312, where Mr. Kennedy was killed."

The MP laughs. "I shoplifted some nappies when I was a young single mother with Sharon. I hardly think that makes me a murdering criminal mastermind."

"Then how do you explain your DNA in the sink?"

"Harry pulled me in there one day to talk about the housing estate plan again. The room was dirty and dusty, so I washed my hands before leaving."

"How did he come by the key to the room?"

Carla shrugs. "I have absolutely no idea. Why would I?"

"The animosity between yourself and Mr. Kennedy is well known. You can claim you were really friends all you like now that he can't contradict you, but the public evidence shows that he and you had many arguments. I believe you lured Harry Kennedy into that storeroom, killed him there, then shoved him off the balcony and washed off the blood before returning to your Tai Chi class."

"That is a preposterous fantasy," she says, "and I won't dignify it with a response."

"You don't have to. Sergeant, arrest Ms. Nesbitt."

• Turn to **196**

107

Watching the swollen river water rush over the bridge's surface, you decide today is no day to take unnecessary risks.

"Turn around, Sergeant. I know you're a good driver, but this is a fool's errand. We'll wait out the storm at the house."

McAdam sighs, obviously disappointed. "Right you are. It'll pass soon enough, I'm sure."

You wish you shared her confidence about that. Regardless, it's clear now that you'll be safer inside Finchcote Manor than outside—so long as no more of the roof collapses, that is.

The car slips a couple of times while McAdam turns it around, strengthening your conviction that you made the right decision. Finally she drives back up to the house, a little faster than the journey down, parks in the space you vacated only a few minutes ago, and turns off the engine.

You both brace yourself for a moment, then fling open the doors and run up the steps to reenter the house. Even though you're only exposed to the rain for a few seconds, once again it's enough to soak you through. At least you're both still standing.

Jennifer passes you towels from the extensive collection she's amassed at the front desk, and sighs.

"I'm sure we can find you all rooms for the night, Inspector," she says. "Or, if worse comes to worst, we'll put you up in the waiting room with some spare bedding."

"Thank you, but let's hope it won't come to that," you say, drying yourself as best you can.

The prospect of being forced to spend the night at Elysium doesn't appeal—especially with a potential killer somewhere in the house.

Could the murderer strike again? You're beginning to narrow down your list of suspects, but whether they're a danger to anyone else very much depends on their motive for killing Harry Kennedy. Guess wrong, and you might have another corpse on your hands.

• Turn to **67**

108

"Why didn't you tell us this before?" you ask.

Alina shrugs. "Because it looks bad, yes? I can't risk losing this job, Inspector. I need the money."

"Surely there are other places you could work."

"I don't want to move away. I have family here."

That's understandable, especially for someone who moved their whole life here from another country.

"That's not the only thing you didn't tell us, though, is it?" you say quietly. "Yesterday you said that Harry Kennedy left your session at ten thirty to conduct a phone call."

Alina looks confused by this apparent change of subject. "Uh, yes. That's right."

"You're absolutely sure he didn't have a call while he was in here with you?"

She turns away to place the hot stones back on the heater, avoiding eye contact. "I'm sure. No phone call."

"So how do you explain that Mr. Kennedy's phone records show he took a call at ten twenty, for three minutes?"

"I don't know. There must be a mistake."

"The only mistake here is yours, for lying to us," McAdam growls. "The call was from someone called Robert Graham. Do you know him?"

Stone clatters on metal as Alina fumbles with the tongs, dropping one of the hot stones onto the heater. She puts them away and faces you, looking defeated.

"Yes, OK. Robbie is married to my sister, but it wasn't him who called. Not this time. Mr. Kennedy's phone rang while he was on the table. I told him this was a place of relaxation, and he should turn it off, but he would not. So he took the call, and I kept working. I could tell he was arguing with a woman, but it wasn't until he called her 'Roxana' that I knew it was my sister. And then I realized who he was."

"What do you mean?" McAdam asks. "Surely you already knew Mr. Kennedy's name."

She shrugs. "I didn't know he was the same useless bastard Kennedy who built her house. Why should I?"

A picture starts to form in your mind. "And he in turn didn't know you were Roxana's sister, did he? But I bet he soon found out . . . when you *deliberately* burned him with the hot stones. It wasn't an accident, was it?"

Alina hangs her head. "No. I lost my temper. But that—that pig, he was a criminal! A no-good bastard man who would let a baby sleep in a house with leaking windows. Roxana has been fighting him for months, but he will not repair the house. I'm not sorry for what I did."

"That's the real reason he left early, isn't it?" McAdam ventures. "Just like our friend a minute ago—he stormed out after you burned him."

Alina nods silently.

• Turn to **87**

109

"There's only one person here with sufficient motive and cunning to have killed Harry Kennedy," you say. "A man already well steeped in lies and deceit . . . and the last person to see the victim alive. Isn't that right, Tank?"

The so-called tech mogul looks completely shocked by the accusation.

"Harry was my friend," he says, offended. "We were going to be business partners. Why would I kill him?"

It's a good question. Do you have the evidence you need to make a successful accusation?

Check your notebook for clues in the following order:

- If you have T5 written down, turn to **22**
- If you have T4 written down, turn to **85**
- If you have S2 or S6 written down, turn to **188**
- If you have J3 written down, turn to **66**
- Otherwise, turn to **138**

110

"It's quite simple," you say, addressing the crowd. "What many of you may not know is that Alina's sister, Roxana, has been in a dispute with Harry Kennedy for months. Roxana and her young family bought a Kennedy Homes house, only to discover the windows leak. It's not the only house on the estate with that problem, either."

Flora sniffs. "The houses on Burrowlands are beyond the defects insurance period. They should contact their insurers."

"Nobody mentioned Burrowlands, Mrs. Kennedy," McAdam points out. "So it's interesting that you knew which houses we meant, isn't it?"

"I'm familiar with both the complaint and the complainant," Flora says dismissively. "I didn't know her sister worked here, though. My God, did she really kill Harry just because her sister's too stupid to understand the law?"

"No!" Alina protests. "Though maybe I wanted to. You are a criminal just like him."

Not wishing to see Flora give Alina a second black eye, you step between the women.

"I think this was about justice, not law," you say. "Something Roxana and her family were unlikely to get from Harry Kennedy. Alina lied about the time of the phone call because she didn't want us to make the connection between her sister and Kennedy. But that call happened while he was still on Alina's massage table, and when she realized he was the same man who was making her sister's life hell, she was incensed. She deliberately burned him with hot stones, leaving marks on his body that we discovered at the postmortem."

A collective gasp goes up around the room.

"But that wasn't enough, was it, Alina? Harry Kennedy stormed out of the room, and you followed him to finish the job. You killed him, pushed him off that balcony, then claimed to have been in your room the whole time."

"It's not true!" Alina protests. "You said he was killed in that storeroom, but I don't have a key. How would I get in?"

"We can find that out down at the station. Sergeant, arrest Ms. Martinescu."

• Turn to **185**

111

Without fully understanding how you got here, you find yourself standing in a bookstore before a selection of crime fiction. In your hands is one such book. Turning it over, you read the title: *Can You Solve the Murder?* by Antony Johnston.

"Never heard of him," you mutter, skimming the description on the back cover.

"What was that?" asks the bookseller, looking up from her desk. "We have nonfiction crime, too, if that's more your thing." She points out a signed hardcover entitled *Tougher than Tarmac: Killer Cases* by Ruth McAdam, a police detective.

"No, thank you," you reply, "I'm just browsing . . ."

You trail off, returning to the book you're holding. An *interactive* story? What an extraordinary idea. You skim the introduction to see how it works, learning about its numbered sections and how you shouldn't read the book from start to finish—or visit sections you aren't directed to.

If only you could remember how you got here! But you're sure it'll come back to you later. For now, watched carefully by the bookseller, you turn to section **1** and begin reading . . .

112

"For example," you say, "let's talk about your relationship with Harry Kennedy, and this 'mutual investment' you've mentioned. It hadn't actually happened yet, had it? We know that no money had changed hands."

Tank shrugs. "He agreed to invest in my new AI startup, and in return I'd invest in his new housing plan. Nothing unusual about that. We were both just waiting till the time was right. There are contracts to draw up first."

"More likely you were both waiting for a cash windfall. The only large payment Kennedy Homes made recently was to a different company entirely, owned by Carla Nesbitt."

"Nesbitch again," Tank spits. "I should have guessed she'd get his money before I did."

- Write **T5** in your notebook, then turn to **180**

113

At last, after stumbling through the dark for what feels like an age, Jennifer turns a corner and lets out a triumphant cry.

"Aha!"

You follow and take in the sight of a diesel generator pushed against a wall, silent and squat, with a flexible silver pipe leading from its exhaust up into the ceiling (and, you hope, eventually out into open air). Beside it are stacked half a dozen fuel canisters. You lift one experimentally and hear fuel sloshing around inside.

"Well, here goes nothing."

You fill the generator's tank while Jennifer checks the controls. She locates the start button, then pulls the choke handle and presses the button. You hold your breath . . .

It works! The generator rattles and sputters into life, soon settling into a working hum. You hurry back through the cellar and up the steps, delighted to find an illuminated doorway at the top. Inside the relit lobby, Jennifer is more excited to find that her computer now has power. You don't know how long it will last, and it's only one floor, but the restoration of light and power brings you some small comfort, ready to face what you must do next:

Catch a killer.

• Turn to **80**

114

You fix Flora with a steady gaze. "You accused Jennifer Watts of being attracted to your husband's money, and we know you were planning to divorce him. Was the Viagra really such a shock to you?"

"I don't know," she sighs. "I suppose it's one thing when I could shout at him about it, but now to see it from, well, beyond the grave . . . She's just his type, you know. Young, blond, boobs."

It's hardly an unusual taste, and would have described Flora Kennedy herself in her prime. Perhaps that recognition is why she accused Jennifer.

"Mrs. Kennedy, we have CCTV footage of your car heading in this direction yesterday morning. So I'll ask you again: Did you come here after meeting with your solicitor? Did you confront your husband and demand a divorce?"

"I don't like your tone, Inspector."

"And I don't like being lied to. For the last time: Did you come to this house yesterday morning?"

Flora defiantly returns your gaze.

"*Hypothetically*, let's say I did. Let's say I made up my mind to divorce Harry in my solicitor's meeting, and came here to tell him. I might have sneaked in so that nobody would see me and warn him. But when I realized I had no idea where he was, and that the longer I hung around the more chance there was I'd be seen, I gave up and left."

"And so, *hypothetically* speaking, you didn't see Harry?"

"Not at all."

It's a plausible story, but it's also rather convenient. By claiming to have deliberately evaded everyone else in the house, nobody can corroborate Flora's story. You only have her word for it.

- Write **F4** in your notebook, then turn to **175**

115

"I believe you had ample motive to kill Harry Kennedy," you say to Jennifer, "and so does Flora. It was she who realized you were having an affair with her husband, which I assume is why he came here under the guise of taking a break. Did he suspect that Flora knew? Were you worried that news would get out about the affair, putting your job at risk? Sleeping with Friends of Elysium is bad enough, and doing it *at* Elysium is surely worse. Or were you simply jealous when you realized he was also trying to bed most of the other female staff?"

"Neither," Jennifer protests. "I already told you, I wasn't sleeping with him! You saw the bruise I gave him!"

"A bruise is just a bruise," you reply. "It could have been made while you were intimate, or from something else altogether. Need I also point out that you have unfettered, unmonitored access to room 312's missing key. You're the one person who could easily have taken it and used it without anyone else knowing. It would then be simple for you to hide it and claim it was stolen."

Jennifer looks confused. "That makes no sense. Why wouldn't I just put it back?"

"To cast suspicion on others. With the key in its place, only yourself and Stephen Cheong could possibly have entered the room. But the 'stolen' missing key sent us on a wild-goose chase, placing many other people under suspicion."

"This is absurd," she says, bewildered. "I'm not a shareholder or anything, you know. I enjoy my job, but I wouldn't kill someone to keep it—whether I was sleeping with him or not!"

"We'll get the truth down at the station. Sergeant, arrest Ms. Watts."

• Turn to **157**

116

Checking the timetable, Jennifer tells you that Tank Destroyer doesn't currently have a class scheduled, and hasn't booked a private room anywhere. She gives you his bedroom number, but as you're about to send Sergeant McAdam to see if he's there, a passing member of staff overhears. They saw Tank enter the swimming pool changing rooms a few minutes ago.

You thank them and head for the pool area on the converted ground floor of the manor's east wing. It runs most of the building's length, forming a long and narrow pool with loungers positioned along the internal wall. The opposite exterior wall features the windows that look out onto the grassy courtyard. It's only now that you're here inside the pool area that you realize how small and dim those windows are. The view of the opposite wing isn't as clear as you'd hoped, though you can make out the white forensics tent still in place under the balcony from which Harry Kennedy fell. It's just as well the body is now in Dr. Wash's mortuary, and all the ground evidence gathered already, as today's weather would destroy anything that remained.

In the shallow end of the pool, under a large wall clock, an Elysium staffer leads a mixed group of Friends through aquatic exercises. Petals surround them, floating on the water's surface. You scan the group for Tank, but don't see him.

"Maybe he finished already," McAdam says, frustrated.

But then you look down to the deep end and see someone doing widths. Someone with tattoos all over their body.

"Perhaps group therapy isn't Mr. Destroyer's style," you say, and walk down to intercept him at the pool's edge.

- If you have T6 written in your notebook, turn to **32**
- Otherwise, turn to **71**

117

You may get a chance to ask Tank what's going on sooner than you expected. As you're about to leave the waiting room, you hear tense whispers from the other side of the door. One of the voices sounds like his, while the other is a woman's.

They sound so close, they must be directly outside the door. If you press your ear to it, you could probably make out what they're saying. Alternatively, you could open the door and face them directly.

- To eavesdrop, turn to **88**
- To announce yourself, turn to **169**

118

While McAdam asks Jennifer at the reception desk for Mr. Kennedy's timetable, you mount the stairs to the top floor. This time you walk past the old storeroom and make directly for the bedroom door. The police officer guarding it confirms the room was Kennedy's.

"I saw you arguing with a guest here earlier," you say to the constable. "Tall chap, tattoos. What did he want?"

The officer shrugs. "Trying to get in the room. He said the deceased had borrowed some of his possessions. I told him he'd have to wait until we'd finished examining everything before he could claim them."

"How did he take that?"

He smirks. "About as well as you'd expect. Are you wanting inside yourself? I've been told forensics are on their way."

"So they haven't been over this room yet? Has anyone else been inside?"

"Definitely not. I've been here since we arrived."

"Very good. Well, before the team gets here I'm going to take a quick look around."

Pulling on a pair of nitrile gloves, you enter the room. It's bigger than the storeroom and feels curiously sparse. The decor is another collision of old and new, where a four-poster bed and wood paneling butt up against a smooth pine desk, ergonomic chairs, built-in wardrobe, and gleaming en suite. The window looks out over the grounds. Presumably this is normally a green and verdant view, with a grassy area leading to trees, but thanks to the summer weather the grass and leaves are both starting to brown. To one side you see the main driveway, leading down through the avenue toward the bridge and estate entrance.

The impression of sparseness continues as you look through Kennedy's possessions. He appears to have brought a week's worth of the most normal clothes and toiletries you could imagine. Polo shirts, chinos, jeans. Gillette razor. You wonder if this was a dead end after all. Perhaps you should have sent McAdam to give this room a cursory once-over, while you checked out Kennedy's timetable. But you can't help feeling there's a lot you still don't understand about him, and in your experience getting to know a victim is often the key to solving their murder.

It's at that moment you spy a small gray backpack tucked at the bottom of the wardrobe, behind a jacket. You remove and open it, finding a laptop inside. Potentially much more interesting. Unfortunately, when you open it you're confronted with a password screen and can't go any further. You place the computer on the desk, ready for forensics to bag up, and turn to the jacket.

Inside are Kennedy's car keys and wallet. The wallet has a few credit cards, coffee shop loyalty cards, his driving license (which confirms his identity, not that you doubted it), and sixty pounds in cash. Nothing out of the ordinary . . . until you replace one of the loyalty cards, and feel something else tucked deep inside the same slot.

You carefully remove it and discover an old photograph, cut down to fit inside the wallet. In the picture two young, good-looking people smile with their arms around each other. It's at least twenty years old, but there's no mistaking the subjects: Harry Kennedy and Carla Nesbitt.

- If you have C3 written in your notebook, turn to **141**
- Otherwise, turn to **59**

119

"Why didn't you tell us this before?" you ask.

The therapist shrugs. "Because it looks bad, yes? I can't risk losing this job, Inspector. I need the money."

"Surely there are other places you could work."

"I don't want to move away."

You consider this. "Martinescu is a Romanian name, is that right? Your accent fits."

She narrows her eyes in suspicion. "So?"

"I just wondered what ties you have to this area, given you already moved across a continent to work here. Are you married?"

"No. Roxana, my sister, she is family. We look after each other."

McAdam looks around the room. "This is where you had that morning session with Mr. Kennedy?" she asks, and Alina nods in agreement. "Where did you go after he left?"

"Nowhere. I saw the tattooed man, Tank, talk to him in the corridor, but then I closed the door and stayed here. I—I should have told Jennifer I was free again, so someone else could book me. But I took the free time instead."

"Did you hear what Harry and Tank were discussing?"

"No." Alina looks offended. "I do not listen to other people talking."

"Were you worried that Mr. Kennedy might tell Stephen about the burns?" you ask. "I assume that's the real reason he left early, just like our friend a minute ago."

She shrugs. "If he had told Stephen, I would just have to deal with it, you know?"

"Did you tell him after he found Mr. Kennedy dead on the lawn?"

"No, only that Mr. Kennedy had left early. There were more important things to think about."

• Write **A5** in your notebook, then turn to **87**

120

You return to the main entrance hall and cross to the reception desk. You're just beaten there by a small group of older guests, each wheeling a suitcase behind them.

"We're checking out early," the man at their head tells Jennifer Watts. "It's not safe." He casts a disparaging glance in your direction.

The receptionist puts on a sympathetic smile. "We're sorry to see you go, Mr. Jones. You do understand we can't refund you for the days remaining on your stay?"

"Of course you can," Mr. Jones insists. "There's a man dead out there, for goodness' sake!"

You take this as your cue. "Actually, Mr. Kennedy is no longer on the premises," you explain. "What's more, I'm afraid we can't allow you—or anyone else—to leave. First we must take everyone's statements, and investigate what happened."

"We know what happened." A short, gray-haired woman stands beside Mr. Jones, wagging a finger at you. "A man got stabbed, and now what if one of us is next? The killer might still be in the building!"

"Precisely why we must keep everyone here, madam. We have officers throughout the house, so you're quite safe. If it helps, I suggest you always travel in groups, or at least in pairs."

"You can't stop us from leaving," Mr. Jones says angrily. "We're not suspects."

"But you are potential witnesses, and I know you all want to help us apprehend Mr. Kennedy's killer. Isn't that right?"

A discontented murmur ripples through the group, but you can see acceptance gaining ground. Grumbling but obedient, they leave, taking their suitcases with them. You can't blame them, really. The manner of Kennedy's death suggests he was deliberately targeted, but you can't yet be sure his killer won't strike again.

"Do you really need everyone to stay?" Jennifer asks you when they're out of earshot.

"I'm afraid so, at least until we can take everyone's statement. Staff can return home overnight, of course, but we'll need you all back here tomorrow. Do you have any guests—sorry, Friends—who are actually due to leave today or tomorrow?"

"Let me check." She clicks around on her computer. "Yes, six people." She prints off a list for you. One name immediately stands out: Carla Nesbitt, MP.

You turn to look around the lobby for Constable Zwale. This would be a good task for him. But you don't see him anywhere—

"Just tell me who's in charge, for heaven's sake! I'm his wife!"

The shout came from the front entrance. You walk to the doors and find a heavyset blond woman arguing with Zwale outside, under the portico. She wears a riot of gold jewelry: fingers festooned with rings, necklaces, bangles, and ostentatious earrings. You wonder how much it all weighs. The constable is attempting to prevent her from entering the building, though it's a battle he seems destined to lose.

"Can I help?" you say, approaching them. "Whose wife are you, exactly?"

"I'm Flora Kennedy," the woman says. "Harry's wife. Who are you? What's going on?" Up close you can see she's heavily made-up, and wears false eyelashes.

"Constable, let her through. It's all right."

You quietly give Zwale the list from Jennifer, asking him to inform those unlucky guests they can't yet leave, and instruct McAdam to remain in the lobby to prevent any more walk-outs. Then you lead Flora Kennedy past the stares of staff, and a few guests no doubt hoping to overhear something salacious, until you find an empty waiting room off the entrance hall and usher her inside, closing the door behind you.

When the manor was still a family home this room would have been a reception, with tall windows looking out over the driveway and grounds. Now it's lined with cushioned bench chairs and coffee tables of unvarnished wood, scattered with brochures for Elysium and other local attractions, as well as a smattering of the "celebrity businessman" biographies Stephen Cheong seems to enjoy. A large screen mounted on one wall silently plays a video of someone doing yoga in a flower-filled garden. Every space between the benches is filled by plants and flowers in pots, though you notice that some are wilting.

Flora sits on a bench, tapping her foot nervously. She's no fool, and has by now realized that something isn't right.

"What's going on?" she asks. "I just wanted to surprise Harry. Where is he?"

You sit beside her. "Surprise him? So your husband wasn't expecting to see you here?"

"No," she says cautiously. "No chance of a surprise now, I suppose. Why can't I see him?"

You take a deep breath. "Mrs. Kennedy . . . I'm sorry to tell you that your husband was found dead this morning."

Everyone receives such news differently. You've delivered it many times throughout your career, and can never predict how those left behind will react.

Flora Kennedy appears stunned, unable to speak for a while. She doesn't ask if you're sure, or for you to repeat yourself. Then she breaks down, distraught and sobbing, her cries echoing around the room.

You prepare to leave and order a constable to look after her, but as you stand up Flora pulls herself together and asks, "How did he die?"

"That's what we're here to find out, and I'm afraid we're treating his death as suspicious." You sit back down. "Mrs. Kennedy, I must ask: Can you think of anyone who would want to harm your husband?"

"No!" she protests. "Harry was a charming man, always ready with a smile . . ." She hesitates. "Well. I mean, sometimes he charmed people and later they regretted it. But it was just business! Nobody would want to kill him." She sniffs.

"I'm afraid somebody did."

"Really, I can't believe it . . ."

"I understand. I'm very sorry for your loss."

The widow shakes her head. "No, I mean I can't believe he was staying here. This place isn't his kind of thing at all."

"You mean Elysium? He didn't frequent wellness retreats?"

She sits a little straighter and regards you carefully. "Inspector, my husband is—was—what I believe they call an 'unreconstructed male.' Steak and Mercedes, not yoga and aromatherapy. I didn't even know he was here. He just said he wanted a break, and packed last week. Then this morning, a brochure arrived in the post."

"Did he often take holidays without telling you where he'd be?"

The widow looks up at the garden yoga video looping on the TV screen. "I know it might seem odd to you, Inspector, but we often took breaks by ourselves. We weren't joined at the hip."

"What about you, Mrs. Kennedy? Is Elysium the sort of place you'd frequent?"

She sniffs. "If someone else was paying, perhaps."

"Could that explain your husband's visit? Was he scouting it for you?"

"I don't know. Maybe . . . I don't know." She sighs, then suddenly remembers something. "Oh God, the company. I'll have to run everything now."

You nod in sympathy. "So you're a partner in his business? He was a house builder, is that right?"

"We prefer *construction entrepreneurs*," she corrects you. "Kennedy Homes is the foremost local estate designer. We offer a full solution, from concept to construction."

"I see. So you'll now take over?"

She looks offended. "Now hang on. I didn't kill Harry for it, if that's what you're implying."

"No, of course. And I imagine you'll have plenty on your hands, with the new housing development being blocked."

"Um, yes. Yes, naturally."

- If you have C3 written in your notebook, turn to **174**
- Otherwise, turn to **72**

121

The document that Constable Zwale found in Stephen's office drawer contained an invoice number. Did you note it down? If so, *reverse* it and turn to the section matching the new number.

- Otherwise, turn to **105**

122

McAdam whistles. "I don't care how much she earns as an MP, seven grand is a decent amount. And Kennedy was short of cash himself, so he must have been desperate for whatever he wanted to buy with it."

"A bribe of some kind fits with the message, doesn't it?" you suggest. "'You knew what that seven grand was for,' indeed."

There's something else tingling in your mind, something connected . . .

"Consulting!" you gasp.

"Best wait till you've retired, don't you think? Might be against regulations."

"No, not me. Kennedy Homes recently paid seven thousand in consultancy fees to Standard Umbrella, remember? This message is a threat about that same payment."

- If you have C1, C8, or C15 written in your notebook, turn to **179**
- Otherwise, turn to **12**

123

Before you can decide on your next course of action, a flash of lightning illuminates the sky, quickly followed by a rumble of thunder. With the perpetual rain and darkening clouds overhead, you've been expecting a major storm all day. Yesterday you hoped for some respite from the heat, but you didn't intend something quite this extreme. Be careful what you wish for.

Suddenly you hear another thunderous crash, followed by yells of shock and surprise from the lobby area. You exchange a worried glance with McAdam, wondering what could have caused this sudden uproar. She doesn't hesitate to run toward the commotion, with you following. Soon you arrive and see something you could never have expected.

The entrance hall's grand old chandelier, one of the main features of Finchcote Manor's previous life, has fallen to the floor and smashed in a maelstrom of metal and glass, topped with sodden pieces of splintered wooden joist. From the shattered ceiling rose where it previously hung pours a thin but steady waterfall.

"Was anyone hurt?" McAdam calls to Jennifer, who stands frozen behind her desk.

"I—I don't think so," she gasps.

You lean over the chandelier, craning your neck to look up through the ceiling while trying to avoid the falling water. It's hard to make out, but you're pretty sure you see daylight up there. Something in the roof appears to have given way under all this rain and started a chain reaction down through several floors, culminating in the chandelier's destruction. From the moment you stepped inside Elysium you knew the manor house was in need of repair, but you didn't expect to be proven right so quickly.

"Well, that's a fine way to round off one's week." Carla Nesbitt stands on the wide staircase, mid-descent, staring down at the wreckage.

Staff and Friends alike crowd into the lobby, attracted by either the crash or the shouting. Tank Destroyer saunters in from the pool area, toweling himself down. Finally Stephen Cheong runs in from the rear of the house, dripping wet.

"What the hell happened?!" he cries.

You explain your theory about the roof, which only makes him more upset.

"How did you know anything *had* happened?" you ask. "You couldn't have heard the crash from outside in the polytunnels."

"Jennifer texted me," he says. She nods in confirmation.

"I was getting changed when I heard the crash," Tank says, unprompted.

"And I was on my way down to see when you're planning to let us leave at last," Carla adds acidly.

Alina Martinescu rushes downstairs behind Carla, out of breath. "The room next door to mine is ruined!" she sobs. "I heard a terrible sound through the wall and went to look. There's a hole in the ceiling and floor, like something fell through. It was so close to me!"

"Good lord, I was only a few doors down from there myself," Carla says, shivering.

"Was anyone in that room?" McAdam asks, ready to spring into action.

Alina shakes her head. “No, thank God. It wasn’t being used.”

Murmurs of amazement and gossip move through the crowd like ripples as everyone wonders what to do next. You notice a steady stream of people turning around and heading back upstairs, and words like “deathtrap,” “dangerous,” and “killer” reach your ears over the hubbub. The mood in Elysium is growing tense.

Meanwhile, the thin but steady stream of water continues to fall through the ceiling. Jennifer brings out a bucket from a storage cupboard behind her desk, and sends other staff for towels to form a water barricade around the soaked chandelier.

Stephen pulls himself together and takes out his phone. “I’ll call Ted,” he says, moving aside. Jennifer explains to you that Ted is their regular handyman.

“But he’s not on-site,” she says, “and I don’t fancy his chances of getting here in this weather.”

You’re inclined to agree, and while you can’t hear Stephen’s conversation, his facial expression and body language tell you Jennifer’s assumption is correct.

“Right, well,” the manager says, ending the call with a look of bewilderment. “Ted’s road is flooded, so he can’t drive anywhere. I’ll have to do it myself.”

Stephen’s words make you think of Constable Zwale, driving Flora Kennedy to the police station through the rain. You hope they’re OK.

As if on cue, the main doors burst open and Zwale staggers inside with Flora Kennedy in tow. They’re both soaked through and stand inside the entrance, looking wretched.

“What the hell happened?” McAdam says. “Did you decide to walk her to the station, or what?”

“No, ma’am,” Zwale splutters. “The road down to the bridge is running like a river. I didn’t want to risk it, so I turned around and came back. I’m sorry, I should have tried to leave earlier. Does anyone have a towel?” He glances at Flora’s bedraggled countenance. “Maybe two.”

The staffers that Jennifer sent are now returning. One of them hands towels to Zwale and Flora. Jennifer directs the others to roll theirs into cylinders and place them around the edges of the chandelier wreckage, to soak up the spreading water.

"You should get out of those clothes," Jennifer says to Zwale, adding quickly, "both of you, I mean. I'm sure we've got spare workout kits you can borrow. Come with me."

Jennifer leads them down a corridor to a staff-only room. Flora and the constable follow, drying their faces and hair. As they pass by, you instruct Zwale to keep the widow in that room until the storm clears and he can take her to the station. He nods, then resumes following Jennifer. You're intrigued by how much of Elysium seems to run through the receptionist. She's almost more of a maître d', and you wonder if Stephen realizes how vital she is to the smooth running of his operation.

"Maybe we should leave while we still can," McAdam says to you quietly. "This storm doesn't look like it's going to let up. If we don't go now, we might be stuck here."

"It may already be too late. Constable Zwale felt it wasn't safe."

"All the more reason to try right away. Wait too long and we'll be trapped for sure."

She has a point, and if you can make it back to the station you can probably get home from there. On the other hand, you'd be putting yourself at risk—and could potentially be leaving everyone at Elysium trapped with a killer. At least here in the manor house everyone is, so to speak, in the same boat.

- To leave immediately, turn to **15**
- To wait out the storm, turn to **67**

124

"The woman who killed Harry Kennedy is perhaps the one who seems least likely," you say. Many of the crowd turn to look at Carla, but you shake your head. "No, not our upstanding, if occasionally deceitful, MP. I'm talking about the woman who knew him best, but perhaps wished she didn't. Isn't that right, Flora?"

You fix your gaze on Harry's widow.

"That's outrageous!" she protests, her jewelry rattling. "All right, I admit that I was planning to divorce Harry. So then why would I need to kill him?"

It's time to answer that question. Do you have the evidence you need to make a successful accusation?

Check your notebook for clues in the following order:

- If you have F4 written down, turn to **83**
- If you have F3 written down, turn to **186**
- If you have C12 written down, turn to **49**
- If you have F2 written down, turn to **151**
- Otherwise, turn to **18**

125

Greenleaf Lane is well named; situated in a tree-lined suburb on the other side of town from Finchcote Manor, the road is sufficiently narrow and winding that even McAdam is forced to drive slowly.

"Do you still think Flora Kennedy could have done this trip in twenty minutes?" you ask. "Ferrari or not, this isn't a fast road."

"It's not about the engine, it's about how you drive it. If she takes this route often, she'd know how to take it at speed."

"So she still might have been able to reach Elysium in time to kill her husband. Let's see if we can find the right Mr. Proctor to corroborate Flora's alibi."

McAdam parks outside the offices of Proctor, Proctor and Proctor. Grateful for the shade of the surrounding trees, you marvel at how quiet it is here. The only sounds are birdsong and the occasional passing car.

You enter and greet the receptionist, showing your warrant cards. "We'd like a word with whichever Proctor deals with Mrs. Flora Kennedy."

"Oh, yes, that would be Mr. Proctor," she says with a light Scottish burr. "May I ask what it's concerning?"

"Just tell him it's a police matter," McAdam says, dialing up her accent a notch. "Aye, and be sure we get the right Mr. Proctor, too."

This attempt at patriotic bonding collapses like a house of cards. The receptionist looks down her nose at the sergeant, an impressive feat given she's sitting down and McAdam is standing up.

"There is only one Mr. Proctor," the receptionist says imperiously. "The other partners are Mrs. Proctor and Ms. Proctor."

You smirk and nudge McAdam. "One mustn't make assumptions, Sergeant. It's the twenty-first century."

McAdam turns a shade of red, though you're not sure if it's embarrassment at being dressed down by the receptionist, or irritation at being blamed for an assumption you also made.

Moments after the receptionist calls through, Mr. Proctor steps out of the back offices to greet you. He's short, round, and entirely bald, with a bulldog gravitas to his jowly face.

"How can I help?" he asks, extending a hand, which you decline. "Something about Flora Kennedy, was it?"

"I'm afraid so. I regret to inform you that her husband Harry Kennedy has been found dead in suspicious circumstances. Was he a client of yours as well?"

"Good heavens!" Mr. Proctor reels, seemingly shocked by the news. He leans on the front desk for support, gathering himself. Finally he says, "No, Mr. Kennedy wasn't a client. That would be . . . difficult to reconcile."

"I see. Shall we talk privately?" You gesture toward the door leading to the offices. Proctor hesitates, checking the time on his watch, so you add, "We won't take long."

"Well . . . I suppose, in the circumstances . . . all right, but I can't give you much time."

He leads you along a short corridor, past several closed doors. At its end, you mount a set of stairs to find yourself in a plush office occupying the entire first floor.

"How would it be difficult to reconcile having both Mr. and Mrs. Kennedy as clients, exactly?" You take a seat in a leather chair while

Sergeant McAdam closes the door behind you. "They're both partners in their business, aren't they?"

"Oh, we don't handle Kennedy Homes. Good heavens, no. I am Mrs. Kennedy's personal solicitor."

McAdam nods, her suspicions confirmed. "She was planning to divorce her husband, wasn't she? Therefore you couldn't represent them both."

"I couldn't possibly comment," Proctor replies. "It's a matter of privacy, you understand."

"Where were you between ten and eleven this morning, Mr. Proctor?"

"I don't see why I should answer that. Surely I'm not a suspect?"

"You may not be," you reassure him, "but your client is. With Harry Kennedy dead, Flora Kennedy no longer requires a divorce. She'll now inherit Kennedy Homes in its entirety, rather than settling for whatever portion of the business she might have been hoping for in a separation. Not only does this give her a reason to want her husband dead, but she's also given you as her alibi between those times. So I'd appreciate some answers."

Proctor clears his throat and glances out of the window. "I understand your position, Inspector, but I'm still bound not to disclose the circumstances under which I represent Mrs. Kennedy. However, given the situation I can confirm we had a meeting here this morning. She arrived at nine thirty, and left a little before ten thirty. Does that corroborate my client's statement?"

You exchange a glance with McAdam. If she's right about driving times, that still leaves just enough time for Flora to reach Elysium, kill Harry Kennedy, and be home by eleven.

"You said 'the circumstances under which I represent Mrs. Kennedy,'" McAdam points out. "That's very specific, and implies she engaged you for a single task. When did she first hire you?"

It's a good question. Hiring a solicitor so recently may not prove by itself that Flora was seeking a divorce, but it's strong support for the theory.

Proctor checks his watch again, then relents. "In February of this year. Now, is there anything else? I do have other appointments, and as I said, if you want to know any more you must ask Mrs. Kennedy herself."

You doubt you'll get anything further out of Mr. Proctor without an airtight warrant. But as you make to leave, you hear the distinctive sound of a loud, well-tuned performance engine approaching. Proctor glances nervously at the window. McAdam walks over and looks out.

"Maybe we'll do that," she says with a smile, "and sooner than expected."

You join her at the window and see Flora Kennedy parking her Ferrari. One of the solicitor's "other appointments"? Or an impromptu visit following the death of her husband? Mr. Proctor may remain tight-lipped, but Flora herself might talk—unless advised not to by her solicitor, of course. How should you approach her?

- To wait in Mr. Proctor's office for Flora to enter, turn to **171**
- To intercept her before she enters the office, turn to **68**

126

Jennifer shrugs. "I don't know if it means much, but Joseph—sorry, I mean Constable Zwale—mentioned how Harry Kennedy hadn't paid for his stay, which surprised me. I thought I'd check how often Stephen gave out freebies to other Friends without telling me."

"What did you find?" you ask.

"He does it every so often, but what stood out to me was that there are two this week. Harry Kennedy, and an upgrade for Tank Destroyer."

This could go some way to explaining Elysium's seemingly perpetual money problems. "What kind of upgrade?"

"Tank normally books the basic Rose package," the receptionist explains. "That's more of a pay-as-you-go program, with a lower standing fee. But this week Stephen put a note on his admission to upgrade him to Lotus Flower, free of charge."

"How often does Mr. Destroyer stay here?"

"Five days at a time, every month or so."

McAdam grumbles. "Why does a tech millionaire need a free upgrade?"

Constable Zwale shrugs. "Some people are just tight, ma'am. My uncle's loaded, but he gets all his clothes from charity shops. With him, I think it comes from having been poor as a boy."

Tank Destroyer may be worth millions now, but perhaps he also grew up without money. The question remains: Is it a coincidence that Stephen Cheong gave Harry Kennedy a free stay and Tank Destroyer a free upgrade at the same time? Or is there something more to it?

"This could be useful information," you say to Jennifer. "Thank you for checking. There is one more thing I have to ask, and please forgive me: Was Mrs. Kennedy right? Were you sleeping with her husband?" When she hesitates, you quickly add, "I must remind you that lying to the police is an offense."

"Oh, come on," Zwale says, defending her. "Kennedy was a sleazebag, everyone says so. Jennifer wouldn't!"

"Be quiet, Constable!" McAdam barks.

"He's right, though," Jennifer says. "Mr. Kennedy tried it on, like he did with every other woman in here, but I told him where to stick it. Not in a million years."

- Write **T2** in your notebook
- If you already have J3 written down, turn to **37**
- Otherwise, turn to **136**

127

"Answer me this, then," you say. "A man matching your description was seen watching—in what could be deemed an intimidating fashion—a young family on the Burrowlands estate, who just happen to be in dispute with Kennedy Homes over shoddy building practices. What can you tell me about that?"

Tank eyes you carefully. "Seen by whom?"

"You're on camera, so don't try to deny it. What I don't understand is that you said you met Harry Kennedy for the first time this week, but this intimidation has been going on for more than a month. Now, please don't insult me by claiming it's all a coincidence."

The tech mogul sighs. "All right, fine. I actually met Harry about six months ago at a business mixer. We got along well, and agreed to make mutual investments."

"How well?" McAdam asks.

"Why, are you jealous?"

"Mr. Destroyer, you've just admitted you lied to us about when you first met a man who was murdered not a hundred yards from here. I suggest you grow up, and tell us why."

Tank looks away. "Because I didn't want any trouble from you lot, all right? I had nothing to do with his death, and no, I didn't see anything from here in the pool yesterday morning. But I knew if I told you me and Harry were already friends, you'd get suspicious. Just like you are now, aren't you?"

You don't deny it, because it's true—although part of your suspicion is now founded on Tank's reluctance to tell you the whole story.

"Did you plan your visits to Elysium at the same time? Given it was Mr. Kennedy's first time here, that also seems unlikely to be a coincidence."

"No, it wasn't a coincidence. I mentioned Elysium to Harry when we first met. He'd never heard of it at the time, but then a couple of weeks ago he called and told me he was coming. We agreed to meet and discuss business."

"So what were you doing in Burrowlands?" McAdam asks. "A favor for a friend?"

"Something like that, sure. Just to let those troublemakers know someone was watching them."

- Write **T4** in your notebook, then turn to **161**

128

While you continue taking in the estate, McAdam calls the agent selling that row of four houses. It's not a bad area; the estate is paved over but the edges are lined with trees, giving plenty of green space for children to play. Birdsong fills the air, and traffic noise from the main road is muted. It's not hard to see why young families would come to live here.

"Can I help you?"

A young woman with an infant in a stroller, thankfully shaded by a large parasol, calls out to you from the other side of the road. You're about to politely decline, but then decide to ask her some questions after all.

"Actually, perhaps you can. Do you know who's buying that field across the road?"

She shakes her head. "No, it's been fenced off for months. Are you builders?"

"Police, actually. Have you seen anything unusual happen over there recently?"

"Like what? It's a field."

Indeed it is, and yet it seems to have carried a significant importance for Harry Kennedy.

"Tell you what," she continues, "if you're police, you want to have a word with the company that built this place. Bunch of cowboys."

"Oh? How so?"

"My windows leak whenever it rains hard, and I'm not the only one. The sod who built them says it's nothing to do with him because the houses are a few years old. Kennedy Homes, they're called. They all belong in jail."

You look around the estate, taking it in with a new eye.

"This estate was built by Kennedy Homes? Are you sure?"

"Yeah, of course I am," the young mother says slowly, as if talking to a child slow on the uptake.

"It's the same company," you explain. "Kennedy Homes applied to build another estate on that field."

"Shouldn't be allowed. Do you know they're only liable for the windows for two years? What kind of warranty is that? None at all."

You find it hard to disagree. But could Harry Kennedy really have been killed over leaking windows? It would be a very extreme reaction.

"You want to catch some criminals, just take a pair of handcuffs round their offices," she says, resuming her walk. "Crooks, the lot of them."

As the woman leaves, McAdam finishes her phone call.

"Well, well," she says, grinning. "This is a turn-up for the books. First of all, guess who built this estate?"

"Kennedy Homes."

"Oh." Her grin fades.

"I was just told, in no uncertain terms, by that young mother. She also said Harry Kennedy was a cowboy builder who should be arrested and locked up. Apparently several of the houses on this estate have leaking windows."

McAdam's grin returns. "That might explain what I found out about that row of houses up for sale."

- If you have C1 written in your notebook, turn to **43**
- Otherwise, turn to **96**

129

As you walk on through the cellar, past empty shelves storing nothing but dust, you consider what Jennifer said about Harry Kennedy and try to fit the pieces together.

"So Kennedy really did try it on with every female member of staff?"

"He really did," the receptionist says. "Especially the massage therapists. So predictable."

"Including Alina Martinescu?"

Jennifer thinks for a moment. "Maybe not, because yesterday

morning was his first booking with her. Everyone he'd already had a session with begged me not to let him see them again. Trouble is, there's only so many 'Roses' at Elysium. Sooner or later I'd have had to send one of them back in. I wasn't looking forward to it, believe me."

"But now you might say the problem has been solved," you point out.

To your surprise Jennifer laughs, then quickly stifles it.

"Inspector, if you think Harry Kennedy was the only man who got handsy with the staff, you're more naive than you look. The big spenders do whatever they like around here."

"Surely you could complain to the management?"

"Stephen? He's the one who lets them get away with it. Doesn't want to risk them taking their money elsewhere, does he?"

• Write **J2** in your notebook, then turn to **166**

130

You reach out and remove the central plant, which blocks your view of Carla, placing it on the floor.

"Shortly before he died, Harry Kennedy paid seven thousand pounds in consultancy fees to a firm with which he'd never previously done business: Standard Umbrella. I understand you're familiar with them?"

Carla eyes you carefully. You can almost see cogs whirring behind her eyes as she tries to guess how much you already know. Finally, she counters your question with another question.

"Why do you ask?"

"Because that's a significant sum, even by your high standards, and an unusual transaction to make with a man you claim to have disliked. We know Standard Umbrella is your company. We also know that through it you own several houses on Burrowlands, originally purchased from Kennedy Homes, which you're now trying to offload in a quick sale. Houses that, if Kennedy's new plan had been approved, would be in the path of potential flooding—making them harder to sell."

Carla blinks, taking in this barrage of evidence, and her skin pales. But you don't let up.

"So I'll ask you again," you say, "and this time I'd appreciate an answer. Why did Mr. Kennedy pay you seven thousand pounds?"

- Turn to **82**

131

Over his protestations of innocence, McAdam arrests Tank. Later, when the storm has died down, you take him into custody at the police station.

But while further research proves the so-called tech mogul's credentials and life story are fake, it doesn't uncover any physical evidence tying Tank to the crime. You can't place him at the crime scene, or put the murder weapon in his hand. All you have is your own speculation—and that's simply not enough.

The case is a bust. Losing faith in you, the detective chief superintendent reassigns you to a different, simpler case and calls in another inspector to take over the Elysium killing. Harry Kennedy's murder may yet be solved . . . but not by you.

Later, you consider what went wrong. Were you right that Tank did it, but simply failed to collect the right evidence? Or was the killer someone else altogether?

- To find out, don't despair. Simply wipe your notebook, return to **1**, and try again.

For now, though, this is . . .

THE END

132

"This is a case of fraud and blackmail," you say simply. "Floral therapy, with flowers grown here on-site, is Elysium's 'unique brand promise,' as Stephen puts it. But he's been struggling to grow enough flowers because of the poor weather. Going without isn't an option, so instead he's been buying plants and precut flowers from a nursery, to pass them off as his own."

Stephen says nothing, waiting for you to provide evidence.

You oblige. "We know this for a number of reasons—not least that we have a firsthand eyewitness. Don't we, Mr. Destroyer?"

Tank looks surprised to be called on, but nods in agreement. "I saw him at the nursery, buying plants and piling them into the back of a van. It was Harry who told me to follow him."

"Indeed he did," you agree, turning to Stephen. "With confirmation of your fraud, Mr. Kennedy then blackmailed you. That's why you gave him a free VIP stay at Elysium, and Tank a free upgrade; it's why you let them both behave like brats."

"Hey!" Tank objects, but you ignore him.

"Harry Kennedy had you over a barrel," you say to Stephen, "until you sensed an opportunity to rid yourself of this turbulent businessman. You weren't in the polytunnels yesterday morning at all, were you? You were here in the house, and saw Harry leave Alina's session early. You lured him into the storeroom, then silenced him once and for all. The rose in his mouth was a poetic symbol of why Harry Kennedy had to die."

Stephen reels from the accusation. "All right, I admit that I bought in a small number of flowers. You people have no idea how hard it is to keep this business running! My God, if I could start again I'd ditch the flowers entirely. Or maybe ditch the retreat entirely, and go back to owning a garden center. So what if some of the flowers weren't grown here? They're the same bloody flowers!"

Carla tuts loudly. "You sell Elysium as a holistic retreat, Stephen. What are we all paying for, if not that special touch of knowing all the plants are hand-grown here in the grounds? It's a disgrace!"

"They're only flowers," Tank says.

"That is *not* the point!" Carla insists.

The room devolves into shouted arguments. Ignoring them, you direct McAdam to arrest Stephen Cheong.

• Turn to **76**

133

You emerge from the waiting room into the lobby, where Jennifer is sweeping up the crushed Viagra pills. With dustpan and brush in hand, she chats to the East Asian man who helped Constable Zwale to restrain Flora Kennedy.

"Have you arrested Mrs. Kennedy?" Jennifer asks.

"I have."

"Good," the man says. "Don't want people thinking they can come in here and start a fight."

You offer your hand to him. "Thank you for your help with Mrs. Kennedy, by the way. Even though I'd prefer you didn't put yourself at risk, it's appreciated."

"Just being a good citizen," he replies with a firm handshake. "Besides, I didn't want Stephen to be saddled with a cleaning bill if things got bloody."

"That's very considerate of you, Mr. . . . ?"

"Cheong. Bill Cheong. I lead the Tai Chi classes." He beams with pride and saves you from having to make an assumption. "Yes, we're related. Stephen's my son."

Jennifer nudges him playfully as she passes to empty the dustpan. "Let's hear it for nepotism," she jokes.

"I'm sure that's not true," you say, though you had the same thought. "How long have you worked here, Mr. Cheong?"

"Three years. Since the day it opened."

"And where did you teach Tai Chi before that?"

Bill shuffles closer and says quietly, "Nowhere, but don't tell our 'Friends' that. I learned on the job, if you know what I mean."

So the jab about nepotism was true after all. McAdam shakes her head in disbelief.

Bill looks in Jennifer's direction. "Got some tips off that one, too. She knows her karate."

"Judo, actually," Jennifer says, replacing the cleaning tools in the cupboard behind her desk. "It's for self-defense, not like Tai Chi."

"That's OK," Bill says with a smile. "They don't know that."

- If you have C3 written in your notebook, turn to **26**
- Otherwise, turn to **81**

134

The sun shines through the waiting room's large windows, nourishing the plants lining its walls. You sit in silence for a moment, then move on to a difficult question. "Forgive me for asking, Mrs. Kennedy, but where were you between ten and eleven this morning?"

Flora takes a tissue from her handbag, dabs at her eyes, then blows her nose. Finally recovered, she says, "With my solicitor. Proctor, Proctor and Proctor, on Greenleaf Lane. I had an appointment at nine thirty, left at half past ten, and was home by eleven."

"Where is home? We haven't yet determined your husband's details," you explain.

"One of our larger properties, on Monkroyd Avenue."

"Then I'll have an officer drive you there."

"Nonsense," she protests. "I'm perfectly capable, and besides, I'm not leaving my car here."

You find this reaction odd until, still trying to persuade her not to drive, you emerge onto the main steps and see a bright red Ferrari convertible parked behind the row of police cars. Perhaps Flora Kennedy and Sergeant McAdam would get along, talking fast cars.

Regardless, no matter how stoic she may seem, you can't let the widow drive herself home after such an emotional shock. Eventually you compromise: an officer will drive her sports car. You expect Constable Zwale to jump at the chance to get behind the wheel of a Ferrari, but to your surprise he demurs. Instead another young officer steps forward, practically rubbing his hands with glee, and with Mrs. Kennedy safely inside, you watch the car speed down the avenue toward the bridge.

Returning inside the house, you gather McAdam and Zwale in the lobby. You ask Zwale to look up Greenleaf Lane and Monkroyd Avenue, and McAdam to request any CCTV from this morning covering the route between them.

Zwale notes that according to his phone, Greenleaf Lane is a thirty-minute drive from here, while Monkroyd Avenue is less than ten minutes away. "Looks like her alibi holds up," he says.

McAdam peers over his shoulder at the map. "Not so fast. Those timings assume you're in a normal car, which Mrs. Kennedy's is definitely not. Say the meeting with her solicitor ends ten minutes early, and she's out of there by ten twenty. She could put her foot down, get here by ten forty, sneak in, and kill her husband. Plenty of time to be home by eleven."

With no CCTV at Elysium, it's true Flora could have sneaked inside—but with more than a hundred staff and guests on the premises, wouldn't someone have seen her? Besides, how would she steal the key to the old storeroom? How would Flora even know where it was, if she'd never been here before? And how did she lure Harry out of his massage therapy session? These and many other questions remain unanswered.

"The spouse is always a prime suspect when it comes to murder," you agree, "though Flora Kennedy did seem genuinely distraught. Let's see if the traffic cameras can shed any light on her movements." Suddenly a thought strikes you. "*Flora* . . . a connection to the rose in Kennedy's mouth, perhaps?"

"I don't know about that," McAdam says, "but while you had her tucked away in the waiting room, I took a look around her car."

She holds up her phone, showing you a series of photos. The first is of the front passenger seat of Flora's Ferrari, where a brochure for Elysium sits atop a plain brown envelope. McAdam swipes, and the next photo shows the envelope open to reveal its contents: literature with titles such as *Your Rights in a Divorce* and *Divorce Proceedings Explained*.

"It was only on the front seat, so I took a peek inside," she explains. "Maybe Mrs. Kennedy isn't as cut up about her husband's death as she claims."

Constable Zwale looks over McAdam's shoulder. "You opened the envelope?" he asks, wide-eyed. "Isn't that an illegal search?"

"It's certainly against regulations," you agree.

McAdam shrugs. "She's a murder suspect. Besides, the top was down so I didn't need to open the door. And I used a glove to open the envelope. Good thing, too, eh? This puts things in a different perspective."

She looks at you expectantly.

- To compliment Sergeant McAdam on her initiative, turn to **60**
- To reprimand her for making an illegal search, turn to **156**

135

You and McAdam walk into the manager's office, in the main part of the house facing the courtyard. In contrast to the elegant, minimalist ambience of the public areas you've seen so far, this room is a maelstrom of folders, files, letters, archive boxes, and reference books, balanced between plants and flowers. One shelf contains biographies of successful businessmen, mostly American, some of whom you recognize as having been charged with fraud. The floor and shelves are crowded with pots containing a variety of greenery.

Nobody could work somewhere this cluttered by accident. But looking more closely, you theorize that it may also be to cover up problems with the house. Bubbling paint above the shelves and faint black sprays of mold behind flowers suggest issues with damp and even rot. Old buildings like Finchcote Manor require continual maintenance and upkeep, and Elysium appears to be falling behind on those responsibilities.

At the center of all this sits a dark-haired man—younger than you expected, in his thirties—wearing an Elysium-branded polo shirt that's too large, hanging off his wiry frame, and a chunky digital smartwatch. He stops chewing his nails, stands, and offers his hand.

"Stephen Cheong," he says. "God, this is awful. We've already had a coach from Southend cancel, they were supposed to be coming tomorrow. And I've had people all morning telling me they're leaving and want a refund. You'll be gone soon, won't you? No need to hang around once you've taken him away."

"On the contrary, Mr. Cheong, we have every reason to 'hang around.' Mr. Kennedy's death was no accident."

Stephen stares at you and McAdam, blinking in confusion. Then realization sets in and he pales, collapsing into his chair.

"But I thought—who—for God's sake, we're just a spa! I mean, how—?"

"One thing at a time. First of all, I believe it was you who found Mr. Kennedy?"

He rubs a hand over his face. "That's right. I'd been in the greenhouses, watering the plant beds. Everything's so parched at the moment. I finished up and was walking back here for an eleven o'clock call, so I came through the courtyard and . . . well, there he was."

"Did you touch him?" you ask.

"Yes, sorry. I know you're not supposed to, are you? But it was just so surreal. I couldn't quite believe it at first." He gestures at his ill-fitting shirt. "One of your lot took my clothes away. I've had to get spares until I can go home and get changed."

"So you saw he had the garden fork embedded in his chest. Didn't that suggest to you that it wasn't an accident?"

Stephen stares out of the window into the courtyard. "When you put it like that, it makes me sound stupid. But at first I thought maybe he'd tripped, and then when your officers said he'd fallen from the balcony, I thought that explained it."

"Did you hear or see anything unusual before you found Mr. Kennedy?" asks Sergeant McAdam, taking notes. "Someone crying out, a sound, anything at all?"

"I don't think so. I wasn't paying attention, to be honest, because of the plants."

You remember the flower placed in the victim's mouth. "Was there anything strange about the body?"

"What, you mean apart from the fork sticking out of him? God, I don't remember. I don't think so."

So the manager didn't see the flower . . . unless he placed it there and is now lying.

"There are a lot of plants." You gesture to the pots around you. "And I couldn't help noticing the polytunnels beyond the gardens earlier. I assume you have an interest?"

Stephen blinks again, then explains. "Sorry, I thought you knew. Elysium is a pioneer in holistic floral therapy: corollic yoga, angiospermal homeopathy, pollenated baths, and so on. Plus a strict veganic diet, of course."

"Of course," you agree, with a sideways glance at Sergeant McAdam.

"The flowers we use are all grown here, in the gardens, as part of our unique brand promise. The past couple of years haven't given us the best growing weather, but we're managing. And now we're almost at the end of the season."

"Fascinating," McAdam says, in a tone very much implying the opposite.

"Are you seriously saying someone stabbed Harry, then pushed him off that balcony?" Stephen asks. "It's incredible. I've been meaning to convert room 312 to another bedroom, you know. If I had, he might still be alive . . ."

"Try not to think like that, Mr. Cheong. You can't blame yourself. I understand the storeroom is normally locked, and can only be accessed by staff?"

"That's right. The only key is behind reception."

"Apart from the one you used to open it for our officers," you point out.

The manager blinks nervously. "Oh, well, yes. Apart from mine, obviously."

McAdam walks slowly around the room, examining the shelf contents and peering at plants. "Do you have CCTV inside the house?" she asks.

Stephen shakes his head. "The negative energy would spoil our ambience. Anyway, we've never needed it."

"Until today," she remarks grimly. "If Mr. Kennedy wasn't supposed to be in that storeroom, where should he have been? He was wearing only a bathrobe and underwear."

"He had a session booked with Alina Martinescu, one of our massage therapists. But she said he left early."

"Have you ever had any trouble with Alina?" you ask.

"No. She's quiet, hardworking, and a good therapist. I sent her to the staff break room. She might still be there, if you want to talk to her."

"How many staff do you have on-site?" McAdam asks.

"Twenty, twenty-five, depending on the day. We can accommodate eighty guests. When they don't cancel by the coachload, that is."

It's understandable that Stephen is worried about his business, and you sympathize. But you can't let it get in the way of a murder investigation.

You cross the room to the window and look out. From here the white police tent is visible, with Dr. Wash now directing removal of the body.

"Who were you calling?" you ask casually.

"What do you mean?"

You turn to face the manager. "You said you were returning to the house for a call at eleven. Who with?"

"That's none of your business, is it?"

"I rather think it is, considering the morning's events."

He stares at you for a moment, then sighs. "OK, fine. I was supposed to have a call with the bank to discuss our mortgage." Seeing your questioning expression, he explains. "This isn't just my business; I own the place. When Finchcote Manor came onto the market I sold my old nursery business, bought the house, and opened Elysium."

"That must have been expensive."

Stephen grimaces. "Less so than you might think, because the place needed a lot of repairs. The trouble is, it still does. The roof is a nightmare, the stonework is shot, there's dry rot in the rafters . . . I sometimes think I must have been mad. Anyway, obviously I've had to reschedule that bank call. Look, will you be here for long?"

"For as long as we have to be," you say noncommittally. "I must also ask everyone here, including you and the staff, not to leave the area for a while. Do you have any guests due to check out tomorrow?"

"Not many, I should think; most people stay weekend-to-weekend. Jennifer at reception will know for sure. Why?"

"Because they'll have to stay at least one more day while we look into Mr. Kennedy's death."

Stephen groans. "Listen . . . don't speak ill of the dead and all that, but you should probably know that Harry wasn't the most popular Friend."

"A friend? So you knew him well?" you ask.

Stephen looks confused, then explains. "No, that's what we call our customers. We think of them as our Friends."

"I see. But you're saying Mr. Kennedy didn't have many? Friends, that is."

"That's right. Oh, he could turn on the charm when he wanted to, especially with women like our Roses. Despite being in his fifties, Harry seemed to be a wide boy at heart. Including being loud and entitled, which annoyed a lot of people. The only person he really got on with around here was Tank Destroyer."

McAdam almost chokes. "I beg your pardon?"

"Another Friend. One of our regulars, actually. Tank made a lot of money in websites, and legally changed his name."

The sergeant makes a note. "Is Mr. . . . Destroyer . . . still here?"

"You just said you won't let anyone leave, so I assume so. Ask Jennifer, she can access his timetable."

You turn to go, then pause at the door. "How about Ms. Nesbitt, the

MP? We ran into her earlier, and she assumed Mr. Kennedy had killed himself. How did they get along?"

"From what I saw, they avoided each other like the plague, and if they did run into each other there was always an argument," Stephen says, shaking his head. "They had a big blow-up yesterday evening, in fact, near the tennis courts."

"What time was that?"

"Around seven, after dinner."

You thank the owner-manager for his time and leave. Outside, you confer with McAdam.

"Roses, roses, everywhere," you say. "Interesting, isn't it? Did you notice he even used that nickname for his staff? 'Women like our Roses,' he said. Stephen Cheong is certainly committed to his 'unique brand promise.'"

McAdam shakes her head. "I missed that. And then I was too busy wondering why a man would change his name to Tank Destroyer."

You're surprised the sergeant would overlook such a detail. And she's already rubbed some people the wrong way. Have you been lumbered with a dud for a partner?

"Details, Sergeant. Always look and listen for the details. We can find out about Tank Destroyer soon, anyway. More importantly, we need to ask whether being a rogue and generally disliked was enough to make someone stab Harry Kennedy with a gardening fork . . . or if there's more to this murder than meets the eye."

- If you have P4 written in your notebook, turn to **79**

Otherwise, decide on your next course of action:

- To question Alina the massage therapist, turn to **48**
- To question Carla the MP, turn to **177**
- To question Tank the tech mogul, turn to **73**

136

You return inside, leaving Jennifer to finish her vape break, and speak quietly to Zwale.

"I know everyone loves a man in uniform, Constable, but remember you're on duty and Ms. Watts is a potential suspect."

"I know," he protests. "But Jennifer sees almost everything that goes on around here, and being friendly is a way to get her to open up."

You don't believe for a moment that's the only reason he's keen to spend time with the receptionist, but he does have a point.

"All right, but be careful what you say around her. It's important we keep our cards close to our chest. Now, when this rain eases off, I want you to drive Flora Kennedy to the station yourself and book her in. She'll likely get off with a caution, but it'll bring her to her senses."

With Zwale briefed, you discuss your next move with Sergeant McAdam.

"Flora might get a caution for the assault," she says, "but what about her husband's murder? She had plenty of motive, and there's the CCTV of her car."

"It does seem that way," you agree. "I can't help thinking there's more to this than marital strife and inheriting a business, though. Especially given that taking over Kennedy Homes will be something of a poisoned chalice."

"Aye, but if she didn't know that—" McAdam's phone buzzes, interrupting her. She checks it and smiles. "Oh-*ho*."

"Something good?" you ask.

"Turns out Carla Nesbitt has a record. Apparently she was a single mother to her daughter, Sharon, and in her twenties was nicked for shoplifting baby supplies."

"A desperate young mother stealing nappies is a long way from cold-blooded murder twenty-odd years later, Sergeant."

She shrugs. "Once a criminal, always a criminal, in my experience. Not quite the upstanding pillar of the community she'd have us believe. Anyway, that's not all. Digital forensics have also come through."

"I was hoping we'd hear from them today. What have they found?"

McAdam reads from her email. "Penny got into Kennedy's laptop. Most of it is standard business stuff, accounts and whatnot, which she's digging into. One thing she found right away, though, was an old photo collection of him and . . . guess who?"

The smirk on her face can mean only one thing. "Carla Nesbitt?"

"In one. They look rather friendly, don't you think?"

McAdam holds up her phone and swipes through pictures of Harry and Carla, both young and fresh-faced. In two of the photos they have their arms around each other, smiling. One shows Carla alone, dressed to the nines and sitting in what appears to be a nightclub. The final picture is more recent, though still not quite present day, and appears to have been scanned from a newspaper article reporting her election to Parliament.

- If you have C14 written in your notebook, turn to **74**
- Otherwise, turn to **149**

137

You return to the lobby with its smashed chandelier. A barricade of towels now surrounds the wreckage, absorbing much of the water that fell from the roof and hemming in the rest. The bucket is full, but the impromptu waterfall it was set to catch appears to have stopped, despite the storm still going strong.

In his borrowed workout clothes, Constable Zwale crosses the lobby to speak with Jennifer. She notices you looking up through the ceiling's ragged hole.

"Mr. Cheong went upstairs to repair the roof," she explains. "I think he's just hammered a board over the gap, but it's better than nothing."

"At least that's one thing we don't have to worry about," McAdam says. "Now, Ms. Watts, I have a question. When exactly did you give Harry Kennedy that bruise on his arm?"

It's a gamble—there are several other people with the strength to have left a mark on Mr. Kennedy, like Tank Destroyer or Stephen Cheong—but it pays off, as she doesn't try to deny it.

"I don't remember exactly," Jennifer says with a shrug. "Two or three days ago? He cornered me as I was coming out of the bathroom and tried it on. I told him to get lost."

"Gave him a nice bruise, too," McAdam adds. "All that judo is good for grip strength, I assume?"

The receptionist is defiant. "I won't apologize for standing up to him. Men like that need telling. I only wish it had stopped him from—"

But you never find out what she wishes, because at that moment the lights go out in Elysium.

Not just the lights, you quickly realize. The screens mounted on the lobby walls are suddenly blank, Jennifer's computer has powered down, and the perpetual background hum of modern living is absent.

"If it's not one thing, it's another," McAdam grumbles.

For a moment Elysium is completely silent, as if the house itself is holding its breath. Then, all at once, people call out to one another and shout in panic. Several screams of alarm sound from upstairs. It's still technically daytime, but the storm clouds and rain make it feel like dusk, and the tension you felt rising earlier now fills Elysium's halls. You send a couple of uniformed officers to check on the screamers and make sure they're all right.

McAdam takes a flashlight from her pocket and casts the beam about the lobby.

"We can't even use wi-fi calling with the power out," Jennifer complains. "We're completely cut off. I'll have to go and fire up the generator."

"The house has one?"

"In the cellar," she confirms. "Although I'm not sure when it was last used, or even checked, to be honest. Definitely before I started working here. But let's hope it's still working." Jennifer activates the flashlight on her phone and opens the key lockbox behind the front desk.

"Constable, go with her," you say to Zwale.

The receptionist bristles. "I'm quite capable of doing it myself," she says. "No offense, Joseph," she adds to Zwale.

"I'm sure you are. But judo or not, I'll feel safer if someone accompanies you."

"Is that wise?" McAdam says quietly. "Those two have been making puppy eyes at each other since we arrived. His mind isn't entirely on the job, and now he's not even in uniform."

You lower your voice so only the sergeant can hear you. "We can't be entirely sure the killer won't strike again, and this power outage could give them a perfect opportunity."

"I could go with her instead," McAdam suggests, but you disagree.

"No, I want you here with me in case something important turns up. There are people we still need to talk to."

"I doubt you'll be doing much of that until the power returns," a woman says from close behind you. Startled, you turn to find Carla regarding you with a surprising expression—she's smiling.

"Ms. Nesbitt. What can I do for you?"

The MP's smile doesn't falter. "I thought we could chat. Given my position within the community, it would be appropriate to be kept abreast of developments, don't you agree?"

In other words, she wants to know what you've found out so far. As Carla herself is a suspect, you'll have to tread carefully. But this friendly attitude is a new development, and you don't want to look a gift horse in the mouth.

"Perhaps that's a good idea, Ms. Nesbitt. As it happens, I wanted to talk to you again anyway—"

Before you can continue, Constable Zwale's voice calls out:

"Um . . . don't look now, but I think Tank Destroyer's making a run for it."

Zwale stands by a window near the reception desk. You rush over to see, and he points outside to the unmistakable form of Tank Destroyer, fighting against the rain and wind to walk down the steps and along the driveway.

"How's the eejit think he's going to get out?" McAdam asks rhetorically. "I don't fancy his chances trying to get across the river."

"More to the point, what could motivate him to leave in the middle of a raging storm?" you wonder. "What's happened to suddenly make him need to go?"

"Shall we go after him?"

You're inclined to say yes, given the appalling weather, but behind you Carla Nesbitt clears her throat. With the MP seemingly in a friendly mood, you may not get a better chance to question her. Perhaps Constable Zwale can handle Tank by himself.

- To leave Carla and chase after Tank, turn to **164**
- To send Zwale after Tank while you question Carla, turn to **28**

138

The room waits for you to explain why you accused Tank . . . but the truth is, you're not sure yourself. You feel confident he did it, but you have no real evidence to back up your assertion, or suggest what his motive was. You have your suspicions, but without evidence they're just speculation.

Perhaps you hoped that accusing Tank would cause him to spontaneously confess, but if so it hasn't worked.

The moment drags on, until McAdam clears her throat. You tell her to arrest Tank, with a promise that once the tech mogul is in custody at the police station you'll explain your reasoning. Disappointed, the crowd disperses from the room, whispering doubts about your deductive skills.

- Turn to **154**

139

Constable Zwale returns to his post at the entrance. You and McAdam move to one side of the lobby—not coincidentally, close to the vent of an air conditioning unit you noticed earlier—to discuss your next steps.

"Talking to Flora Kennedy just now made it clear there's a lot about her husband we don't know," you say. "To understand someone's death you must first understand their life, as the saying goes, so let's get on that. I want the team to pull Harry Kennedy's financial records—statements, credit cards, all the usual."

McAdam takes out her phone to make a call and says sarcastically, "Are you sure that's within *regulations*?"

"A little less snark, please, Sergeant."

She frowns. "What about Kennedy Homes' business records? Should we apply for those, too?"

"Yes, good thinking. We can't overlook that Flora Kennedy stands to inherit the company. Her surprise could all be a front, and whether this was a crime of passion or a matter of money remains to be seen. We must learn as much as we can about every side of Harry Kennedy's life."

Check your notebook in the following order:

- If you have A5 written down, turn to **14**
- If you have C3 written down, turn to **51**
- Otherwise, turn to **162**

140

"I met your sister yesterday," you say to Alina. "She told me you had . . . problems at your last job in Romania, and that's why you left. What can you tell me about that?"

"You spoke to Roxana? Why?" asks Alina, confused.

"She's not in any trouble," you reassure her. "In fact we went there to speak to Robbie, her husband. We had no idea who Roxana was until we arrived." You notice Alina hasn't addressed the original question. "So, leaving Romania . . . ?"

"No man harasses me."

Seeing her normally friendly expression turn cold, you pity any man who would try. Whatever occurred in her past, Alina looks determined to make sure it never happens again.

"Is that the real reason you stayed in your room after Mr. Kennedy walked out, and didn't tell Jennifer you were free?"

Alina does her best to maintain her cold composure, but you sense a slight crack in her demeanor. She nods, looking away from you.

- Turn to **173**

141

You move to the window for a better look at the photo. Carla Nesbitt was very clear that she and Harry Kennedy didn't get along. Yet here's an old photo of them together—happy, smiling, and friendly, having a good time—which he kept not just tucked into his wallet, but hidden away.

Evidently there was a side to their relationship, at least historically, that Carla didn't feel the need to mention. You wonder if the MP knew Harry carried this photograph. If not, how will she react to finding out?

- Write **C5** in your notebook
- If you already have T8 written down, turn to **104**
- Otherwise, turn to **7**

142

There's no subtle way to ask this question, so you come right out with it.

"Ms. Nesbitt, was Harry Kennedy the father of your daughter, Sharon?"

To your surprise, the MP laughs.

"Absolutely not. Sharon was born before I even met Harry. No, I met her father when we were both at university, and he took off the moment he learned I was pregnant. Last I heard he was somewhere in Bangkok, and they're welcome to him."

- If you have C4 written down, turn to **184**
- If you have C1 written down, turn to **55**
- Otherwise, turn to **93**

143

You lean back, massaging your temples. "I think that's enough decoding for now, don't you? Why don't we take a look at those emails Penny sent through?"

"Already on it," McAdam says, reading from her phone. "Her summary was on the nose. Look, these emails from Harry to Tank make for interesting reading. Kennedy was furious."

She shows you the messages. Kennedy becomes increasingly angry with each email, and Tank's refusal to reply only makes things worse. Eventually Kennedy resorts to threats, and in an email just last week warned the tech mogul he would "expose" Tank to other investors.

"I wonder what sort of 'exposure' he meant," you murmur.

"No idea, and he doesn't explain anywhere. That's the last email from Kennedy, sent a couple of days before he came here. Perhaps he and Tank continued the conversation in person."

"I hope it was less one-sided than those emails. What do we really know about Tank Destroyer, apart from being a man who got rich from technology?"

McAdam shrugs. "Not a lot. Most of these types hog the limelight, but Tank seems to actively avoid it. His Wikipedia page is pretty short, and I didn't find many interviews. The news stories about Google buying his company all read like PR puff pieces, no real substance. I did find a website for his new AI startup, but it's as short on detail as it is long on stock photography."

"Is that unusual? I'm far from an expert, but technology companies often operate in secrecy to avoid others beating them to . . . whatever it is they're doing."

"Aye, that's true. Still, it makes me wonder what our Mr. Destroyer is up to."

- If you have T7 written in your notebook, turn to **75**
- Otherwise, turn to **117**

144

"Ms. Nesbitt, is there anything else you'd like to tell us? We learned about your prior relationship with Mr. Kennedy, and be assured we'll find out more. It's better that you tell us yourself."

"Actually, there is something," Carla says. "But not about me. The receptionist."

"Jennifer Watts?"

"That's her, with those wretched keys jangling on her belt everywhere she goes."

"Go on."

Carla lowers her voice, even though the door is closed. "I wouldn't be surprised if she was going the extra mile with Harry, if you know what I mean."

"Do you have any reason to believe so?"

"I know Harry, and his type. What do you think all that Viagra was for?"

"Ms. Nesbitt, this is quite an accusation to make without evidence. Are you suggesting Jennifer killed Harry in a lover's spat?"

"Don't be fooled by her looks. Did you know she's some kind of martial artist? And if you're looking for the key to that storeroom, Jennifer has a full set. Honestly, she acts like it's her who owns this place, not Stephen."

Sergeant McAdam consults her notes. "As far as we know, Ms. Watts was at the reception desk during the time Mr. Kennedy was killed. She couldn't have done it."

"I'd look again if I were you. Ask her how many ten-minute vaping breaks she takes."

Resuming her lotus position, Carla raises the volume on her phone and the sound of crashing ocean waves once again fills the small room. Evidently, she considers this conversation to be over. You stand and brush yourself down.

- Write **C4** and **J3** in your notebook
- Have you decoded the *second* text message retrieved from Harry Kennedy's phone? If so, write **P9** in your notebook. Then *multiply* the number found in that message by *14* and turn to the corresponding section.
- Otherwise, you exit the room and leave Carla to her meditation. **Add 1** to your INTERVIEW number and turn to **65.**

145

You read the decoded message again, deciphering not just the words but its meaning.

"Three weeks ago, an anonymous person sent Harry Kennedy a message about a 'flower boy' buying four pallets of . . . something . . . from a nursery."

"Presumably not children," McAdam quips.

"Don't give up your day job, Sergeant. No, the obvious answer is flowers. And 'trying to be invisible' implies whoever it was didn't want to be seen."

You both ponder this for a moment, before realization hits you.

"Remember the invoice that Constable Zwale found in Stephen Cheong's office? It was from Green Fingers Nursery."

"Flower Boy," McAdam says, understanding. "Someone saw Stephen buying those flowers, ready to pass them off as his own."

"Not just anyone. Who's the only other person we've heard call Stephen 'Flower Boy' . . . ?"

She grimaces. "Tank Destroyer. Of course. But why would he be watching Stephen in the first place? He must have suspected something."

"Or Kennedy did. Look at the first part of the message again."

"'You were right,'" McAdam reads. "It suggests Kennedy had his suspicions, and asked Tank to keep an eye out."

"Not only that, but told him to encode the message upon sending, ensuring nobody else could read it." You recap what you now know. "Stephen Cheong has been secretly buying in flowers and passing them off to guests as his own. Somehow Kennedy came to suspect this, and had Tank watch Stephen. Sure enough, Tank observed him making a big purchase at the nursery and texted Kennedy to let him know. That gave Kennedy a hold over Stephen, something that could very easily turn into threats or blackmail. It might explain why Stephen gave Kennedy the Lotus package for free."

"And upgraded Tank, too. Blackmail, eh? One of the oldest motives for murder you'll find. Like I said before, we're all carrying secrets. There isn't much a person won't do to protect them, especially when his livelihood's at stake."

That's true. Could Stephen have killed Kennedy to prevent his secret from being revealed?

"One question remains," you say, looking again at the message. "How come this text was sent three weeks ago?"

McAdam looks confused. "I don't follow."

"Harry Kennedy had never been here before, and by all accounts wasn't normally one for wellness retreats in the first place. How did he even know who Stephen Cheong was, let alone suspect him of lying? And why would he care?"

"I've no idea. Go on."

You laugh. "That's just it, I don't know either. But hopefully we can find out . . ."

- Write **S7** in your notebook, then return to **100** and skip to the end of that section

146

"For example," you say, "let's talk about your relationship with Harry Kennedy, and this 'mutual investment' you've mentioned. It hadn't actually happened yet, had it? We know that no cash had changed hands, and earlier I heard you badgering his widow for money."

Tank's expression darkens. "Harry agreed to invest in my new AI startup, and in return I'd invest in his housing plan. But the money never came through, so I reminded Flora to hold up her end of the bargain."

"Perhaps you need to hold up your own end first, so she can then pay you with your own money. Kennedy Homes is in dire financial straits, you see. The only large payment the firm made recently was to a company owned by Carla Nesbitt."

"Nesbitch again," Tank spits. "I should have guessed she'd get his money before I did."

- Write **T5** in your notebook, then turn to **180**

147

You shake out your umbrellas and return them to the stand by the front door, nodding your thanks to Jennifer behind reception. It's only then that you realize Constable Zwale is once again standing at the desk, casually chatting to her.

Before you (or more likely Sergeant McAdam) can reprimand him, however, the constable preempts you.

"Inspector," he says, hurrying over. "I found something you should see."

He leads you to a corner of the lobby where you can't be overlooked and takes out his phone.

"I used my initiative," he says, "just like the sergeant with Mrs. Kennedy's car. Jennifer told me you were interviewing Stephen in the greenhouse, so I took the opportunity to have a nose around his office. Look what I found, stuffed at the bottom of a drawer . . ."

He calls up a photo of a document and zooms in so you can read it:

```
Invoice #981
From: Green Fingers Nursery
FAO: Stephen Cheong
Goods: Assorted whole and stems
Amount due: £1,630
VAT: £326
Total: £1,956
```

"I knew there was something off about this place," McAdam says with a smirk. "All grown on the premises, my foot."

You nod in agreement. "So Stephen has been buying in flowers, then passing them off as being from his own greenhouses."

"That's fraud, isn't it?" Zwale says.

"I think it's more likely to be a simple breach of the Trade Descriptions Act. Regardless, it's not good. Notice how the invoice is made out to Stephen personally, too. Presumably to avoid a paper trail leading back to the business."

McAdam snorts. "But surely he's not paying amounts like that out of his own pocket to keep the business going. Is he?"

"That's a good point. Either the company means that much to him . . . or he could be taking the money from Elysium itself by other means."

"Would that still be embezzlement, if he steals from the company to pay for goods the company uses?" McAdam shakes her head. "This is beyond me, but it smells fishy."

Corporate wrongdoing is far from your area of expertise, too. Fortunately, there are specialists in the police force who can much more accurately determine whether or not this is an offense. You make a note of the invoice details in order to pass on the information later.

"Good work, Constable," you say. "We'll make a detective of you yet." Zwale beams with pride, though you cut that short. "But don't let it go to your head. Stop flirting with the staff and get on with your work."

"Absolutely," he says seriously, though he can't quite hide his smile.

Meanwhile, you must determine your next move.

- Write **S1** in your notebook, and **add 1** to your INTERVIEW number
- Then turn to **65**

148

"Oh, I told you before," Jennifer says to you. "About Tank Destroyer getting a free upgrade this week, from the Rose plan to the Lotus package."

"That's right, and the Rose package is the cheapest, isn't it? Tell me, how often does Mr. Destroyer stay here?"

"Five days at a time, every month or so."

McAdam grumbles. “Why does a tech millionaire need a free upgrade?”

Constable Zwale shrugs. “Some people are just tight, ma’am. My uncle’s loaded, but he gets all his clothes from charity shops. I think it comes from having been poor as a boy.”

Tank Destroyer may be worth millions now, but perhaps he also grew up without money. The question remains: Is it a coincidence that Stephen Cheong seemingly gave Harry Kennedy a free stay and Tank Destroyer a free upgrade at the same time? Or is there something more to it?

“Forgive me, but there’s one more thing I have to ask,” you say to Jennifer. “Was Mrs. Kennedy right? Were you sleeping with her husband?” When she hesitates you quickly add, “I must remind you that lying to the police is an offense.”

“Oh, come on,” Zwale says, offended on her behalf. “Kennedy was a sleazebag, everyone says so. Jennifer wouldn’t!”

“Be quiet, Constable!” McAdam barks.

Jennifer sighs. “He’s right, though. Mr. Kennedy tried it on, like he did with every other woman in here, but I told him where to stick it. Not in a million years.”

- If you have J3 written in your notebook, turn to **37**
- Otherwise, turn to **136**

149

“So it seems Harry Kennedy carried a torch for Carla Nesbitt,” you say. “Plus we still have the bizarre text message he sent her. Has Penny figured out what it says yet?”

“No, but she’s found something else,” McAdam replies. “Two more text messages from Kennedy’s phone. Another from Kennedy to Carla, sent two weeks ago, and a third sent by persons unknown to Kennedy three weeks ago. They're both garbled like the others, but she's more certain now that they're a code."

She shows you the messages:

Text Message #2: Harry Kennedy to Carla Nesbitt, 13 days ago

biwm vi huaa mecib ewm O'uu veclq bog mehb, qi'uu veti byeli oua vi oo qi twufb fqec'b puum oua qov

Text message #3: Unknown to Harry Kennedy, 20 days ago

HUA FIAI AOPQC, SABC BEF OUUFIA KUH CAHOWP CU KI OWEOBOKUI OW E EEW AUAWM CQI WAABIAH. KUAPQC OUAA YEUUICB

"Penny's hopeful that, given time, she can figure out how to decode them all," McAdam says.

You don't doubt Penny's code-cracking abilities, but you're running out of time, and at least two of these messages were between Kennedy and Carla Nesbitt. If only you knew what they said, they might give you more ammunition with which to question the MP before you have to let her leave. You copy them into your notebook and decide that at some point soon, you should take a moment to try and decode the messages yourself.

"What exactly was going on between Kennedy and Carla?" you wonder aloud.

"Something fishy, I'm sure of it," McAdam says. "The photos, the text messages . . . if it's all unrelated, I'll eat my hat."

"You don't wear a hat."

"Precisely."

You're inclined to agree with her, but the answers are still tantalizingly out of reach. Surely the answer to this mystery, and the others facing you in this case, lies right here in Elysium . . . if you can just ask the right questions.

- Write **C2** in your notebook, then turn to **65**

150

Reading Kennedy's timetable, you recall that Alina said her massage therapy appointment with him ended thirty minutes early, when he walked out saying he had to make an important phone call.

This timetable confirms that the session wasn't supposed to end until 11 a.m., fifteen minutes after his body was found in the courtyard. You really need to see his phone records.

- Write **A6** in your notebook
- If you already have T6 written down, turn to **86**
- Otherwise, turn to **16**

151

"You've answered your own question," you say. "A divorce could take months, even years, to finalize. At the end of it you might get half of Kennedy Homes to yourself. But the business was already in dire straits, with very little money in the bank."

Flora protests. "I had no idea about the financial troubles. Harry told me the business was doing well."

"Do you expect us to believe that you simply took him at his word? A man you admit you were planning to divorce? Even if you did, your solicitor certainly wouldn't. I think you discovered that Kennedy Homes was in trouble—perhaps also that Harry paid a large sum he could barely afford for a mysterious 'consultation'—and decided enough was enough. After all, even if you came away owning more of the company in a divorce, your ex-husband would still be running it."

"Running it into the ground," the widow grumbles.

"Perhaps. But with him dead you inherit the entire business, which you can now run as you see fit. Isn't it true that you believe the new housing plan is solid, if only Carla Nesbitt would cooperate and intervene on your behalf? Harry clearly hadn't persuaded her to do so. Do you believe you can succeed where he didn't?"

Flora turns to Carla, but the MP merely shrugs.

"I still haven't seen a compelling case," she says. "Besides, I have more important things on my plate."

"But that's not an outright *no*," you point out. "That ghost of a chance is why Flora killed her husband."

The widow's eyes dart from side to side nervously. "You're forgetting two things," she says. "First, I didn't know for sure Harry was here. Second, how could I have done all this without being seen? Check the CCTV cameras in town—they'll show me driving home from my solicitor's office."

McAdam nods. "They do . . . before you divert to come in this direction. There's a ten-minute gap until you return on camera, at which point you're heading away from the manor and back to your house."

"Well, I took a scenic route," Flora says, close to tears. "I had a lot on my mind. But none of it involved killing Harry!"

"Didn't it?" you say. "You had sufficient motive to want your husband dead. Your car disappears from CCTV, giving you enough time to rush here, sneak through the house—where there are no cameras at all—and kill your husband, before returning to your car and driving home."

Carla Nesbitt speaks up. "That sounds like a lot of effort, Inspector. Does Flora really look like a woman who'd do that? No offense, Flora," she adds.

"Still waters run deep, Ms. Nesbitt. Earlier today, Mrs. Kennedy climbed out of a window to escape confinement. And the more unlikely the plan, the better chance it won't cast suspicion."

Flora Kennedy moans quietly and bursts into tears. You're not convinced they're any more real than her alibi.

"Also, there's the matter of the rose placed in the victim's mouth. A flower . . . or should I say *flora*."

The widow sniffles. "You can't possibly think that points to me. Why . . . why would I leave a clue like that?"

"Some criminals subconsciously want to be arrested and punished," you say. "And I'm happy to oblige. Sergeant, arrest Mrs. Kennedy."

• Turn to **172**

152

"Alina is fine," you reassure the woman. Now that you know, you can see the family resemblance. "I assume from your question that you've heard what happened at Elysium?"

She nods. "Alina told me. How is she?"

"A little shaken up, that's all. Can you confirm your name, please?"

"Roxana Martinescu," she says, shifting the baby to her other hip. "Why are you here?"

"We were actually looking for Mr. Robert Graham." You cast a glance at McAdam. "Do we definitely have the right house?"

Roxana nods. "Robbie is my husband. Why do you want him?"

"We just have some questions relating to the incident at Elysium," McAdam says. "Can we please come in?"

Roxana hesitates, then turns and walks farther into the house. "You must be quiet. Valeria needs to sleep."

You follow her through to the lounge. As you'd expect from a young family, every inch of the house is dedicated to the baby's needs and comfort.

Roxana lowers Valeria into a rocker, and herself onto a cushioned stool beside it, gently rocking the frame while she talks to you.

"Is your husband at home, Mrs. Graham?" McAdam asks.

She corrects the sergeant. "I am still called Martinescu."

"Yeah, I'm here," says a man descending the stairs. "What's going on?"

Robbie Graham is a heavyset man, wide of shoulder and long of limb. He could have been a boxer; perhaps he still is. He stands by Roxana, but doesn't sit down, so neither do you.

"Harry Kennedy was found dead this morning at the Elysium wellness retreat," you explain. "We're treating his death as suspicious, and his phone records show that you called him shortly before he died. Can you tell us what you talked about?"

"There must be some mistake," Robbie says, with a confused expression. "I haven't spoken to him in weeks."

"There's no mistake, sir," McAdam says. "The call came from this number. What was your relationship to Mr. Kennedy?"

The couple's expressions remain stony. "How did he die?" Robbie asks.

"He was murdered," you say, taking a firm tone. "And you are one of the last people to have spoken to him before it happened. So I'll ask again: What did you talk about?"

"Please, be quiet," Roxana says. You look down and realize the baby is already asleep. "Let's go outside." Roxana slides open the room's patio doors and leads you all into a small, north-facing garden, shaded from the afternoon sun.

She quietly slides the door closed behind you and explains. "Robbie works nights. He was asleep upstairs when I called Kennedy." She practically spits the victim's name.

"It was you who called him? Why?"

"Because he is a crook, and a liar, and does nothing."

Roxana's accent grows stronger as she becomes angrier. Seeing her frustration, Robbie elaborates.

"Our windows leak when it rains heavily," he says. "And we're not the only ones—half the estate's got the same problem. It's not so bad now, but once we get to winter it's horrible. Trouble is, Kennedy reckons the house isn't his responsibility anymore because it's four years old. Ten-year warranty, but only a two-year 'defects insurance period,' so he won't pay. But why should we have to, when it's his builders who messed up? Not like we can afford it anyway, with the mortgage and energy bills."

You experience a moment of growing revelation, like a candle flame illuminating darkness.

"These are Kennedy Homes? Did his company build this estate?"

"Yeah. Took the money and ran. They should have him on that program, with the cowboy builders."

"More likely to be on a true crime show, now," McAdam says quietly.

"That is why I called," Roxana says. "To try again to convince him. But he shouted at me and said, 'Get lost.' Well, he used different words."

You can well imagine. "Do you remember what time you called him?"

"I will check," she says, sliding the door open a crack and slipping back inside.

McAdam turns to Robbie. "Your wife said you work nights?"

He nods. "Security guard at the shopping center. I tried out for your lot once, but I just failed the exam by a couple of points." He doesn't elaborate, but is obviously hoping to enjoy some camaraderie with you.

"I'm sure you'd have been a fine addition to the force," McAdam reassures him. "So where were you between ten thirty and eleven this morning?"

"Got home just gone seven, haven't left the house since." Robbie folds his muscular arms, though you're not sure if it's defensive or meant to be threatening. "I'm not sorry he's dead, you know. Kennedy. He was a right tosser. Even sent someone to spy on us after we said we'd take him to court."

"Spy on you? What do you mean?"

Roxana returns to the patio, cordless phone in hand. Robbie turns to her.

"Tell them about the bloke you saw outside the house."

She shudders. "I was very worried. He was a big man, shaved head and tattoos. He came first a month ago, then more times since. Only when I am alone with Valeria. If Robbie was here, or even Alina, he wouldn't come."

"We've got a doorbell camera, look," Robbie says, holding up his cell phone. "I saved these in case we had to call you lot." He shows you several short clips of a man walking on the other side of the street, occasionally stopping to stare at the house. Even seen from a distance, you're confident you're looking at a man you already saw this morning at Elysium . . .

"Leave that with us," you say. "I have an idea who that might be. Now, Ms. Martinescu, did you check the time of your call with Mr. Kennedy?"

Roxana nods. "Ten twenty this morning. I knew it was after I fed Valeria, when she was sleeping."

That matches the time in the phone records, which means her sister Alina is either mistaken or lying about her session with Kennedy.

"You came over from Romania at the same time as Alina, is that right?" McAdam asks, knowing the therapist told you something different. This is a test.

"No, she was first," Roxana says, correcting her. "Alina escaped and came here for a better job. When she told me what it was like, and that she was happy, I followed."

"Alina's the big sister," Robbie explains. "Roxana follows her a lot."

Roxana nudges him in mock protest. "We look after each other. Until I met you, of course. Now you look after me."

Seeing them side by side, with Roxana barely coming up to Robbie's chin, it's not hard to understand why a petite woman like her would feel safe with a burly man like him.

"What do you mean, 'escaped'? Was Alina in trouble in Romania?"

"Oh, no. I mean—not police trouble." Roxana's voice drops. "She was assaulted, but her boss called her a liar and made things very difficult for her. He thought she would stay anyway, because she needed the work. But he was wrong. She left, and now she is free."

A soft wailing emanates from inside the house, quickly growing louder. Instinctively you all turn to the window, and Roxana goes to tend to her daughter.

"Who's going to fix the house now?" Robbie asks, shaking his head. "If Kennedy's not around, we're completely screwed."

"I gather his widow will take over the business," you say. "Perhaps she'll be more amenable to your plight."

"Yeah, and I might win the lottery," Robbie says with a sigh.

You leave them and return through the estate. "Now we know who built these houses, but does Kennedy still own them?" You pass the row of houses with For Sale signs. "Sergeant, call the agent and find out who's selling those."

McAdam does, as you walk back to her car. You can only hear one side of the conversation, but occasional murmurs of, "Well, well," tell you she's found something interesting. Finally, she nods with satisfaction and ends the call.

- Write **T3** in your notebook
- If you already have C1 written down, turn to **43**
- Otherwise, turn to **96**

153

"We know you were more than just friends," you say. "In fact, you and Harry Kennedy were lovers, as you've already admitted to us."

A collective gasp goes up around the room.

"You, Carla?!" Flora Kennedy cries. "How could you?"

McAdam places a sympathetic hand on the widow's shoulder, as all eyes turn to Carla.

"No comment," the MP says, her lips pressed into a firm line.

"We don't need one," you say. "We know you and Harry Kennedy arranged to 'coincidentally' be here simultaneously, as a way to spend time together without your spouses knowing. In public you kept up a pretense of disliking each other so that nobody here would suspect. You even saw an opportunity to reinforce Flora's suspicion that Jennifer was the one sleeping with him."

"I told you it wasn't me," the receptionist says quietly.

You continue: "Sneaking around this house wasn't difficult thanks to the lack of security cameras, but something went awry. Did you think one of the staff might suspect what was going on, and expose your affair? Or were you simply worried Harry would feel compelled to confess to Flora?"

"Where are you going with this nonsense?" Carla asks.

"To murder, Ms. Nesbitt. If your relationship with Kennedy was revealed, you'd find yourself in the headlines for all the wrong reasons, fending off calls to resign. Depending on your husband's attitude toward such matters, you might also be facing divorce."

The MP regards you with contempt. "Do you really think I'd kill Harry for that? Why wouldn't I just tell him it was over?"

"Because then he'd have even less reason not to go public. He could even sell that story for a tidy sum to the press, which would go some way toward solving his cash-flow problems. So you took a break from your Tai Chi class, lured him into the storeroom, stabbed him, then shoved him off the balcony before returning to the lawn. Your DNA was found in the sink of room 312, presumably from where you washed off Kennedy's blood."

"That is a preposterous fantasy, and I won't dignify it with a response."

"You don't have to. Sergeant, arrest Ms. Nesbitt."

• Turn to **196**

154

You return to the station, confident you can extract a confession in the interrogation room—but your confidence is unfounded, and soon you're forced to release the suspect without charge.

When you're subsequently called in front of the detective chief superintendent, you find McAdam standing at his side. She avoids eye contact with you. Whatever friendship and respect you and the sergeant were building has wilted like old flowers.

The DCS has likewise lost all confidence in you, and removes you from the case. Harry Kennedy's murder may yet be solved . . . but not by you.

Later, you consider what went wrong. Did you accuse the right killer, but failed to gather enough evidence? Or should you have accused someone else altogether?

- To find out, don't despair. Simply wipe your notebook, return to **1**, and try again.

For now, though, this is . . .

THE END

155

"I believe Harry Kennedy's killer was one of the last people to see him alive," you say. Many people turn to look at Tank, but you shake your head. "No, not the *very* last person. I'm talking about the woman whose massage session he stormed out of shortly before his death. Isn't that right, Alina?"

The therapist is taken aback. "Yes! I mean no, I didn't kill him. He left, I saw him talk to Tank, and then I didn't see him again until he was lying in the courtyard. Why would I kill Mr. Kennedy?"

It's time to answer that question. Do you have the evidence you need to make a successful accusation?

Check your notebook for clues in the following order:

- If you have A7 or A3 written down, turn to **92**
- If you have A1 written down, turn to **110**
- If you have A4 written down, turn to **29**
- Otherwise, turn to **61**

156

"I don't know how you did things in Northumbria, Sergeant, but this is unacceptable," you say. "You've violated Flora Kennedy's right to privacy, without any mitigating circumstances that would hold up in court. If she *is* our killer, those pictures will be inadmissible as evidence, and anything derived from them would also be at risk."

McAdam defends her decision. "In my experience, knowing whether a murder suspect planned to divorce the victim is damn useful."

You shake your head. "I understand you want to make a good impression on your first case with me, but this isn't the way. Remember, we represent the law. If we violate it in the course of our duties, what trust can we expect the public to place in it . . . or us?"

McAdam looks downcast. "Sorry. I suppose I got overexcited. It won't happen again."

"See that it doesn't," you say. "I'll overlook this occasion, and it won't appear in my report. But in future I won't be so forgiving." You look between the sergeant and the constable. "Are we all clear on that?"

"Absolutely." Zwale nods. He's young and keen, hoping for promotion, and you're confident you won't have any trouble from him.

"Yes, crystal clear." McAdam is more reluctant, but acquiesces to your authority.

"Good. Now I suggest you delete those photos immediately, while we all do our best to forget what we saw and proceed with the investigation."

• Turn to **139**

157

McAdam arrests Jennifer, and when the storm has cleared you take her into custody at the police station. Constable Zwale objects, and refuses to help with the arrest. His disappointment in you is clearly written on his face, but this is a lesson he has to learn.

Later at the station, though, you begin to wonder if you still need to learn a few things yourself. The receptionist sticks to her story, and her solicitor quite rightly points out that you have no physical evidence tying her to the crime scene or the murder weapon. There are also no witnesses placing Jennifer anywhere near the storeroom at the time of the murder. Flora may have suspected them of having an affair, but she has no proof . . . and neither do you.

The case is a bust. Losing faith in you, the detective chief superintendent reassigns you to a different, simpler case and calls in another inspector to take over the Elysium killing. Adding insult to injury, Constable Zwale asks the DCS to excuse him from working with you ever again.

Harry Kennedy's murder may yet be solved . . . but not by you.

Later, you consider what went wrong. Were you right to accuse Jennifer, but you simply didn't have enough evidence? Or was the killer someone else altogether?

- To find out, don't despair. Simply wipe your notebook, return to **1**, and try again.

For now, though, this is . . .

THE END

158

"If the plans weren't made public, who would know about them?" asks McAdam. "For example, Carla Nesbitt certainly did. She was the one who first told us about them."

Mr. Baker steeples his fingers. "You're right, she did, but I don't know how. Certainly, nobody here would have told her. Perhaps Mr. Kennedy mentioned it at one of those dreadful fundraisers she's always holding."

"Considering the choice words Ms. Nesbitt had about him, I doubt he'd be donating money to her," the sergeant says.

"He may have been hoping for a quid pro quo," you point out, explaining to Mr. Baker: "Carla Nesbitt told us that Harry Kennedy asked her to intervene with you on his behalf."

- Write **P11** in your notebook, then turn to **90**

159

Your thoughts return to the decoded text message about a "flower boy" secretly buying from a nursery, as well as the invoice Constable Zwale found in Stephen Cheong's office. Those strongly suggest the manager is buying in flowers and passing them off as grown on-site. Now, hearing Carla Nesbitt talk, you realize this could be how Kennedy came to learn about it in the first place. The first part of the text message he received, "You were right," implies Kennedy already suspected Stephen of wrongdoing.

Everything you've learned about Harry suggests he wouldn't have been above indulging in a spot of blackmail. If he had Stephen Cheong over a barrel, it would explain how he was able to book a place despite Elysium being busy, and why he was given the Lotus package for free.

Most importantly, it would give the manager a powerful motive to protect his business by silencing Kennedy. Perhaps permanently.

• Write **S4** in your notebook, then turn to **25**

160

Sergeant McAdam calls ahead to make sure someone's in to meet you. With Carla Nesbitt in town, albeit on holiday at Elysium, her secretary is on-site at her constituency office and gives you directions.

You drive through the local town and out again, to a small converted house in a semirural area that you suspect isn't well served by public transport. If this is where Carla Nesbitt holds her town halls, you wonder how many of her constituents can actually make it out here. Perhaps that's the point.

Her secretary, a young woman with brightly dyed red hair and collarbones that could take an eye out, is waiting for you inside. "Sharon Gibbs," she says, introducing herself. Something about her seems familiar, but you can't quite put your finger on it.

The secretary guides you and McAdam into a bookshelf-lined room with a desk in one corner and several chairs facing it. "No town hall today, so we can use the main office. I heard about what happened with Mr. Kennedy, of course. Terrible business. How can I help?"

Ms. Gibbs takes the chair behind the desk, presumably where Carla Nesbitt normally sits to receive constituents, and you get the impression she's very comfortable doing so. You almost expect her to put her feet up.

"I understand that Ms. Nesbitt and Mr. Kennedy didn't get on," you say. "And yet he was hoping she'd intervene with the council on his behalf concerning a plan to build a new housing estate. What do you know about that?"

Ms. Gibbs looks blank. "Nothing at all. Harry Kennedy isn't a subject that comes up often. I know one shouldn't speak ill of the dead, but I expect you'll struggle to find many to speak well of him."

"Did Ms. Nesbitt mention anything about the estate earlier?" you ask. "When she was telling you about Mr. Kennedy's death, I mean."

"No, Mummy didn't say a word. A new housing estate, eh?"

"That's right—oh, wait a moment." You exchange glances with McAdam, as it dawns on you why Ms. Gibbs looks familiar. "Did you say 'Mummy'?"

"Yes," the secretary says, evidently amused that you didn't recognize her right away. "I'm Carla's daughter. I run the office for her. Sorry, I assumed you knew. Being the police, and all."

Sergeant McAdam forces a smile. "The surname threw us off," she says. "So you took your spouse's name?"

"That's right. I didn't want people treating me like a nepo baby."

A bold statement from someone managing her mother's office, but you let it pass.

"I suppose there isn't much you don't know about your mother's life," McAdam says gently. "If you're the engine that keeps things running around here."

"Well, she's a busy woman," Ms. Gibbs replies, unable to completely resist the flattery. "Someone has to stay on top of things."

"So did you book her stay at Elysium, as well? When was that arranged?"

"Oh, a couple of months ago. I'd need to check my email to give you a precise date."

You and McAdam both smile and wait until Ms. Gibbs gets the hint.

"Perhaps you should come through to my office," she says, and leaves the room without waiting for you. So much for the daughter's power trip behind her mother's desk.

Back in reception Ms. Gibbs sits at her own rather cluttered desk, sweeps some printouts off her laptop so she can open it, and checks her email. A couple of the pages drift off the desk, but you catch them before they can hit the floor. They're from an estate agency website, showing houses for sale.

"Thinking of moving?" you ask, handing them back to the secretary.

"Selling, actually. Those are Mummy's, but she's looking to move them out of her portfolio. I could call the agent to arrange a viewing, if you're interested?"

"No, thank you. Just the dates for that booking, if you don't mind."

Ms. Gibbs returns to her screen and peers at it. "Elysium . . . here we are. Mummy's stay was booked seven weeks ago, at the end of July."

"Was there anything unusual about this particular booking?" McAdam asks.

"She's stayed there before, so it was fairly routine."

"I just wondered if perhaps it might have been timed to coincide with Mr. Kennedy's stay at the same facility. Or any other guests."

"No, and I don't think it could have been. Originally Mummy wanted to book the last week in August, but Elysium was full on those dates so we had to make do with this week instead. It's a bit tight before returning to Parliament after recess, but she was determined to enjoy a break."

The secretary is right; if she had to unexpectedly change her booking dates, Carla Nesbitt couldn't have planned to stay at Elysium at the same time as Harry Kennedy.

- Write **C14** in your notebook, then check it in the following order:
- If you already have C15 or P5 written down, turn to **50**
- If you already have P7 written down, turn to **10**
- Otherwise, turn to **97**

161

You take a moment to frame your next question. "Are you quite sure you don't know what time you came here to swim yesterday morning?"

"I told you, I don't wear a watch," Tank replies impatiently. "My therapist says it's an expression of my rejection of societal norms."

"Does that rejection extend to reading a clock?" You turn to gesture at the far wall, where the Elysium staffer leads a group of Friends in the water. Above them is the large wall clock you saw upon entering.

"If you like." Tank shrugs. "Anyway, I didn't look at it. I wasn't on a schedule. Now, have you finished giving me the third degree?"

- Have you decoded the *third* text message retrieved from Harry Kennedy's phone? If so, write **P6** in your notebook. Then *multiply* the number found in that message by *14* and turn to the corresponding section.
- Otherwise, turn to **89**

162

"It does seem Harry Kennedy was something of a complex character," you say to McAdam, "even if some here would have us believe otherwise."

"Aye, few people see every side of a person. We're all of us carrying secrets."

"Very philosophical, Sergeant. I wasn't sure you had it in you."

"Which only proves my point, Inspector."

You laugh quietly. "You've got me there. Well, hopefully those records of Kennedy's will expose a few of his secrets. We need to know more about the man, and why someone wanted him dead. I wonder if it's worth taking a look over his bedroom."

"Surely forensics will be all over that. I was thinking maybe his timetable could tell us something."

Forensics will indeed search Kennedy's bedroom, but it might still pay to take a look yourself. On the other hand, finding out what the victim was doing during his stay at Elysium would also be useful. Time being of the essence, you decide to do both and split the tasks with McAdam.

- To search Kennedy's bedroom yourself, while McAdam checks his timetable, turn to **118**
- To check Kennedy's timetable yourself, while McAdam searches his bedroom, turn to **40**

163

The room waits for you to explain why you accused Stephen . . . but the truth is, you're not sure yourself. You feel confident he did it, but you have no real evidence to back up your assertion, or suggest what his motive was. You have your suspicions, but without evidence they're just speculation.

Perhaps you hoped that accusing Stephen would cause him to spontaneously confess, but if so it hasn't worked.

The moment drags on, until McAdam clears her throat. You tell her to arrest Stephen, with a promise that once the manager is in custody at the police station you'll explain your reasoning. Disappointed, the crowd disperses from the room, whispering doubts about your deductive skills.

- Turn to **154**

164

You make your decision. "He wouldn't run without good reason. Let's get after him."

McAdam grabs two umbrellas from the stand in the lobby and

tosses one to you. Zwale is already ahead of you both, throwing open the main entrance door and running headfirst into the rain, shouting after Tank. Visibility in this weather is poor, and you're rapidly losing sight of the tattooed mogul. Even if he was inclined to obey the constable, he probably can't hear Zwale over the storm.

You and McAdam follow, umbrellas braced against the driving rain. Your legs are soaked before you even reach the bottom of the entrance steps.

The sergeant puts on a burst of speed you couldn't hope to match, and before long she and Zwale are comfortably ahead of you. That's OK. Where can Tank go, anyway? The grounds are enclosed by the high estate walls, leaving the main gate as the only exit. That means crossing the river, which is now impassable. So you jog doggedly on, knowing you'll catch up eventually.

When you do, you're surprised to see McAdam and Zwale keeping their distance from Tank, who stands in front of the swollen, raging river not far from the bridge. The water is so high you can barely see its stone walls, and the road surface is long since submerged. Tank is wet through, but even in this sodden state you witness a desperate fear in his eyes.

"I'm telling you, he killed Harry and now I'm next!" he yells over the rain. "If I don't leave now, he'll get me!"

"We can protect you!" Zwale calls back. "Don't do anything stupid!"

A thunderclap booms overhead.

"You can't protect me from him! I've got to get out!"

And with that, Tank dives into the river.

You, Zwale, and McAdam all rush forward, getting as close to the water as you safely can. Tank is undoubtedly a big man and a strong swimmer, but immediately he struggles as the fast current tries to sweep him away. You don't fancy the water much yourself, but without help he might drown. Then again, anyone going in to try and rescue him risks drowning, too. You must make a quick decision:

- To risk the waters yourself and dive in after Tank, turn to **2**
- To send young, fit Constable Zwale in after Tank, turn to **42**
- To prioritize the lives of your officers over Tank and leave him to sink or swim, turn to **181**

165

"Two weeks ago, Harry Kennedy told Carla to 'send me your dates' so he could 'match six days,'" you read aloud. "How long did he book to stay here at Elysium?"

"Six days," McAdam confirms with a smile. "Maybe it's no coincidence that they're both here at the same time."

"I'll wager it's very far from a coincidence."

"Who's 'he,' do you think? As in, 'he'll make space for me if he knows what's good for him.'"

If you're right about the context of this message, it can surely only be one person. "Stephen Cheong. We know he appears to have given Kennedy a VIP package free of charge, which implies the threat worked."

"'If he knows what's good for him,'" McAdam muses. "Did Kennedy have organized-crime connections that we don't know about? Would he really send round some bruisers with a baseball bat just because Stephen couldn't fit in the dates he wanted?"

"That doesn't feel right to me. No, I suspect it's something more subtle but no less damaging. Perhaps Stephen has a secret he doesn't want getting out."

"No shortage of those around here, is there?" McAdam sighs.

- If you have C5 or C9 written in your notebook, turn to **182**
- Otherwise, turn to **45**

166

Jennifer sounds more resigned than bitter about this state of affairs. But, thinking of affairs, you wonder how much of what she's telling you is true. Not about Kennedy being a serial molester—she has little motivation to lie when you can easily verify that with the other staff—but about her own relationship with Harry Kennedy.

Extreme as it might be, is the receptionist disparaging him to disguise her true feelings? Could Flora be onto something with her accusation that Jennifer was Kennedy's lover, and she killed him to save her job? She has a great deal of responsibility at Elysium, and seems to enjoy her job.

Or could the motive be much simpler? If the staff all gossiped about Kennedy to Jennifer, she'd quickly learn that he obviously wasn't satisfied with her alone.

There's also the matter of Kennedy being a "big spender," when you know he in fact wasn't. He was enjoying a VIP package here at Elysium free of charge, thanks to Stephen Cheong's generosity. Is that connected to his death somehow?

- If you have A4 written in your notebook, turn to **20**
- Otherwise, turn to **113**

167

For all Constable Zwale's willingness, you can't ignore that he's young and inexperienced. After a rocky start yesterday, McAdam impressed you with some insightful questions and observations, so you decide to trust her instincts and leave the CCTV footage for later.

"Keep a lid on things until we can get there," you tell Zwale over the phone. "Reassure Mrs. Kennedy that we're on our way, and any argument or objection she has can be taken up with me."

You end the call and hastily fasten your seat belt as McAdam speeds away, activating the "blues and twos"—flashing blue lights concealed behind the car's front grille and an accompanying police siren. Strictly speaking this isn't an emergency that calls for such measures, but at this time of morning it'll allow you to cut through traffic. Pressing yourself back into the seat, you glance over at McAdam. She's in her element, doing her best impression of a rally driver and seemingly loving every minute of it, despite the wet conditions. Maybe because of them.

Vehicles part and pull over as your sergeant thrusts her car through gaps and around corners, until you reach the quieter country roads approaching Elysium. Not that she slows down at this point, but at least you're no longer clutching the dashboard while she races through red lights.

McAdam deactivates the siren as you enter the gates, speeding past the unlucky uniformed officer guarding it in the rain. Crossing the bridge, you see the river is much higher than it was yesterday as it rushes under the stone arches. You wonder who's charged with keeping the bridge in good condition. It's within the manor's grounds, so presumably it comes under Stephen Cheong's purview. As it's the only way in or out, that could be an expensive responsibility if anything went wrong.

You pull up outside Elysium, where waterfalls spout from the mouths of the building's many gargoyles. McAdam parks as close to the entrance as possible, and you hurry up the steps into the lobby. One pleasant side effect of the rain is a drop in the temperature; you wonder if the two combined will help make the plants at Elysium a little happier.

Inside a dozen staff members are gathered, surrounded by twice as many resident Friends. The din of voices combined with the drum of rain outside makes it hard to hear Constable Zwale. From the reception desk he hastily beckons you over, saying something inaudible. You push your way through the crowd, wishing you had the equivalent of blue lights and a siren on foot.

"Why are all these people here, Constable? Don't they have classes and workshops to attend?"

"Someone heard Mrs. Kennedy arguing with me, and word spread," Zwale says. "Now they're all waiting to see if something kicks off, and when I tried to get them to disperse it made them more determined to stay. The good news is, I've calmed Mrs. Kennedy down. I assured her you were on your way and would sort it out." Flora Kennedy herself stands nearby, but is busily involved in a shouting match with Stephen Cheong and can't hear you. "She seems very agitated."

"Divorce or not, the victim was her husband," you remind the constable. "Grief affects everyone differently. In time you'll see that for yourself. Now, where's this parcel?"

Zwale gestures to Jennifer, who reaches for the key ring attached to her waistband. She uses one of its keys to open a locked drawer behind the reception desk and removes a small cardboard box, placing it on the countertop.

"This is my fault," she says. "It never occurred to me it would be evidence, so I just called Mrs. Kennedy automatically."

"It's all right," you reassure her. "Has Mr. Kennedy received mail here before?"

"I'm not sure anyone has, to be honest. The staff often have things sent here rather than home so they don't miss deliveries, but I don't recall a Friend ever doing it."

The parcel is small, six by four inches and two inches deep, sealed with hastily applied packing tape. It's damp, having caught some of the morning rain, but you can clearly see it's addressed to *Harry Kennedy c/o Elysium at Finchcote Manor* with a preprinted label and postage. However, the return address doesn't give a company name, only the unit number on an industrial estate in Wolverhampton.

"Whatever it is, it was intended for Harry, so I'll inherit it," Flora Kennedy says, appearing suddenly at your side, her argument with Stephen either forgotten or paused. "You've no right to keep his personal property. There are laws, you know."

"I'm well aware of that, Mrs. Kennedy. But given the circumstances of your husband's death, this parcel is potential evidence." You can see she's about to launch into another argument, so you preempt her with a question. "Who would be likely to send Harry something? Who knew he was here?"

She thinks for a moment. "Nobody, as far as I know. I told you, even I didn't until yesterday. Why would anyone send something here, rather than to our home?"

"Seems obvious to me," someone says from behind you. You turn to see a familiar tattooed figure in sweat-stained workout gear, toweling himself down.

"What do you mean? Who are you?" Flora says, regarding him with distaste.

"Tank Destroyer," he says, introducing himself. "Whatever's in that parcel, I'm betting Harry didn't want you to know about it. Makes me wonder what's inside."

Now Carla Nesbitt joins the conversation, stepping out of the crowd. "We're all wondering that, you simpleton. Why do you think everyone's gathered here?" She turns to you. "Are you going to open it, or not?"

"For God's sake, Carla, do you have to be so smug all the time?" Flora snaps. "Show some respect."

You expect the MP to dismiss this plea for civility in her characteristic fashion, but instead she falls silent and turns away, the remark seeming to cut deep. You wonder how much history there really is between the two women.

Sergeant McAdam produces a small knife from her jacket and offers it to you, along with a pair of nitrile gloves.

"It's not ticking or anything, so we might as well open it."

You pause. Whatever the box contains will surely fuel the gossip mill at Elysium, and among the suspects, potentially hampering the investigation. Perhaps it would be better to open it in private.

But the decision is taken from you—as is the parcel. When you turn to address McAdam, Flora grabs the box and makes to prize it open with her bare hands. You try to take it back, and for a moment the two of you are locked in an undignified tug-of-war—until, weakened by the damp, the cardboard bursts open and scatters its contents over the floor.

The lobby falls silent. An Elysium staffer reaches down to pick up one of the silver foil packets, sniggering when she recognizes the blue diamond shape.

"It's Viagra!" she shouts, loud enough for everyone gathered to hear. "Someone sent him Viagra!"

The silence breaks. Everyone reacts and talks at once, equally divided between mocking laughter and scornful tutting.

"I think that's enough," you say loudly to the watching crowd. "Could you all please disperse now!"

The reaction is a general grumbling, and some people do leave. But most of them simply move back a few meters, then continue watching.

Flora Kennedy is confused and appalled. "Is this some kind of joke?" she says, barely audible.

But you've already guessed that it isn't, and can now answer the question of how someone knew Harry Kennedy would be here to receive a delivery. This isn't a gift from a friend. Kennedy ordered it himself, timing it to be delivered during his stay.

His widow reaches the same conclusion. With cheeks the color of an Elysium rose, she turns and yells at Jennifer.

"What is this, some kind of brothel?! Oh, I know your type, can't resist a bit of money! Well, you won't get it! Not now!"

The accusation seems to confuse Jennifer as much as offend her.

"Believe me, nobody here wanted to—" she begins, then thinks better of it and bites her tongue. A home truth or two about Harry?

"I assure you Mr. Kennedy wasn't sleeping with anyone here," Stephen says, stepping in to calm things down. "The idea runs counter to every standard of professionalism we have. Isn't that right?" He turns to the staff for confirmation. Some nod vigorously, while others roll their eyes.

One, though, is incensed. Alina Martinescu steps forward, wearing a venomous expression. "You don't even know your own husband," she says to Flora. "He tried with us all, hands everywhere. But nobody would be with that pig! Disgusting!"

Flora punches her.

Shocked gasps ripple through the gathered staff and clientele as Alina wavers, then collapses to the floor. Tank Destroyer laughs out loud. Constable Zwale swiftly moves in to restrain Mrs. Kennedy, helped by an East Asian man who steps out of the crowd. Together they prevent any further attacks while you and McAdam approach Alina. Jennifer helps the therapist to her feet. She already has the beginnings of a black eye.

"Arrest her!" Stephen shouts. "That's assault, that is, and I'll press charges!"

"That's a decision for the crown prosecutor, Mr. Cheong, not you." You turn to Zwale and the older man, still holding on to Flora. All the fight seems to have abandoned her, and she sags in their grip. "Nevertheless, Mrs. Kennedy, he's right that you've committed assault, not to mention tampered with evidence. That must be answered for."

Perhaps sensing the action is over, the crowd disperses. Jennifer leads a tearful Alina away, while Zwale holds on to Flora.

You suspect both women have more to tell than they've let on. Should you let McAdam and the constable deal with the widow, while you check on Alina? Or do you want to interview Flora now, while Jennifer takes care of the injured therapist?

- To question Flora, turn to **8**
- To check on Alina, turn to **53**

168

"We have to try. Go on, Sergeant."

McAdam grimaces, shifting the car to a low gear and slowly but steadily moving toward the bridge. Water quickly surrounds you, pressing against the car and forcing her to compensate with constant adjustments to the steering wheel and throttle. Her expression is focused, determined to maintain control as you crawl through the rushing river water overflowing the bridge. If a car can be said to *wade*, that's what you're doing.

Unfortunately, cars weren't meant to wade, and for all that Sergeant McAdam is an excellent driver, she underestimated the sheer force of the torrent you face. The first sign something has gone wrong is when the heating sputters and dies, while the interior lights strobe on and off.

"That's not good," McAdam whispers, gritting her teeth. "Come on, girl, just a wee bit more . . ."

The car suddenly slides to the left, its tires aquaplaning as the fast-flowing water drags you along with it. McAdam spins the steering wheel and furiously pumps the pedals, but the car rotates and glides across the surface water as smoothly as if it were on skis.

Your head snaps forward as the car's rear end slams into the low bridge wall with sufficient force to break through it. The air bags deploy to force you back against the seat, holding you in position as the car plunges backward into the river's cold embrace.

Panicking, you glance at McAdam. Blood runs from her nose, and she appears to be unconscious. Your teeth begin to chatter, and you realize you can't feel your own feet. Looking down, you see the freezing river water quickly rising over your ankles. The car is sinking!

You release your seat belt, then McAdam's, and pull on the door handle. But the water is now halfway up the window, and no matter how much you strain, it won't budge. *Of course*, you think. *Equalize the pressure.* You recall emergency training from years ago, explaining that you must counterintuitively let water in. Only when the pressure inside the car is close to the water outside can you open the door. You press the window control to lower it . . . but nothing happens. The car's power is out, and you don't know if there even is a manual override in this vehicle, let alone where it might be.

McAdam is still unconscious. There's no time. Reaching down into the icy water, you pull off a shoe and slam it against the glass, again and again. You yell as loudly as you can, hoping that somehow the officer guarding the gate might hear you, or have seen the car as it attempted to cross the bridge. But nobody comes.

A wave of water buffets the car, jerking you around and throwing you out of your seat. Your head slams against the dashboard. Your vision blurs. You're dimly aware that the water is already up to the glove box, and you must try the door again. But your limbs are heavy and your head is spinning. As you reach for the handle, the car sinks farther and you swallow a lungful of bitterly cold water. Reflexively you cough and try to breathe, which only ingests more water . . .

Tomorrow, when they find your bodies, Dr. Wash will shake her head and wonder what you were thinking trying to cross a flooded bridge.

You and Sergeant McAdam will be mourned by your colleagues—but not for long, as there is still work to be done and cases to be solved.

A new detective will be assigned to Harry Kennedy's case, hoping to bring justice to his killer.

- You can now wipe your notebook, return to **1**, and try again—maybe next time placing more trust in your own instinct for self-preservation.

For now, though, this is . . .

THE END

169

You open the door as casually as you can, pretending that you have no idea anyone is on the other side.

Tank sees you and immediately turns tail, hurrying across the lobby and up the wide staircase. To your surprise, the person he was talking to is Flora Kennedy. She wears the workout clothes Jennifer found for her, though they don't seem much drier than the wet clothes she changed out of.

"Mrs. Kennedy, shouldn't you be locked in a staff room somewhere?"

Flora recovers her composure. "I don't see why I should be held prisoner. I'm hardly going anywhere in this weather, am I?"

"That's not really the point. Where's Constable Zwale?"

"I have no idea. Still standing outside the door, I should imagine."

McAdam stifles a laugh. "You climbed out of a window, didn't you? Well, I never."

The widow declines to answer.

"What were you and Tank talking about?" you ask her.

She hesitates. "He . . . offered his condolences on Harry's death."

"That seems almost as unlikely as you climbing out of a window."

Flora shrugs. "Perhaps you're simply a bad judge of character, Inspector."

On the contrary, you feel you have the measure of both Tank and Flora pretty well. "Do please come with me, and don't wander off again." You turn to McAdam. "Fetch Constable Zwale, would you? Don't be too hard on him—I doubt any of us expected Mrs. Kennedy to pull off a daring escape."

- Turn to **137**

170

"For example," you say, "let's talk about your relationship with Harry Kennedy, and this 'mutual investment' you've mentioned. His records show that he hadn't paid anything to you, nor you to him. How do you explain that?"

"These things take time, Inspector," Tank says in a patronizing tone. "You don't just shake on it and hand over a hundred grand. There are contracts to draw up, lawyers to pay, all that stuff."

"But even if he'd wanted to, Harry Kennedy didn't have that kind of money to invest in your company anyway. In fact the only large payment he made recently was to a different company entirely, owned by Carla Nesbitt."

"Nesbitch again," Tank spits. "I should have guessed she'd get his money before I did."

McAdam tuts at the insult, before posing a question of her own. "Your own investors seem rather small-time. How come a man with your track record doesn't have the big tech companies lining up to invest?"

"They don't have the vision," Tank sniffs. "They just wait for people like me to innovate, then buy us out."

You wonder about that. There's something about Tank Destroyer that you can't help but feel is performative, like he's putting on an act for you and everyone around him. But given the paucity of information online, it's difficult to verify anything. You assume Google doesn't buy just any old company . . . do they?

"You should be talking to Stephen, not me," Tank says. "He's the madman taking a run at people with a hammer."

Before you can correct Tank again, a loud scream reverberates through the lobby—then is just as quickly cut short.

• Turn to **69**

171

Using Mr. Proctor's desk phone, you call down to the front desk and ask the receptionist not to mention to Flora Kennedy that you're here.

"Inspector, if you're hoping to stand there while my client and I discuss private and personal business, I tell you now that I won't tolerate it," the solicitor says, offended.

No doubt he knows that technically he could eject you from the premises. This is private property, nobody is under arrest, and you are without a warrant. But Mr. Proctor also knows that doing so would only invite further scrutiny and suspicion, something he seems keen to avoid. For a specific reason, or just a general distrust of the police?

"It's not our intention to intrude, sir. But you've been checking your watch since we arrived, so I'd like to know if this is a scheduled appointment?"

"Of course. I don't see just anyone who walks in off the street, you know." He quickly adds, "Present company excepted."

"*When* was it scheduled?" McAdam asks. It's a good question.

Proctor grumbles. "About half an hour ago. She said it was an urgent matter, but wouldn't say why. Now I know."

At that moment the door is flung open by a breathless Flora Kennedy, who gasps, "Good news—!" before the sight of you and McAdam brings her to a screeching halt, and a look of panic crosses her face.

"Mrs. Kennedy," you say, smiling. "How nice to see you again. Could you simply not wait to see Mr. Proctor after our constable drove you home?"

"I, I was just coming to begin the necessary arrangements around Harry's death," she says, re-forming her expression into one of grief. "I didn't expect to see you here."

"That much seems obvious. Can I take it that you're not quite as distraught over your husband's death as you led us to believe? Perhaps the 'good news' is that you'll now inherit Kennedy Homes in its entirety, rather than settling for whatever share of it you'd have won in a divorce?" You decide not to mention the company's precarious financial state.

"I've already told the police that's none of their business," Mr. Proctor interrupts before Flora can answer. "You don't have to answer any questions."

McAdam approaches Flora and says gently, "He's right, you don't. But look at it from our point of view. We suspected you were considering divorce, and now you rush in here all overjoyed. Perhaps there's an innocent explanation, but it doesn't look good."

Flora looks from McAdam to you to Mr. Proctor, then lets out a deep breath and falls into a leather chair.

"Yes, all right. I was going to divorce Harry. I'd had enough of the affairs. Twenty-five years, and I doubt there was one where he wasn't carrying on with some girl or other."

"Your husband was a serial philanderer?" McAdam asks.

"Harry was weak, is what he was. Our business is filled with pretty young things: real estate agents, secretaries, marketers . . . he couldn't help himself. At one time he had three on the go at once, all half his age with the brains to match. Oh, afterward he'd always tell me he was sorry and swear it was the last time. I know he meant it, too. But then another would catch his eye and he'd be off again."

"Flora, nobody could blame you for wanting to be rid of him," Mr. Proctor says gently. Then he seems to realize what he's said and quickly adds, "In a legal sense, I mean. Inspector, you can't think Mrs. Kennedy would resort to violence."

Despite his confidence, you know that many people are capable of violence when pushed hard enough.

"Is my assumption correct, that Mrs. Kennedy will now inherit Kennedy Homes in its entirety?" you ask the solicitor.

He spreads his hands. "I have no firsthand knowledge of the late Mr. Kennedy's will."

"Yes, I will," Flora says. "We don't have children, so we drew up wills leaving everything we have to each other. I might sell the company," she adds. "I'm not sure I could face running it."

"Aren't you already a partner?" McAdam asks.

"I'm a director on paper, and Harry talks to me about big decisions. But I don't really have anything to do with operating things. I wouldn't know where to begin."

"I'm sorry to inform you that selling it may not be easy, either," you say. "According to Kennedy Homes' financial records, the company is carrying significant debt. Did you know?"

Flora looks deeply unsettled by this news. "I don't . . . debt? Really? But Harry always had . . . no, surely you must be mistaken."

"I'm afraid not. Perhaps your husband hoped the new estate would set things right, and you'd never need to find out. But the council was on course to formally reject the plans, leaving Kennedy Homes in the red. You've inherited an albatross, Mrs. Kennedy."

Flora looks to Mr. Proctor with wide eyes, searching for help. The solicitor steps out from behind his desk, places a reassuring hand on her shoulder, and fixes you with a disdainful expression.

"I think you've had your moment, don't you, Inspector? Now if you'll excuse us, my client and I have private matters to attend to."

You're confident you've got as much out of Flora Kennedy as you can at this time. You and Sergeant McAdam take your leave, walking out into the afternoon sun and back to her car.

"Flora seemed genuinely surprised by the state of the business," McAdam says. "It makes sense Harry would have kept it to himself, so as not to upset her."

"It does—if we assume she's telling the truth. Regardless, it feels thin as a motive. If she was going to divorce him anyway, why go to the trouble and risk of murder?"

Neither you nor McAdam can answer that question—yet.

- Write **F3** in your notebook, and **add 1** to your LOCATION number
- Then turn to **30**

172

McAdam arrests Flora Kennedy, and after the storm clears you take the widow into custody at the police station.

But she does not, in fact, have a guilty conscience and secretly believes she deserves to be caught. Instead Flora maintains her innocence, and her solicitor rightly points out that you have no physical evidence tying her to the murder. You can't place her at the crime scene, or put the weapon in her hand. All you have is your own speculation—and that's simply not enough.

The case is a bust. Losing faith in you, the detective chief superintendent reassigns you to a different, simpler case and calls in another inspector to take over the Elysium killing.

Harry Kennedy's murder may yet be solved . . . but not by you.

Later, you consider what went wrong. Were you right to accuse Flora, but you lacked the right evidence? Should you have looked more deeply into her potential motivation? Or was the killer someone else altogether?

- To find out, don't despair. Simply wipe your notebook, return to **1**, and try again.

For now, though, this is . . .

THE END

173

"Any woman here can tell you what Kennedy was like," the yoga instructor says. "I count myself lucky he only tried it once, and when I gave him a slap he didn't come to my class again."

"Same here," the other staffer agrees. "He kept calling me his 'little rose,' like we were on a date. Horrible." She shudders.

The women exchange knowing glances between themselves, but nobody says anything more—perhaps because of your presence. They don't need to; their silence speaks for them.

Just then, your phone rings with a call from McAdam. "Flora Kennedy's shut down," she says. "She won't talk, and insists Kennedy must have been sleeping with the staff here. You might have more luck, but I wouldn't bet on it."

"Thank you, Sergeant. I'll be with you shortly."

The yoga instructor has finished tending to Alina, and leans back to admire her handiwork. "There, done. It's not so bad," she says, repacking her makeup bag.

"Thank you," Alina says quietly, tucking a stray dark hair behind her ear. "Now, I have a booking. I must go to work."

Jennifer places a hand on her arm. "You probably shouldn't. I can find someone to sub for you, nobody will blame you."

Alina smiles, but shakes her head. "No, it will help me. I can forget what happened." She leaves with her head held high.

"I suppose I'd better go sweep the little blue pills off the floor," Jennifer says, rising. The other staffers also stand, and you take the hint. Bidding them goodbye, you decide to see if you can indeed get anything more out of Flora Kennedy.

- Write **A3** in your notebook, then turn to **101**

174

She makes a quick recovery, but it seems clear that Flora Kennedy doesn't know what you're talking about.

"You were unaware the council wouldn't approve the new estate?" you ask.

"Um . . . Harry hadn't told me that yet. I'm sure he would have once he returned home."

You wonder what other secrets Kennedy kept from his wife.

"Did you know your husband had asked the MP, Carla Nesbitt, to intervene on his behalf?"

Flora looks confused. "Intervene? What do you mean?"

"To persuade the council to approve the plans. He seemed keen to emphasize that it would create new jobs, which it must be said politicians normally like to endorse. Can you think why your husband wouldn't have told you about that?"

She gazes out of the window. "Harry often protected me from the rough and tumble of business, Inspector. I helped him with big ideas, but I didn't get bogged down in the nitty-gritty of running the company."

"How would you characterize your relationship with Ms. Nesbitt?"

"There isn't one, really," the widow replies. "Harry and Carla have known each other a long time because they both grew up around here, but we're not close. We attend her fundraisers now and again because it makes good business sense, but that's all."

- Write **F6** in your notebook, then turn to **134**

175

"Mrs. Kennedy, you must understand my position," you explain. "If you knew your husband was having an affair, not only is that grounds for divorce, it's also an excellent reason for you to want him dead. Vengeance, plus total inheritance of the business. Admittedly, the business isn't worth much at the moment, but it seems you didn't know that."

"But I *didn't* want him dead," she protests. "I had no idea Harry was running the business into the ground."

"Aren't you a company director?" McAdam asks.

"For tax purposes, Constable." The sergeant twitches at the unconscious insult to her rank, but says nothing. "I'm not sitting there with a spreadsheet watching the finances. That was Harry's job."

"He doesn't appear to have been very good at it," you suggest.

"He used to be. Who do you think bought me a Ferrari?"

McAdam did initially say Harry Kennedy was regarded as a successful local businessman. Perhaps he was, once.

"So why couldn't he get the council to approve his new planned development? What went wrong?"

The widow shakes her head. "I don't know, but I'm not surprised. They've always been jealous of Harry in that place, everyone from the mayor on down." She runs a hand through her hair. "I know he could rub people up the wrong way if he didn't get what he wanted. But inside he was a good man."

You're not sure the staff of Elysium would agree.

"Maybe I'll have more luck with the council myself," Flora says. "I might as well continue trying to get the plans approved. They might give me a sympathy vote."

"There's still the question of murder. And we've already seen that you're capable of violence when provoked." You look her in the eye. "Mrs. Kennedy, let me be direct. Did you kill your husband?"

"No," she says firmly. "I told you I haven't seen him since last week, and that's the truth."

She could simply be lying. While you don't have any firm evidence either way, the circumstantial case is getting stronger by the minute. With little choice after what she did to Alina, you get to your feet and deliver the bad news.

"Flora Kennedy, I'm arresting you on suspicion of assault by beating, contrary to Section 39 of the Criminal Justice Act 1988. You do not have to say anything . . ."

As you caution her, you're surprised to see Flora's reaction. Most people break down and grow listless upon being arrested, but Mrs. Kennedy regains her strength and poise, sitting upright with a defiant expression. A moment ago she was in despair; now she seems ready to face the world.

You direct Constable Zwale to arrange for her to be taken into custody. First, though, you check in regarding the witness statements taken yesterday.

"I'm afraid nobody saw anything," he says glumly. "Most people were in classes at that time, they weren't looking at the courtyard. As far as we know, Alina and Tank remain the last people to see Kennedy."

He leads Flora away.

"What if she's right?" McAdam frowns. "About Kennedy sleeping with Jennifer Watts, I mean."

"It could lend more weight to the hypothesis that Flora killed him. She may claim it was only a suspicion, but if it's true and she found out, it strengthens her motivation."

"Aye, but . . ." McAdam trails off, something clearly bothering her.

"Speak your mind, Sergeant. I don't know what your previous colleagues were like, but I'm always open to hearing new ideas."

"Well, I was thinking—who has the key to the old storeroom?"

"Nobody does. It's missing."

"Is it, though? Jennifer Watts oversees the lockbox where it's normally kept. She could easily have taken the key herself, then claimed it was stolen. There's no CCTV to prove otherwise."

She's right. The receptionist claims she didn't know the key was missing until after Kennedy's death, but . . .

"Are you suggesting Jennifer was sleeping with Harry, and killed him to keep it secret? To preserve her reputation?"

"Perhaps to keep her job, too. Or maybe she's just hanging on to the key rather than admit she took it. She might be embarrassed about the affair and not want his widow to find out."

"But surely Jennifer could have replaced the key just as easily as she took it. Nobody would be any the wiser."

McAdam shrugs. "Aye, but then she'd be one of two suspects, wouldn't she? If only she and Stephen have a key to that room, and neither key is missing, we'd be looking at those two and nobody else."

Once again, the sergeant is right. Your respect for her is increasing.

"I wonder where that key is now?" you ask aloud. "And how was it stolen in the first place?"

Your mind swirls with possibilities. Could Jennifer Watts be the killer? Or is it still more likely to have been Flora Kennedy? You need more evidence to even eliminate people, much less make an accusation.

- Write **J3** and **F2** your notebook, then turn to **133**

176

"I believe you had ample motive to kill Harry Kennedy," you say. "One you told us yourself, in fact. You told us that Elysium's most prominent Friends are allowed to get away with bad behavior, because Stephen is desperate for their repeat business. In the case of someone like Carla that means she gets to treat the staff like servants, always beat them at tennis, and generally walk around like she owns the place."

"I beg your pardon?!" the MP gasps, but you ignore her.

"But with male clients, that freedom becomes something more sinister. Even in his short time here at Elysium, Harry Kennedy quickly gained a reputation among the female staff as a molester. 'Handsy,' I believe was the word you used."

"That's true," Jennifer says. "He tried it on with everyone, and Stephen did nothing about it."

"You should have brought your concerns to me," Stephen protests.

A collective rolling of eyes sweeps through the assembled female staff like a breeze.

"We did, Stephen," Jennifer says coolly. "You ignored them. You even accused one therapist of 'overreacting,' so she quit. The fact you don't even remember shows how *concerned* you were." She turns to you. "Harry Kennedy was far from the only one, you know. Men like that aren't used to being told no."

"But that's what you did, isn't it? First when he confronted you coming out of the bathroom, which left the bruise still visible on his arm. Did he then try again? Or did you simply decide to end it once and for all—with a gardening fork?"

"Absolutely not," she protests. "He knew what would happen if he tried it on with me a second time."

Everyone in the room looks at the receptionist, who realizes what she's just said.

"I meant give him a good slap!" she protests. "Not stab him and throw him off a balcony. I'm not a psycho, for God's sake."

"That's for a jury to decide," you say. "Sergeant, arrest Ms. Watts."

• Turn to **157**

177

When you saw Carla Nesbitt earlier she was wearing tennis whites, pristine enough that you presume she was on her way to a game rather than coming from one. You ask a passing staffer, identified by the Elysium logo on their polo shirt, for directions to the tennis courts. The young man directs you through the east wing, past the entrance to the swimming pool, and out into the grounds. You pass a lawn with a wide gazebo, shading a group of resident "Friends" from the sun. They stand at rows of wooden tables, each with a pestle and mortar in hand, apparently grinding flower petals. Two members of Elysium staff walk among them, monitoring their progress.

Beyond the lawn stand two tennis courts. Carla plays on one, handily beating another staffer. With each strike of the ball on the ground, dust billows into the air. You can't quite tell if Carla is just that good, or if the staffer is letting her win.

Sergeant McAdam tuts disapprovingly. "I know she didn't like the man, but I'm surprised at how quickly everyone seems to have resumed going about their business."

"Perhaps that's the power of angiospermal homeopathy," you reply sarcastically, and wave to Carla.

She's clearly annoyed by the interruption, but pauses her game to speak with you. "How can I help, Inspector?"

"I'll get straight to the point," you say, confident that even here at a leisure retreat, the MP values her time. "Where were you between ten and eleven this morning?"

Carla watches you carefully. "I thought Harry threw himself out of a window."

"On the contrary, it appears that someone killed him."

"Really! Well, I never. So now you're checking alibis, are you?"

"That is the method we follow," you say patiently.

She tuts. "Well, you're out of luck with me. I was doing Tai Chi on the lawn, along with a dozen other people and Bill the instructor. They'll all back me up."

"I'm delighted to hear it. Tell me, how did you know Mr. Kennedy? I gather you didn't get along."

"That's one way of putting it. The man was a boor; a patronizing sexist who thought his looks were a free pass to do anything, and that any problem could be solved by waving money around."

"Is that what you were arguing about yesterday evening?" The look of surprise on Carla's face pleases you. You suspect the MP isn't used to other people catching her out. "Here by the tennis courts," you add, to jog her memory.

She scowls. "I see someone has a big mouth. Yes, Harry and I argued. He had a harebrained scheme to build a housing estate on a local field, but the planning department wouldn't approve it. He was outraged that they wouldn't just let him waltz in and do whatever he wanted, and asked me to intervene on his behalf."

"But you refused."

"I did. The field in question is a floodplain, and covering it in tarmac will send water rushing down onto the Burrowlands estate next door instead."

"Mr. Kennedy didn't see it that way?"

Carla sniffs impatiently. "Really, Inspector, I don't see what any of this has to do with Harry's death. In case you hadn't noticed, I was in the middle of a game when you came over. Can't we talk later?"

"I'm sure we will, but time is of the essence. I wouldn't presume to tell you how to do your job as an MP."

"You'd be unusual, then."

"It has been said. Now, please tell me: Why did Harry Kennedy think he could convince you to change the council's mind?"

"He promised to install drainage to divert the runoff into the river, bypassing both the old and new estates. He also played the old saw about how building houses creates jobs. But the council wasn't convinced on either point, and neither was I."

McAdam is taking notes, but you can tell she's also trying to get a question in. Given her aggressive approach, you worry she might offend Carla Nesbitt further. But you have to give her a chance, so you let her interject.

"Ms. Nesbitt," she asks, "if you and Mr. Kennedy didn't get along, why were you both staying here at the same time?"

To your relief, it's a good question. You wish you'd asked it yourself.

"That wasn't deliberate," Carla replies, frowning. "I'm only here this week because I couldn't get in at the end of August. My options are limited, with Parliament returning soon."

If she thinks reminding McAdam of her political status will shut down the sergeant's questioning, Carla's mistaken.

"But could Mr. Kennedy have known you'd be here?" McAdam asks. "Perhaps he thought it would be easier to persuade you in an informal setting like this."

"I wouldn't put it past him," Carla sighs. "Is there anything else?"

"Almost," you reassure her. "Did you see Mr. Kennedy again, after you argued?"

"No. He started a game with that tattooed chap, and I retired to my room. I didn't see him after that."

"Not even in the courtyard this morning?"

She fixes you with a skeptical eye. "You may enjoy gawping at corpses, Inspector, but I was quite happy to let everyone else do that. Now if you don't mind, I should like to return to my game."

"Thank you for your time, Ms. Nesbitt. If you think of anything, do let us know."

Casting a doubtful expression back at you, she returns to the tennis court.

- Write **C3** in your notebook
- If you've already questioned either Alina or Tank, turn to **120**

Otherwise, choose one of them to interview:

- To question Alina the massage therapist, turn to **48**
- To question Tank the tech mogul, turn to **73**

178

It doesn't seem like you'll get any more information out of Tank Destroyer at this time.

"Thank you, that's all for now," you say, turning to leave. Then you pause and ask: "Actually, there is one more thing, if you'll forgive my curiosity. What prompted your choice of new name?"

A sly smile forms on Tank's face. "Long story. Let's just say it involves a bachelor party with some old school chums, a decommissioned tank range in Dorset, and a little too much champagne."

McAdam snorts. "How the other half live, eh?"

You thank Tank for his time and let him return to his yoga class.

- Write **T6** in your notebook
- If you've already questioned either Alina or Carla, turn to **120**

Otherwise, choose one of them to interview:

- To question Alina the massage therapist, turn to **48**
- To question Carla the MP, turn to **177**

179

"So three weeks ago, Kennedy paid Carla Nesbitt's company seven thousand pounds in 'consultancy' fees. Then four days ago he texted her, using a secret code, to remind her about the money and demand she hold up her end of a bargain. That really does sound like a bribe, doesn't it?"

McAdam nods. "But what for?"

"Presumably to apply pressure on the council, so they'll permit Kennedy to build on the floodplain. Even though Carla believes the plan is a bad idea, and wouldn't support it."

"She wouldn't be the first politician to do a U-turn after money changes hands. Let's not forget she's also a landlady herself, through Standard Umbrella."

"True enough. But then why hasn't she applied that pressure yet? What's she waiting for . . . ? Oh, of course. Standard Umbrella owns those houses for sale on Burrowlands."

"I don't follow."

You work through the hypothesis in your mind. It feels sound.

"Carla Nesbitt knows that building on the floodplain will divert rainwater onto the Burrowlands estate, which will undoubtedly affect how much those houses are worth and make them harder to sell. But because the council won't approve Kennedy's plan, it's not a problem . . . yet."

"She's trying to sell her houses while they're still worth something," McAdam says, picking up the thread. "Once she's offloaded them, *then* she'll convince the council to change their decision, pocket Kennedy's money, and walk away from it all."

It's quite a scheme, and will be almost impossible to prove. But the theory is sound, and matches with the tone of Kennedy's text message. "Don't think I won't tell if you back out" is a clear threat to Carla's reputation and public standing. You decide to confront her about it next time you speak to her.

- Write **C11** in your notebook, then return to **100** and skip to the end of that section

180

"Your own investors seem rather small-time, Mr. Destroyer," McAdam says. "How come a man with your track record doesn't have big tech companies lining up to give you money?"

"They don't have the vision," Tank sniffs. "They sit back and wait for people like me to innovate, then buy us out."

"You mean like they did before? When Google bought your company for eight hundred million dollars?"

You're not sure where the sergeant's going with this line of questioning, but you let her take the lead.

"That's right," Tank replies.

"Is it, though?" McAdam says. "Because I've checked up on you, and I can't find any record of your previous company being bought out by Google or anyone else. Even the Wikipedia references all point to the same two or three press releases . . . issued by you."

McAdam glances at you. You nod, impressed, and encourage her to go on.

She continues, "Mr. Destroyer, I don't think you're the multimillionaire you'd like us to believe. I think you're a chancer. You convince gullible businessmen that you're a wealthy mogul like them, persuade them to invest in your crackpot companies, then make off with their money."

Understanding the implication now, you pick up the thread.

"Hence you buy the cheap package here at Elysium, and probably a dozen other places, where you can 'fortuitously' meet those businessmen and turn on the charm." You smile at Tank. "How are we doing so far?"

His expression could fell a . . . well, a tank. He says nothing, which is all the confirmation you need.

"Did Harry Kennedy work this out? Is that why he wouldn't invest in your company? Did he perhaps threaten to expose you?"

"Oh my days, what are you saying?" Tank cries. "Harry wasn't just a business partner, he was my friend! He wouldn't do something like that."

"Wouldn't he? You only met a few months ago, and he was quite willing to blackmail Stephen Cheong. Why not you as well?"

"You should be talking to Stephen, not me! He's the madman taking a run at people with a hammer."

Before you can correct Tank again, a loud scream reverberates through the lobby—then is just as quickly cut short.

• Turn to **69**

181

Constable Zwale prepares to dive in, but you stop him.

"I won't risk your life for that of a civilian, especially one who might be a killer. We're not soldiers."

"No, but our duty is to protect the public all the same," Zwale protests. "He'll drown."

"If you jump in after him, you'll both drown! Where's the sense in that? Come on, this was a mistake. Let's get back to the house."

Reluctantly, McAdam and Zwale turn and follow you back to the house. Tank Destroyer has already been swept away and under the rushing water, never to be seen again.

The storm eventually passes, but the cloud cast over your actions stubbornly remains. Zwale and McAdam have lost all faith in you, and when you finally return to the police station that night, you're hauled over the coals by your detective chief superintendent for standing by while an innocent man drowned. Your protests that he may have been a murderer hold no water, and the superintendent reminds you that everyone is assumed to be innocent until proven otherwise.

You are placed on suspension pending an inquiry, and swiftly removed from the case. Will Harry Kennedy's murder ever be solved? Perhaps . . . but not by you.

- You can now wipe your notebook, return to **1**, and try again—maybe next time remembering your duties as a police officer more clearly.

For now, though, this is . . .

THE END

182

"Speaking of secrets," McAdam says, "does this confirm Kennedy and Carla were lovers, even though she insists there was no relationship?"

"Perhaps," you agree. "They secretly arranged to be here at the same time, but even following Kennedy's death Carla strenuously denied she had anything to do with him. She's married, isn't she?"

"Aye, and so was Harry Kennedy."

You'll need more evidence to be sure, but what you've gathered so far suggests Carla Nesbitt and Harry Kennedy may have been conducting a secret affair, using Elysium to explain why they were in the same place together.

Has Carla kept this information secret from you simply to protect her marriage? Or is there another, more sinister reason?

- Write **C12** in your notebook, then turn to **45**

183

"What class is Carla Nesbitt in now?" you ask Jennifer at reception.

She checks the timetables. "Nothing scheduled. Ms. Nesbitt was due to leave today, remember. So she's on personal leisure time."

"Well, she won't be at the tennis courts in this weather," Sergeant McAdam remarks.

"No, but that's a good thought," you say. "Ms. Watts, can you see if Ms. Nesbitt has reserved any other facilities?"

Jennifer does, then nods. "There's a booking for room 2H, one of the Sanctuaries. Our Friends use them for meditation, quiet time alone, that sort of thing," she explains.

You climb the stairs and make your way along a second-floor corridor that resembles the upper floor of bedrooms, lined with doors at short intervals. Some are open, revealing small cozy rooms, identically furnished: each contains a yoga mat, bean bag chair, and low table, plus several of Elysium's ubiquitous flowering plants. While the doors all close, you notice that none have locks.

"These were probably bedrooms before they were converted," you suggest. McAdam grunts.

The door to 2H is closed. From within you hear what sounds like waves crashing. You knock gently.

Carla's voice is muffled. "Is that you, Inspector? Come on in."

You open the door to find Carla sitting cross-legged on the room's yoga mat. In front of her is the low table, with all the room's plants placed upon it. It also holds her phone, which is presumably the source of the crashing waves, and a bottle of water.

"How did you know it was us?" you ask, as McAdam closes the door behind you.

Carla smiles beatifically. "I'm in my astral corolla," she says.

You wait in silence, broken only by the eternally disembodied ocean, but it becomes clear this is all the explanation you'll get.

"I'm glad we found you in a fine mood," you say. "My apologies for interrupting your personal time, but we have some further questions."

She lowers the volume on her phone. The waves now sound like a distant sea. "Your constable made it quite clear that you wanted me to stay on to help with your inquiries, Inspector, and naturally I want to do everything I can to assist the police. Since tennis is impossible in today's weather, I decided to meditate."

"Naturally. Thank you for understanding."

Despite her obvious annoyance at being asked not to leave Elysium, her demeanor is much calmer than the abrasive personality you previously encountered. Perhaps there's something to be said for astral corollas.

Carla invites you and McAdam to sit down. You lower yourselves to the floor, only then realizing the plants on the table now partly obscure your view of Carla. You wonder if that was deliberate, but press on.

- Have you decoded the *first* text message retrieved from Harry Kennedy's phone? If so, write **P3** in your notebook. Then *multiply* the number found in that message by *14* and turn to the corresponding section.
- Otherwise, turn to **95**

184

You look Carla in the eye. "Harry was unaware Elysium even existed until recently. So how would he know that particular storeroom wasn't in use, let alone where to find its key? You, on the other hand, are a regular Friend of Elysium. By now you probably know everyone's habits and routines."

"What are you saying?"

McAdam growls. "You know exactly what the inspector's saying, Ms. Nesbitt."

"You even mentioned it," you add, "when you accused Jennifer of sleeping with Mr. Kennedy. 'Those wretched keys jangling on her belt everywhere she goes,' you said. That was just an attempt to throw us off the scent, wasn't it?"

"Harry and I are both married, for heaven's sake. What do you expect me to say?"

"It still doesn't explain where Harry got the key to room 312. Now, would you care to amend your statement?"

"All right, I took it," says Carla, frustrated. "Every night before she leaves, Jennifer puts the key ring in a box, in a cupboard, behind her desk. You wouldn't find it without knowing where to look."

"Isn't the cupboard locked?" McAdam asks, incredulously.

The MP looks at her with contempt. "This is a health spa, Sergeant, not a bank vault. Anyway, I came down one night when everyone was asleep, retrieved the key ring, opened the cabinet, and took the key to the storeroom. Then I gave it to Harry so I wouldn't be caught with it. I have my reputation to think of."

"Yes, I imagine you do," you deadpan.

- Write **C13** in your notebook
- If you already have C1 written down, turn to **55**
- Otherwise, turn to **93**

185

McAdam arrests Alina, and after the storm clears you take her into custody at the police station. But the massage therapist maintains her innocence throughout, and you struggle to get any admission or further evidence out of her.

One thing you do confirm is that one of the DNA profiles in the storeroom sink is a match to hers. However, the massage therapist has worked at Elysium for several years. She says she used the sink back when the room was in regular use, before it was shuttered, and the DNA must be from that time. You can't prove otherwise, and that means you can't definitively place her at the scene of the crime or even put the murder weapon in her hands. And you still have no explanation for the rose in Kennedy's mouth.

In fact, all you have is your own speculation—and that's simply not enough.

The case is a bust. Losing faith in you, the detective chief superintendent reassigns you to a different, simpler case and calls in another inspector to take over the Elysium killing.

Harry Kennedy's murder may yet be solved . . . but not by you.

Later, you consider what went wrong. You're absolutely sure Alina did it, but you didn't have enough evidence to prove it. Why not? What did you miss? Your oversight will continue to haunt you for many days and nights . . .

- Or at least until you wipe your notebook, return to **1**, and try again.

For now, though, this is . . .

THE END

186

"You've answered your own question," you say. "A divorce could take months, even years, to finalize. At the end of it, you might get half of Kennedy Homes to yourself. But the business was already in dire straits, with very little money in the bank. Everything was riding on this new housing plan, which seems to be going nowhere."

Flora protests. "I had no idea about the financial troubles. Harry told me the business was doing well. I wasn't involved in the day-to-day."

"Do you expect us to believe you simply took him at his word? A man you admit you were planning to divorce? Even if you did, your solicitor certainly wouldn't. I think you discovered that Kennedy Homes was in trouble—perhaps also that Harry paid a large sum he could barely afford for a mysterious 'consultation'—and decided enough was enough. After all, even if you came away owning more of the company in a divorce, your ex-husband would still be running it."

"Running it into the ground," the widow grumbles.

"Perhaps. But with him dead you inherit the entire business, which you can now run as you see fit."

"You're forgetting two things," she says. "First, I didn't know for sure Harry was here. Second, how could I have done all this without being seen? Check the CCTV cameras in town—they'll show me driving home from my solicitor's office."

McAdam nods. "They do . . . before you divert to come in this direction. There's a ten-minute gap until you return on camera, at which point you're heading away from the manor and back to your house."

"Well, I took a scenic route," Flora says, close to tears. "I had a lot on my mind. But none of it involved killing Harry!"

"Didn't it?" you say. "You had sufficient motive to want your husband dead. The CCTV puts you close by, with enough time to sneak through the house—where there are no cameras at all—and kill your husband, before returning to your car and driving home."

Carla Nesbitt speaks up. "That sounds like a lot of effort, Inspector. Does Flora really look like a woman who'd do that? No offense, Flora," she adds.

"Still waters run deep, Ms. Nesbitt. Earlier today, Mrs. Kennedy climbed out of a window to escape confinement. And the more unlikely the plan, the better chance it won't cast suspicion."

Flora Kennedy moans quietly and bursts into tears. You're not convinced they're any more real than her alibi.

"Also, there's the matter of the rose placed in the victim's mouth. A flower . . . or should I say *flora*."

The widow sniffles. "You can't possibly think that points to me. Why . . . why would I leave a clue like that?"

"Some criminals subconsciously want to be arrested and punished," you say. "And I'm happy to oblige. Sergeant, arrest Mrs. Kennedy."

• Turn to **172**

187

You begin: "Looking back, I'm surprised at your reaction to Mr. Kennedy's death when we first encountered you. Yesterday you were dismissive, even dare I say contemptuous, and suggested there was no love lost between the two of you."

Carla unhooks herself from the lotus position and stretches out her legs on the floor. "What's your point?"

"Why didn't you mention that you and he had previously been close?"

"Who told you that?"

McAdam holds up her phone and swipes through images from the archive found on Kennedy's laptop.

"These were found on Harry's computer," you explain to Carla. "They suggest a very different picture to the one you painted."

She shrugs. "That was all a very long time ago. We were young and stupid, which is something of a tautology, isn't it?"

"So it's all behind you now? Water under the bridge?"

"Something like that. Yes, we were an item. It was fun until it wasn't, and in the years since our relationship has been strictly professional. He builds houses, I sometimes buy them, and that's the end of it."

"It doesn't quite explain your earlier attitude."

Carla takes a deep breath. "I always suspected Harry carried a torch for me, to be honest. Or perhaps he just wanted to get his leg over one last time. But I've been married now for twenty years."

She stares at you defiantly, almost daring you to contradict her—but you don't have the evidence to do so.

- Write **C9** in your notebook, then turn to **144**

188

"It's quite simple," you say. "We know you and Harry Kennedy were blackmailing Stephen Cheong over his practice of buying in flowers and passing them off as his own."

A collective gasp goes up around the room, and all eyes turn to the manager. Carla Nesbitt tuts in disgust.

You continue: "I believe this is a classic case of criminals fighting over the spoils. You were onto a good thing with Stephen, and wanted it all to yourself. Therefore, Harry Kennedy had to die."

"But we weren't getting money from it," Tank protests, "just freebie Lotus packages here at Elysium."

"For now, perhaps. But with blackmail there's always more potential money in the future, isn't there?"

Tank looks confused. "Then why not accuse Stephen? He's got the most to lose. I wouldn't kill Harry over a few quid like that."

"I've seen worse for less," McAdam says. "What's more, Alina saw you arguing with Kennedy after he left her therapy session, placing you on the upper floor of the house. Nobody saw you enter the pool, and you claim not to know when you did even though there's a clock on the wall. We also now know you had ample motive to want Harry dead."

Tank glowers at you, and for a moment you fear for your safety.

"That's the real reason you tried to get inside his room, isn't it?" you say. "You weren't looking for a water bottle. You wanted to steal his laptop, in case it contained evidence implicating you. But my officers prevented you, because they know their duty." You turn to McAdam. "Sergeant, kindly do yours and arrest Mr. Destroyer."

• Turn to **131**

189

- If you have T6 written in your notebook, turn to **145**
- Otherwise, turn to **47**

190

"Need I remind you the missing key to room 312 was found buried in a raised flower bed," you say to Stephen. "The polytunnel greenhouses are your domain, as you've previously made clear."

"But why would I steal it, when I have my own key to that room? Even if I did, why bury it in my own workplace? Someone's trying to frame me!"

You've already considered this. "I don't think so. Nobody could know that I or any other police would enter the greenhouses. Why should we? Harry Kennedy had nothing to do with them, and the flower we found in his mouth was taken from the plant on the storeroom's balcony. It was just chance that we came to interview you in the polytunnel at all, even more so that we then found the key. I believe you buried it there yourself, assuming we'd never find it.

"Why you'd take and use the lockbox key rather than your own is obvious. If it wasn't missing, we'd have no reason to believe it had been used. As you have the only other key that can access that room, suspicion would have immediately fallen upon you."

"This is ridiculous," Stephen says. "What possible reason would I have to kill Harry Kennedy? He was one of our Friends!"

"But not a paying one," you remind him. "We know you hadn't charged him for the VIP package he was enjoying. Presumably you hoped he'd become a returning customer. Did he do or say something to convince you he was only out to take advantage? Mr. Kennedy was that sort of person, after all." You nod in deference to Flora, his widow. "My apologies, Mrs. Kennedy, but it's the truth."

She shrugs. "I know Harry was no angel. But he didn't deserve to be killed."

"This is hardly enough reason to want him dead!" Stephen protests.

"I think it is. Sergeant, arrest Mr. Cheong."

• Turn to **76**

191

You pull up near the entrance to Burrowlands and stroll through the estate. To your inexpert eyes it looks like any other modern housing development. Curved rows of semidetached homes curl around one another, no doubt in a pattern optimized to be space efficient and pack in the maximum possible number of houses. The houses have tiny front lawns next to big driveways and identikit wooden fencing surrounding each rear garden. They are all occupied, many with two or more vehicles parked outside, suggesting it's a favorite of young families.

As you round one particular curve, though, you correct yourself. Four houses in a row are unoccupied and for sale, all by the same real estate agent.

"Maybe they know something the others don't," McAdam murmurs. "I don't see any others for sale."

She's right. The only Burrowlands houses on the market are these four, all in a row from the same agent. How odd.

"How old is this estate?" you wonder aloud.

McAdam searches on her phone but finds no immediate answer.

"I'll have to check," she says. "It looks pretty recent, though. No more than a few years, I'd say."

- Write **P5** in your notebook
- If you already have A8 written down, turn to **27**
- Otherwise, turn to **128**

192

Your thoughts return to the invoice from the floral nursery, found in Stephen Cheong's office. At the time you thought it odd that a retreat that prides itself on homegrown flowers would do business with a nursery. Now, hearing Carla Nesbitt talk about it, your suspicions grow.

Is Stephen compensating for this bad weather by buying in plants and flowers from a nursery, effectively defrauding his customers? Did Harry Kennedy suspect this when Carla mentioned Stephen's "miraculous" green fingers? What you've learned about Kennedy suggests he wouldn't have been above indulging in blackmail. If he had Stephen Cheong over a barrel, it would explain how he was able to book a place despite Elysium being busy, and why he was given the Lotus package for free.

Most importantly, it would give the manager a powerful motive to protect his business, by silencing Kennedy—perhaps permanently.

- Write **S4** in your notebook, then turn to **25**

193

"Tank is barely spending his own money, let alone gambling with it," McAdam reminds you. "Jennifer said he normally buys the cheapest package here, remember. He's only on the Lotus this week because Stephen Cheong gave him a free upgrade."

She has a point. Why would someone with Tank's money not get the luxury option every time? Is he a penny pincher despite his millions? Or is there more to his regular patronage of Elysium than he's letting on?

• Turn to **65**

194

By now Jennifer has finished cleaning the skin around Alina's eye. She gives the therapist a reassuring hug. "No broken skin, love."

Another member of staff, a yoga instructor judging by her outfit, arrives carrying a makeup bag and proceeds to work on covering the massage therapist's black eye.

"You said Stephen is desperate for their money," you say, recalling that he was supposed to have a phone call yesterday morning with the bank and was reluctant to talk about it. "Is Elysium in some kind of financial trouble? Running and staffing a place like this must be expensive."

"You wouldn't know it from what he pays us," Jennifer says, returning the first aid kit to its cupboard. "But of course it's expensive. It costs loads to maintain the greenhouses, for a start, but that's our USP. People come here for the floral therapy. They can't get that anywhere else."

"Why not? Surely it's a relatively easy idea to copy."

The women all look at you, offended.

"You don't just grow some flowers and plonk them down on a mat, Inspector," says the one you took for a yoga instructor. "Stephen's got green fingers, but we've all been trained to work with the plants as well. You know, pairing the right flower to a particular mood or season, learning how to mix them for homeopathy. We're professionals."

"Of course," you say, slightly embarrassed by your faux pas. "Naturally it's why people come here. I wonder, is Carla Nesbitt one of these big spenders, too? Does she normally take the Lotus package?"

"Absolutely," Jennifer says. "Stephen chases them because a few regular Lotus Flower Friends are worth more than a minibus of pensioners on the Rose package. But we still need those pensioners, to keep things ticking over."

Recalling what you learned from Kennedy's bank records, you wonder if Jennifer can answer a question that's been on your mind ever since.

"Can you explain, then, why Stephen gave Harry Kennedy a freebie?"

Jennifer is confused. "What do you mean?"

"You told us that clients have to pay in advance. But there's no record of Mr. Kennedy having paid Elysium a penny, much less nine thousand pounds."

Jennifer is left speechless by this revelation.

The yoga instructor shakes her head, confused. "That doesn't make any sense. Stephen told us all to look after Harry Kennedy because he was worth a lot to the business. But how could he be, if he was getting a free ride?"

How indeed? Was there some other financial arrangement between the two men? Did Stephen give Kennedy a gift in expectation of later reciprocation? You'll have to put these questions to the manager.

"There, done. It's not so bad," the yoga instructor says, leaning back to admire her handiwork on Alina's eye. She begins to repack her makeup bag.

"Thank you," Alina says quietly, tucking a stray dark hair behind her ear. "Now, I have a booking. I must go to work."

Jennifer places a hand on her arm. "You probably shouldn't. I can find someone to sub for you, nobody will blame you."

Alina smiles, but shakes her head. "No, it will help me. I can forget what happened." She leaves with her head held high.

"I suppose I'd better go and sweep the little blue pills off the floor," Jennifer says, rising. The other staffers stand up, too, and you sense the moment for questions has passed. You bid them goodbye, wondering how McAdam has got on with Flora Kennedy, and return to the lobby to find them.

• Turn to **101**

195

You read the decoded message again, deciphering not just the words but its meaning.

"Three weeks ago, an anonymous person sent Harry Kennedy a message about a 'flower boy' buying four pallets of . . . something . . . from a nursery."

"Presumably not children," McAdam quips.

"Don't give up your day job, Sergeant. No, the obvious answer is flowers. And 'trying to be invisible' also implies whoever it was didn't want to be seen."

You both ponder this for a moment, before realization hits you.

"Stephen Cheong," you say slowly. "Flower Boy. That's what Tank Destroyer called him, remember?"

McAdam whistles. "But why would Tank be watching out for him at a nursery? Everything here at Elysium is grown on the estate. Stephen said it's their 'unique brand promise.'"

"Exactly. But he also complained that he's been struggling to cope with the recent bad weather. What if he's not coping at all, and has to supplement his own crop with flowers bought from a nursery? If word got out, Elysium's reputation would suffer heavily. It might even be actionable fraud. Look at the first part of the message."

"'You were right,'" McAdam reads. "It suggests Kennedy suspected something and asked Tank to keep an eye out."

"Not only that, but told him to encode the message upon sending, ensuring nobody else could read it."

This text message isn't itself proof. But if you've interpreted it correctly, it's damning evidence against Stephen Cheong. If Kennedy knew Stephen was buying in flowers and passing them off to guests as his own, it would give him a hold over the Elysium manager. A hold that could easily turn into threats, or blackmail—one of the oldest motives for murder there is . . .

"Just one question remains," you say, reading the message again. "How come this text was sent three weeks ago?"

McAdam looks confused. "I don't follow."

"Harry Kennedy had never been here before, and by all accounts wasn't normally one for wellness retreats in the first place. How did he even know who Stephen Cheong was, let alone suspect him of lying to customers? And why would he care?"

"I've no idea. Go on."

You laugh. "That's just it, I don't know either. But hopefully we can find out . . ."

- Write **S2** in your notebook, then return to **100** and skip to the end of that section

196

McAdam arrests Carla, and after the storm clears you take her into custody at the police station.

But she maintains her innocence throughout the interrogation, and you slowly realize that you have no case. The only thing you have is her DNA in the sink, which she claims came from washing her hands after Kennedy dragged her into the storeroom to beg for her intervention. It seems unlikely on its face, but with Kennedy dead you can't prove otherwise.

To make things worse, Bill Cheong turns out to be an unreliable witness; he backtracks, saying he can't be certain about how long Carla's break from the Tai Chi class was, or whether it would have been long enough to kill Kennedy.

You don't have anything else tying the MP to the crime scene, and no way to prove she handled the murder weapon. All you have is your own speculation—and that's simply not enough, especially with an expensive solicitor on her side.

Losing faith in you, the detective chief superintendent reassigns you to a different, simpler case and calls in another inspector to take over the Elysium killing.

Harry Kennedy's murder may yet be solved . . . but not by you.

Later, you consider what went wrong. Were you right to accuse Carla, but you simply didn't have enough evidence? Were you wrong about her motivation? Or was the killer someone else altogether?

- To find out, don't despair. Simply wipe your notebook, return to **1**, and try again.

For now, though, this is . . .

THE END

197

"Harry Kennedy's killer knew him better than anyone," you say. Many in the assembled crowd turn to look at Flora, but you shake your head. "No, not his widow. I'm talking about the woman who knew him long before he was married, and was still in his thoughts until the day he died. Isn't that right, Carla?"

The MP reddens. "Preposterous!" she cries. "All right, maybe Harry and I put on a bit of an act for the public, even though we were old friends. But that's all the more reason I wouldn't kill him."

Is Carla merely dissembling? Or do you have the evidence you need to make a successful accusation?

Check your notebook for clues in the following order:

- If you have C10 written down, turn to **153**
- If you have C13 written down, turn to **38**
- If you have C1 written down, turn to **24**
- If you have C6 written down, turn to **106**
- Otherwise, turn to **63**

198

"Mrs. Kennedy," you say, "I'll ask you again: were you planning to divorce your late husband?"

"No, I—I already told you. I was inquiring on behalf of—"

"Your sister, yes. Perhaps we should call her and verify that. Could you give me her number?"

For the first time since you entered the room, Flora seems truly agitated. "Don't bring her into this. She has nothing to do with it."

"Mrs. Kennedy, I am conducting a murder inquiry into the unfortunate death of your own husband, and I'm starting to get the impression you'd rather I didn't. Sergeant?"

McAdam takes out her phone. "I'll call records and get them to patch me through."

Flora watches her nervously, then suddenly slaps the phone out of McAdam's hand. It clatters to the floor.

"All right! Yes, I knew he had affairs, and yes, I was planning to divorce him. It had been going on for years, and I was tired of it all."

"He was a serial philanderer?" McAdam asks, while retrieving her phone.

"Harry was weak, is what he was. Our business is filled with pretty young girls: real estate agents, secretaries, marketers . . . he couldn't help himself. At one time he had three on the go at once, all half his age with the brains to match. Oh, afterward he'd always tell me he was sorry and swear it was the last time. I know he meant it, too. But then another one would catch his eye and he'd be off again."

- Write **F3** in your notebook, then turn to **114**

199

You are torn between two options.

On the one hand, you were planning to confront Stephen Cheong once and for all about his fraudulent behavior. It's possible he killed Harry Kennedy to cover it up and protect his reputation—as well as that of Elysium itself.

On the other hand, it was evidently a mistake to let Jennifer come down here by herself, and perhaps Flora Kennedy is onto something regarding the receptionist's relationship with the victim. You could send McAdam to interview Stephen while you help Jennifer fire up the generator, taking an opportunity to see what else you can find out.

You must make a choice:

- To leave the cellar and interview Stephen, turn to **102**
- To help Jennifer with the generator, turn to **13**

200

Constable Zwale marches Alina back into the center of the room. The crowd parts to let them through, watching in shocked silence.

Alina fixes you with a defiant stare. "You know nothing."

"On the contrary," you reply. "But let's begin with yesterday morning. Harry Kennedy had booked a session with you from ten until eleven. Why you? Because you were the sole remaining female therapist with whom he hadn't had a session—and none of the other 'Roses' would see him again, after he harassed and molested them during those sessions. You said yourself that Mr. Kennedy's reputation preceded him. Did you warn him off, I wonder? Tell him at the outset that you wouldn't stand for it?"

Alina shrugs. "I shouldn't have to. Nobody should have to, it's obvious."

"Yes, it is. But people like Harry still do it. Did it happen before or after you overheard him speaking to your sister? I suspect the call came first. You lied to us about the time it took place because you're very protective of Roxana, and didn't want us to connect her with Kennedy. In fact, she called him while he was on your massage table, and when you heard him say her name you realized who he was—the man who'd made Roxana's life hell for the past two years. Incensed with anger, you deliberately burned him with hot stones. Those were the marks we discovered on his body at the postmortem."

A collective gasp goes up around the room, especially from the other massage therapists.

"For a while I thought that was your motive; revenge upon the man who made your sister and her family suffer. But there was more to it than that, wasn't there? A stronger motive that connects to your reason for leaving Romania."

Alina doesn't reply.

"Romania is where you trained to be a massage therapist—and also where you were the victim of sexual assault by a client. But when you reported it to your boss, you were appalled to realize he would take no action. Both he and the police dismissed your accusation without a second thought. You decided then that you and Roxana would seek out a better life in England . . . only, when you began working at Elysium, you realized things weren't so different here after all. Stephen Cheong was just another boss who let rich men use his business as their playground to harass female staff."

"That's not true," Stephen protests. "I look into every incident reported."

Jennifer Watts rolls her eyes. "Don't lie, Stephen. Half the time you won't even acknowledge there's been a complaint. When you do, you call it a 'misunderstanding' and ignore it."

"Which is why Alina took matters into her own hands," you explain. "She knew Harry Kennedy would face no consequences for his actions, even though every female staffer here will confirm what he did . . . but we're getting ahead of ourselves. First, we need to know what happened in that room. When did he attack you, Alina? Was it after you burned him? Did he turn on you in a rage?"

The massage therapist looks fit to burst, as if she's desperately trying to hold in something that refuses to be contained. Sure enough, eventually it comes out.

"The bastard pig!" she cries, startling Constable Zwale. "Yes, I warned Kennedy at the start, and he was OK for a while. But then I heard him fight with Roxana on the phone, and I burned him. He jumped up from the table and grabbed me. He started to choke me, and it . . . it excited him! Then he began . . . touching me. So I kicked him, pushed him away, and picked up my tongs. I told him, get out or I would burn him more. He said he would tell Stephen, and have me fired."

"That's when he stormed out and encountered Tank in the corridor, isn't it? No wonder Harry wasn't in the mood to stop and chat. Did you chase after him, Alina? Or did he return to your room?"

She drops her gaze to the floor. "After he left, I knew what would happen. He would tell Stephen, who would fire me instead of telling Harry to get lost. My visa would not be valid, and I would have to return to Romania. I would have to leave Roxana."

"But then you realized there was a simpler way to solve all your problems, didn't you? You could stay here, your sister wouldn't have to deal with him anymore, and you could make sure Harry Kennedy never harassed anyone ever again . . . if only he was dead."

"He deserved it! He only wanted one thing. It was easy to make him think I would let him have me, to keep my job."

"So you went after Harry and seduced him, making him promise not to say anything to Stephen. Was the old storeroom his idea?"

Alina nods. "The key was in his pocket. When we went inside it was obvious he knew it, and had used it before. I told him to lie down, and I . . . massaged him."

Flora Kennedy has been listening with a mixture of horror and surprise the whole time. Now she reddens with embarrassment and looks like she'd rather be anywhere else. But Alina is telling her story with gusto, getting it all off her chest.

"I took off my shirt and told him to lie back," she continues. "He thought this is it, the pig. Well, it was—but not that way! I saw the garden fork on a shelf . . ."

Silence falls across the crowded room as everyone imagines the fatal moment.

"Afterward you picked a rose from the balcony, didn't you?" you ask. "We found it in his mouth."

"Yes," Alina says. "For all the 'little roses' he would not attack anymore. But I looked back inside and he was standing somehow, even though he couldn't balance. He . . ." She struggles to find the word.

"He staggered," you suggest. "Toward you, so you tried to close the French windows on him. He smashed into them, breaking the glass and cutting his arm."

Alina nods. "He fell onto the balcony. His phone dropped out of his pocket. I thought he would die at last, lying there, so I put the rose in his mouth. I wanted Stephen to know why Kennedy had died."

The manager looks suitably chastised, but says nothing.

She continues, "But then he stood up again! I could not believe it. I pushed him away, and this time he fell over the balcony. Then I smashed his phone and kicked it after him."

"Even that wasn't the end, though, was it? You then washed off the blood in the sink, put your shirt back on, locked the room behind you, and hid the key in one of Stephen's polytunnels. Why do that?"

Alina glares at you. "I think you know."

"Yes, I do. But I need to hear you confirm it."

"Because he is a coward!" she cries, pointing at Stephen. "He does not protect us, he does not listen to us. He only wants their money, and he does not care what they do to spend it. I swore when I left Romania that no man would do that to me again." Angry tears course down her face. "But that man did, because of *him*! Yes, I killed Harry Kennedy, but Stephen is the one to blame."

"So you wanted us to think he'd done it. You wanted Stephen to suffer, even though it might have resulted in Elysium closing."

Alina sniffs and wipes away her tears. "Jennifer could run this place instead. She would do it better, too."

"That may be true, Ms. Martinescu. But it doesn't justify murder."

The room falls silent again—truly silent, for the first time this afternoon, as the storm has passed and the rain finally stopped. Soon you'll be able to return to the police station. Soon normality will be restored.

"Sergeant, arrest Ms. Martinescu."

"With pleasure," McAdam says, watching the clouds clear. "Seems the day's brightening up already."

George the goat watches Sergeant McAdam intently, standing between her and Dr. Wash's sheep in a manner that suggests he will brook no nonsense. They appear to be locked in a staring contest.

Nearby, while Dr. Wash pours drinks for you and Constable Zwale, you sit at a picnic table in the pathologist's yard, surrounded by her sprawling farmhouse. A piglet scurries across the yard, heading for one of the many pens inside the tin-roofed barn guarded by George. From inside you hear the quiet sounds of sheep, goats, pigs, and more, all snuffling, eating, and snoring.

Beyond the house lie rolling open fields. The sun is beginning to set.

"We took a diversion past the Burrowlands estate on the way to the station," you say, taking your drink. "No deluge, thank goodness. The floodplain did its job."

"I expect that's the last nail in the coffin for any talk of new houses over there. Oof." Dr. Wash finishes pouring and slowly stands, groaning at her joints. "Joseph, come and give me a hand carrying."

She leads Zwale toward the main house. As they pass McAdam she calls out, "Sergeant, if you stand there much longer, George may have no alternative but to assume a committed carnivore like yourself means to slaughter and roast one of his sheep. I won't be held responsible for any butting that may occur."

McAdam grumbles and concedes, with one last glare at George before she joins you at the table. The goat scratches his hooves in the storm-churned mud, then resumes patrolling the barns protectively.

"Still think she could just get a dog," McAdam mutters, taking a glass of wine. "Why's he called George, anyway? Odd name for a goat."

"Well, his full name is George Washington," you reply. McAdam still looks blank, but you decline to explain further. She can work it out for herself.

Dr. Wash and Zwale return from the house carrying trays of food, and place them on the table. They're laden with burgers and fries.

Sergeant McAdam immediately grabs a burger, but before she can tuck in the doctor says, "I should warn you it's not meat. In case that violates your principles."

McAdam stops and peers at the burger suspiciously. Then she takes a bite, while you all watch to see her reaction. She chews, swallows, then shrugs.

"Aye, it's all right, I suppose."

"Trust me, that's high praise," you say to the others, then hold up your glass for a toast. "To murders being solved, and justice being done." The four of you clink glasses and drink.

Dr. Wash addresses McAdam. "My husband put every fiber of his being into this place. When he passed, my options were to become a farmer, sell it, or close it down. The first wasn't really a choice at my age, but I also couldn't bear to leave all the memories I have here. So I rejected all three choices and forged my own path instead. I see death every day of my life, Sergeant. It therefore seemed appropriate to make my home a sanctuary for life."

"Is that also when you turned vegetarian?" you ask.

"It's never too late," she says with a wink.

"You could charge admission to this place," Constable Zwale suggests. "Get the local schoolkids in to feed the pigs."

"Maybe one day," Dr. Wash says politely, which you can tell is actually a firm *no*. You suspect she enjoys her solitude, and quiet memories of her husband, too much to let the farm become a tourist attraction.

"Now," she says, "tell me what happened with Alina Martinescu. Such a tragic outcome all around, really. You saw the results of the DNA comparison?"

"Yes, thank you. I was confident that her sample would match the third profile you found in the sink, but it's always good to have it confirmed. Thirty-odd witnesses heard her confess at the house anyway, so she had little choice other than to admit what she did. Now she's claiming self-defense."

McAdam snorts. "Her word against that of a dead man, I suppose, but it still gets my goat. No offense, George," she adds, glancing in the baleful buck's direction.

"The other female massage therapists from Elysium have come forward as a group," Zwale says. "Jennifer, too. They all confirm Harry Kennedy was a serial harasser, which might draw some leniency in Alina's sentencing."

"I wouldn't be opposed to that," Dr. Wash says, with a meaningful glance at McAdam. "I think we can all agree that condemning a traumatized young woman would serve nobody."

Around a mouthful of burger, the sergeant grunts in reply.

"It's out of our hands now," you say in conclusion. "Our job was to catch the killer, and that's what we did. Well done, everyone."

Constable Zwale murmurs agreement, then checks his watch and makes to leave.

"Early night, Constable? Bright and fresh for the morning?"

"Um . . . not quite. I have a date. See you tomorrow."

You don't need to ask who the date is with. After he drives away,

Dr. Wash lets her sheep out into a nearby field while McAdam wanders the farmyard menagerie in quiet bafflement.

The doctor returns and asks, "So what's your assessment after her first case?"

"McAdam? She's a simple woman," you answer with a smile. "Definitely a rough diamond, with a—shall we say—healthy disrespect for convention." The doctor sighs. "But she has good instincts, and potential. I think we're going to get along just fine."

You and Dr. Wash turn in contented silence to the surrounding fields and hills, watching her sheep graze as the evening sun sinks lazily to the horizon.

THE END

Scoring

Congratulations—you *could* solve the murder! You'd make a fine detective ("Aye, with a little help," McAdam says).

But *how* fine a detective, exactly? Here's where you find out.

Below are some Clue Numbers you may have found while reading *The Flowers of Elysium*. Check each Clue Number you found, and add the number of points it's worth to your total.

Not all of these clues were necessary to solve the crime, but they reflect well on your investigative powers. Also, note that some clues were missteps, which are worth *minus* points!

Finally, not every clue in the book is listed on this table, as some were benign and don't affect your score either way.

CLUE = SCORE

A1 = +10	F3 = +5	S1 = –10
A2 = +5	F4 = +10	S2 = +10
A3 = +5	F6 = +5	S4 = +5
A4 = +5		S5 = +10
A7 = +10	J2 = +10	S6 = +10
	J5 = +10	S7 = –10
C1 = +5		
C4 = +5	P4 = –5	T2 = +5
C5 = +5	P7 = +5	T3 = +10
C6 = +5	P10 = +5	T5 = +5
C10 = +5	(for bravery!)	T7 = +5
C11 = +5	P12 = –10	
C12 = +5		
C13 = +10		

Encoded Text Messages

If you copied out the encoded text messages by hand when you were first given them, award yourself an extra +**5 points** for diligence.

If you deciphered any of the messages *before* Penny gave you the cipher, award yourself an extra +**10 points per message** that you successfully decoded.

For any that you decoded *after* Penny explained the cipher, award yourself +**5 points per message**.

If you failed to decode *any* of the three messages, deduct –**10 points** (total, not per message) from your score.

And for those of you still struggling, here are the deciphered original messages:

Text Message #1: Harry Kennedy to Carla Nesbitt, 3 days ago

you knew what that seven grand was for. don't think I won't tell if you back out

Text Message #2: Harry Kennedy to Carla Nesbitt, 13 days ago

send me your dates and I'll match six days, he'll make space for me if he knows what's good for him

Text message #3: Unknown to Harry Kennedy, 20 days ago

YOU WERE RIGHT, JUST SAW FLOWER BOY TRYING TO BE INVISIBLE IN A VAN ROUND THE NURSERY. BOUGHT FOUR PALLETS

Now check your score to find out how well you did:

20 or fewer points: AMATEUR

Phew—it's amazing that you solved the murder at all! You must have done so by the skin of your teeth. We suggest you go back to the beginning and try again, to improve your score.

20–60 points: DETECTIVE CONSTABLE

You are a good, hardworking, competent detective. You may not be flashy, but you quietly get solid results. Why not have another go at solving the case? Focus your investigation more on following the right path, and you could potentially score much higher.

60–120 points: DETECTIVE INSPECTOR

You're a great detective! You followed all the right paths, asked all the right questions, and uncovered the killer. What's more, you avoided many of the red herrings and dead ends that were thrown in your path along the way. You are a credit to the police force, and promotion lies in your future.

120+ points: MASTER DETECTIVE

Incredible. You weaved a near-perfect path of deduction by avoiding red herrings, expertly cracking codes, and following the most relevant and correct lines of inquiry. An outstanding, almost impossible achievement—but you did it!

So, how did *you* solve the murder? I'd love to know! You can find me on most popular social media **@AntonyJohnston**, or email me via my website: **antonyjohnston.com**.

The only remaining question is: Could you do better next time?

There's only one way to find out . . .

Acknowledgments

In 1981 I was nine years old, and fortunate to attend a school with a well-stocked library. In there I stumbled across *Choose Your Own Adventure: The Cave of Time* by Edward Packard, a strange and thrilling book with a mind-blowing twist to its format: I, the reader, had the power to decide what the main character in the story would do, and thus how the story would unfold. I was immediately entranced and wanted more, but it was the only book of its kind in the library.

One year later, Steve Jackson and Ian Livingstone published *The Warlock of Firetop Mountain*—another book in which readers controlled the story, but now with rules for fighting monsters and performing feats of skill by rolling dice. I regularly played board games, but this Fighting Fantasy book/game hybrid was beyond anything I'd experienced.

Warlock was a sensation, and "gamebooks" soon became a global phenomenon. Throughout the 1980s I read/played every one I could find, always hungry for new adventures. They were also my gateway into the world of role-playing games like *Dungeons & Dragons*, *Call of Cthulhu*, and *Vampire: The Masquerade* . . . which led to my first professional writing gigs, for the RPG magazine *Arcane* in 1996. A decade later, I began writing video games. I've run that career in parallel with my fiction work ever since, always keeping them separate—until now.

My greatest thanks must therefore go to Edward Packard, creator of the Choose Your Own Adventure series; to Steve Jackson and Ian Livingstone, along with editor Geraldine Cooke, for the Fighting Fantasy books, which truly made me an enthusiast; and to the late Joe Dever, whose unforgettable Lone Wolf series pushed the envelope of what a gamebook could be.

I also want to thank two of my oldest friends, Dave and Jon. In the early 1980s we three were the biggest gamebook-heads around, lending to and borrowing from one another whenever a new title or series was released. I even made them play my own amateurish handwritten attempt—composed at the age of eleven, with the somewhat ambitious title *Hellfire of Death's Caverns*—for which I can only apologize.

Can You Solve the Murder? would not exist without those early experiences, which instilled in me a love of the interactive novel—and prompted me to wonder, many years later, if I could write a murder mystery in the same format . . .

Many thanks to James Thomson and Jonathan Whitelaw, who read my first short experimental prototypes in 2023. Nobody had done anything quite like this before, so their feedback and encouragement was invaluable.

James was also a beta reader and "play tester" for this book, along with Kathy Campbell, Rich Dansky, Heather Fitt, Jonathan Green, and Victoria Hancox. My thanks to them all, particularly Kathy and Victoria, who gave extensive feedback that hugely improved the book.

I pitched *Can You Solve the Murder?* to my agent, Sarah Such, in the freezing rain outside a packed, noisy London pub one cold December night. I do not recommend this approach! But Sarah's enthusiasm for the idea was a testament to her belief in me, and I can't thank her enough for the amazing job she and her team at the Sarah Such Literary Agency have done selling this book all over the world. Thanks also to Jessica Buckman at the Buckman Agency for her sterling work on foreign rights.

To my great surprise many publishers were interested in acquiring *CYSTM?*, but it was Finn Cotton at Transworld who truly grokked the concept and its potential. Finn has championed me and the book throughout the process of getting it into print; huge thanks to him and the team at Transworld for their support and hard work. Thanks also to Jeramie Orton and Bhavna Chauhan, my US and Canadian editors, for enormous help knocking the story into shape. For the US edition, I'd also like to thank Natalie Grant, Brian Tart, Andrea Schulz, Patrick Nolan, Kate Stark, Yuleza Negron, Chantal Canales, Jason Ramirez, Lynn Buckley, Sarah Horgan, Sabrina Bowers, and Randee Marullo, as well as Andy Dudley, Rachel Obenschain, and everyone else on the Penguin Random House US sales team. For the

Canadian edition, I'd also like to thank Amy Black, Megan Kwan, Kaitlin Smith, Keara Campos, Taylor Rice, Ruta Liormonas, Val Gow, and the wider Canadian sales team.

Thanks to you, the readers, for taking a chance on this unusual book. I'm on most social media platforms as @AntonyJohnston—do follow me and, of course, let me know if you solved the murder!

Finally, as always, thanks to Marcia for being there through it all.

Antony Johnston
OCTOBER 2024

Notebook

NOTEBOOK

NOTEBOOK

NOTEBOOK